Eddie was born in Stoke in 1963 and has been employed in the Public Sector all his working life. He lives in Northampton with his wife Dawn who he says is his rock.

He is a keen biker and a charity rider with the Armed Forces Bikers. When not writing, his spare time is filled by being an unpaid groom for his wife's horse!

Dedication

My tolerant wife, Dawn, who has allowed me the time and space to suddenly go to my laptop at all hours of the day and night and also listened to my ramblings as this book progressed.

Eddie Mann

ORDINARILY UNTHINKABLE

AUSTIN MACAULEY
PUBLISHERS LTD.

A CIP catalogue record for this title is available from the British
Library.

ISBN 9781787101654 (Paperback)
ISBN 9781787101661 (E-Book)
www.austinmacauley.com

First Published (2017)
Austin Macauley Publishers Ltd.
25 Canada Square
Canary Wharf
London
E14 5LQ

Acknowledgments

Mark, Dean, Tony, Vicky and Sian – your magnificent support has been invaluable.

To those that have already said they are going to buy a copy, Sean Stapleton, Mark Hammel, Richard Bradley, Dean Miles and Tony Carr.

To the friends who have followed and commented on my (often too many) social network posts, Dee Palmer, Sian Jenkins, Ian Henry Campbell, Carl Pheasant, Tony Carr and many others.

To my daughters, Kelly and Georgie, who both heard their dad say that one day he would write this book. Thanks for believing in me for too many years.

To the main character in this book: I have lived alongside you for the many months it took to write and complete this book. You have been a constant companion, often keeping me awake at night but always happy to see me return to writing another page or two.

'The love and protection you offer in life are often only proved in the actions you take after that life is extinguished'.

Chapter List

FIRST ENCOUNTER   11

MAKING AN IMPACT   28

EVERYONE'S NEW FRIEND   49

PAINFUL MEMORIES   60

A GOOD FRIEND WILL HELP YOU MOVE A BODY   78

RESEARCH AND RECONNAISSANCE   90

POOR PREPARATION – PISS POOR PERFORMANCE   104

THE PEAR OF ANGUISH   118

THE GIRL, THE COP, AND LUMP   127

A CHANGE OF PLAN   144

INTO SECOND GEAR   155

THE CRIPPENS   168

LEVERAGE   185

THE EXCHANGE   201

THREE BECOME TWO   216

ORDNANCE   226

A SPECK OF LIGHT IN A CLOUD OF DUST   237

THE JUDAS CRADLE   257

THE FINAL RIDE HOME   271

First Encounter

The motorcyclist pulled his bike onto the side of the road, a black Yamaha XVS1300 Midnight Star, the chrome gleaming in the morning sunlight, the engine rumbling loudly and smoothly. The rider kept his visor down and looked into his left rear view mirror. The vehicle that had just moments earlier indicated to him that it wanted him to pull over was now stationary about 30 feet behind him, lights flashing, two police officers sat in the front.

He could have easily just floored his bike and put some space between him and the cops but he knew that over a distance his cruiser was no challenge for the police vehicle. Anyway, now was not the time to be getting on the wrong side of the cops, he suspected that this was a routine stop of an innocent biker.

The police officer sat in the passenger seat, made his move and got out of the vehicle, walking towards his quarry with a swagger and the arrogance of an old cop still wanting to be respected by his newer less experienced colleague who remained sat behind the wheel for the time being.

The rider did not get off his bike, lowering the side stand he allowed the bike to lean over to the left, casually and slowly he reached into his angled zipped pocket of his old school leather biker jacket and removed a tin of small cigars and a Zippo lighter, with his other hand he opened his helmet visor just enough to be able to gain access to his mouth. Keeping an eye on the approaching cop in his mirror he lit one of the cigars (not removing or lowering the face mask to do this) and breathed in the warm relaxing smoke, holding and circling it in his mouth before exhaling a long greyish blue plume of smoke. His timing was perfect, the intoxicating fog of smoke hitting the officer directly in his face as he reached the biker.

"Would you mind putting out that cigarette sir?" asked the officer. The rider estimated his age to be in his fifties and despite probably having to pass a fitness test on an annual basis had spent many years letting himself go a bit, his belt strained to keep the chubbiness of his gut from spilling over and his shirt buttons must have been screaming at the amount of pressure they were being put under.

The rider blew out another cloud of foggy smoke, the familiar cigar smell once again wafting into and past the officer's face.

"I didn't realise that I was breaking the law by smoking on a public highway well away from any buildings officer, and I certainly wasn't smoking when you pulled me over. So I'm guessing you stopped me for some other reason?" His voice was quiet and controlled when he replied.

Great, thought the cop, just what he needed, another clever cocksure fucking biker spoiling what should have been a quiet Friday morning patrol. He quickly perused the biker. No patches, nothing to associate him with any known gangs, he couldn't see any long strands of greasy hair hanging out of the back of his helmet either.

"Remove your helmet sir," said the cop casually raising the first finger of his right hand indicating to his colleague that he would like him to join him now.

The biker noticed the cop's attempt to secretly summon his colleague but nothing much passed the attention of this individual. He lifted his visor fully open showing nothing

12

more of his facial features. The cop looked at his face or should I say he looked at a protective half face mask with the pattern of a skull's jaw printed upon it. The rider's eyes still could not be seen courtesy of a set of internal sun shades that were fully lowered protecting the riders' eyes from the sun and whatever else wanted to look into them.

The cop did not respond to his request for the helmet to be removed, at first, instead saying, "Do you know why we stopped you sir?"

The biker smiled unseen beneath the half face mask but it caused just enough movement to cause a deathly smile of bones and teeth to appear on the print. "Now officer, if I knew that it would be me standing there in that smart uniform and you sat on this bike sweating your goddamned ass off, wouldn't it?" The police officer did not smile or react in any way but the biker continued, "Or are you one of those old retired cops who has come back to do them patrols where you play the part of the helpful side of the law and warn people of a broken brake light or to give them directions, cuz if you are that is really useful because I think I am on the verge of being lost."

With his colleague having now arrived and placed himself about 4 feet behind the first policeman he maybe gained a bit more confidence as they now outnumbered the biker or maybe he just wanted to show off in front of him; the older cop repeated himself a little more forcefully than before.

"I told you to remove your helmet, lad."

Slowly removing one short black leather summer glove after another and placing them onto the bike seat the rider casually removed his helmet followed by the skull face protector placing the latter into the former.

Both coppers were now looking at the bald rider, eyes nearly half-closed which sat above a short button nose and a greying goatee beard. *Nothing special or out of the ordinary here* thought the young officer, *just another greasy old biker with nothing in his life other than the bike he rode.* He was pretty accurate with his second thought.

"Where you travelling to?" asked the older, portly cop.

"Was hoping to find hell so I could then go back," said the rider smiling. "You going anywhere nice officer?"

"Name," demanded the officer, becoming totally pissed off with this smartass wanker. "Difficult question officer, you could be named anything, but I think you look like a George"!

"Your fucking name, smartarse," the cop's voice now raised and obviously more irate.

"Well, I do apologise, a slight breakdown in communication there. My name is Grant, what's yours?" said the biker, offering his right hand to be shaken.

"Well Grant, my name is Sgt Murphy. Do you have a driving license or did you lose that along with your last name?"

Grant started to unzip his bike jacket when Sgt Murphy said "careful there boy, nice and slowly." He continued to unzip his jacket reaching into the inside pocket and pulling out his wallet. "Easy yourself, Mr. Murphy, this is Shropshire, not New York."

Opening up the old battered brown leather wallet Grant removed his driving license and handed it to the police officer. As he passed it to the younger officer, Murphy glanced at the licence looking for the drivers name, all it stated was Grant. "Go check that out, Pete." Taking the license Pete walked back to the police car.

"So then Mr. Grant, how come you don't have a surname, you like one of these new modern music stars or something, because to be honest with you, you look a bit too old for that game."

"Firstly, Mr. Murphy, it's just Grant, not Mr. Grant, I have no surname because I changed my name to Grant just a while ago by deed poll and I have to admit that is the one document I don't have with me."

Sgt Murphy led Grant nicely into his second point by asking, "So what was your real name?"

"As I was about to say before you interrupted… and secondly I don't believe I have to tell you my original name unless you arrest me or I'm applying for a passport. Now I ain't done nothing wrong so you ain't going to arrest me and I really don't think you have the authority to issue me a passport."

Grant's cocksure approach and attitude had once again put Sgt Murphy firmly back into the land of pissed off.

"Son, you are heading yourself for a short trip and a long stay in our local police station if you smartass answer me once fucking more, you hear me?"

For the first time, there was a slight reaction from the biker, his neck flushed and he pressed his teeth together, tightening his mouth. Taking a deep breath Grant slowly climbed from his bike, his 6 feet 3-inch frame towered above Sgt Murphy who unwittingly took a step backwards.

"Mr. Murphy, only two people call me son, the first is my father. In fact, that was the last word he said to me eight years ago, the last time we ever spoke to one another. Now as I don't like you as much as I don't like my father that alone doesn't make you my father, understand?"

The size and proximity, coupled with what Grant had just said, had clearly rattled Sgt Murphy who for the first time did not have a reply to give.

"The second was an old squadron sergeant major I had the displeasure of working for several years ago and he was a cunt. Now we have ascertained you are not my father so that must make you…?"

At that moment, Pete, full name Officer Ferguson, returned to join the conversation.

"All checks out Gus, no outstanding warrants, the bike is registered to Grant, no surname," stated Pete.

"So now," said Grant, "what did you stop me for?"

A flustered and surprised Gus Murphy, who had fully expected this lowlife to be wanted for something, coughed to clear his throat and give himself a few seconds of breathing space.

"You took that last corner too fast," he said.

"Really?" replied a quizzical Grant. "Well in that case you will also be arresting young Officer Ferguson here too because leading up to that bend, right through the bend and after the bend he was closing down on me without any lights flashing or sirens sounding, Did you know you were taking that corner too fast Officer Ferguson?"

Officer Ferguson looked down at the ground and kicked the gravel with his feet, "Errr I was in pursuit of you sir," he said rather uncertainly.

"With no lights or sirens Officer Ferguson?" And then once again with that familiar wry smile on his face, Grant said, "You lot put your lights and sirens on just to go and get a refill on doughnuts but you are telling me that you didn't while in pursuit of me, this dangerous felon."

Officer Ferguson decided at this point that there was no point in hanging around any longer and made his way back to the car. He had never wanted to stop the biker in the first place but Gus had insisted on chasing and stopping him so that he 'could have some fun with the prick'.

Murphy had also decided it was time to make a retreat but not without having the last word. "Well son, luckily I am in a good mood so I am going to let you off this minor offence with a friendly warning. Just remind me where you said you were going again."

"Certainly sergeant major," said Grant placing his helmet back on, "I'm going to hell and back and I do believe hell is quite close."

Murphy walked away back to the police car, with a certain feeling that he had just been called a cunt.

Grant started his bike up and it rumbled back into life. The bike was about 15 years old but had been cared for throughout its life by a single hand. While not pretending to be a Harley, its grunting engine stood its own and when she entered a town or village everyone knew that she was there. He let the cop car drive past him giving both the occupants a friendly nod of the head, surprisingly Officer Ferguson raised his hand in acknowledgment but old Gus Murphy didn't even look in Grant's direction.

Grant sat on the roadside for about another ten minutes wondering whether making this journey had been a wise choice, although choice was probably the wrong word. He had never really had a choice to make.

He looked over his right shoulder making sure the road behind him was clear and revved the throttle while slowly releasing the clutch. The Midnight Star moved away smoothly, once again the sun making the chrome glimmer, she really was a bike that had to be looked at when she passed by. The ideal bike for keeping a low profile!

A few miles up the road following his unscheduled, but what could prove useful, brush with the local law Grant rolled into Milton Dryton, a small market town that had seen better days. In 1245 King Henry III had granted a charter for a weekly Wednesday market which had given the town its original name. Riding up and down the rolling road that took you to the centre of town Grant slowed down to take a closer look and quickly decided that the 1245 charter was probably the last positive thing that had happened here. Many shop windows were boarded up, small groups of young teenage boys were hanging around, clearly with nothing to do but with trouble and mischief in mind. As Grant rode past one of these groups one of the lads, who was dressed in what could only be described as a version of that old 1980s classic New Romantic look much loved by the likes of Spandau Ballet, shouted, "Hey old man get yourself a modern race bike you wanker." Grant leaned slightly to his right and put the bike in a position to complete a full circle. Riding past the group of lads, the loudmouth had by now pushed himself to the back of the group in the hope of not being noticed, Grant looked over and shouted, "I prefer the old style lads, heavier you see, easier to crush skulls when you drive over them." The boys said nothing back, preferring to turn on the lad who made the first move.

Completing the circle Grant continued riding in his original direction, laughing at how well his plan to keep a low profile was going.

He followed the one-way system through the town centre coming to a stop at a set of traffic lights. He crawled slowly forward as they changed to green and just as he was going to make a right turn he noticed a garage to his left, swinging the bike left and placing his left foot down to make the turn easier he headed towards the garage.

Pulling up to one of the petrol pumps he unlocked his tank filler cap and reached for the petrol pump hose, he squeezed the handle a couple of times so that the garage attendant would see that he was there and switch the pump on. Instead, a crackly Asian voice squawked from a loudspeaker grill next to the pump, "Remove your helmet please, no petrol until you remove your helmet."

Leaving the petrol pump dispenser in his petrol tank Grant got off his bike and headed towards the door of the garage. Making no attempt to remove his helmet or even raise his visor he approached the counter where, behind a glass built protective bubble, a young Asian youth was stood. Grant slammed a twenty-pound note down on the counter saying "There's twenty quid pal now switch on the damned pump so I can get twenty pounds' worth of fuel. If you don't I will come back in here grab you by the throat and drag you out there where I will force the pump into your mouth and fill you up with twenty quid's worth of prime unleaded, I will then lean you forward and hold my trusty Zippo next to your arse and light the first fuel injected fart that you fucking produce."

As Grant walked back into the forecourt he heard the distinctive click of his fuel pump being activated and just as he had said he pumped exactly twenty pounds' worth of fuel into his tank. Before driving away he nodded towards the garage attendant shouting "Cheers Abdul!" and slowly rolled off the garage forecourt thinking to himself how easy it was to keep a low profile.

Making his way back into the one-way system Grant completed a full circle ending up almost at the place that he had encountered the gobby New Romantic. He had seen an old building on the corner of Cheshire Street, The Old Tudor House Hotel, it looked badly in need of some repair, had the potential to be a right rough old place if it ever managed to get more than six people into its bar and most importantly it appeared to have a few bedrooms up on the first floor. He parked his bike on the side of Shropshire Street right outside the pub; a single yellow line was just about visible having last been painted around the same time that King Henry had bothered his arse to visit this shit hole.

Before entering the establishment he removed his helmet, stashing his gloves and face shield inside it, he unzipped his jacket but kept it on for the time being. He did not want to upset the proprietors of this place, the tactic for this place was polite but memorable in other ways. He found the entrance door and pushed to open. Unfortunately, the door didn't budge, deciding that it must be a pull to open he looked for a handle and was once again disappointed. Looking at his watch the time read 11.08, so with only one thing to do he gave the white wooden door a few bangs with his fist.

He waited for a number of minutes during which a couple of locals walked past openly and brazenly staring at this stranger. One elderly lady in particular, was not particularly unsparing with her opinion muttering the word "Lout," as she walked past Grant and "noisy piece of shit," as she walked past his beloved bike. As he considered giving the door another bang or three in order to distance himself a bit from the crazy locals that happened to be out and about at the moment, a voice sounded from above his head.

"Who's banging the bloody door, we don't open for another hour, is that you Shamrock?"

Grant stepped back a couple of steps and arched his neck back to look up at a window directly above him on the first floor. The window was set back a bit in the wall made of white stone and black timbers which meant, to be seen, the girl leaning out of the window really had to lean forward.

Now Grant had never hidden his preference for the larger, well-endowed ladies but even he gave an inward "Christ almighty," at the view he had been blessed with. The young girl, probably aged around 25 or 26 had been blessed with the firmest and roundest of 42D's that Grant had seen in a very long time. How, with the merest of help from a low cut thin top and a flimsy lacy bra, these four and half pound beauties were defying gravity had him at a loss.

Not that much of a loss though that his mouth couldn't help but say "Newton got it fucking wrong I see."

The girl smiled, winked at Grant and said, "You look for much longer mister and I will start charging. Now, when your eyes have had their fill, go for a walk and come back in an hour when we are open."

He did not want to be walking the streets of this desolate place for a minute never mind a whole hour so thinking quickly he shouted up, "I have booked a room darling, told I could check in from eleven."

"Who booked that for you?" came the reply.

"Never caught the name love, an old fella I think. Really thinking about it I don't suppose you could say it was a confirmed booking, the bloke just said 'yeah that will be fine nobody stays in this dump anymore, ya can turn up from 11'."

"That'd be that damned bloody Shamrock, always answering the bloody phone when I am down in the cellar!" the girl shouted. "Hold on, I'll come down and let you in."

As he waited Grant surveyed the building, especially the rooms at the top from where the girl had previously been looking from. He assumed that they were bedrooms, three would be a fairly accurate guess. The windows were quite small and the drop down to the floor was at least twelve feet if not a bit more. The building looked very old so Grant could only assume that the floorboards were creaky as would be the doors, the stairs and most everything else. All potential problems but this was where the drinkers came, and that was what he needed. He had phoned the pub a week before and if the name Shamrock was anything to go by it was almost certainly that character who had answered the phone, a half drunk middle aged bloke with a very poor attempt at an Irish accent. During the very brief call Shamrock had rattled on about how the

21

place was a dump but yes it had bedrooms but there were a few classier places just outside of town but Grant wasn't listening. He was listening to the background noise and he liked what he heard. A cacophony of shouting and laughing, friendly arguments and lots of people shouting to be served, (maybe the girl had been down in the cellar) and Shamrock occasionally shouting "Serve yerself fella, the stupid cow has got lost downstairs."

Grant could tell that Shamrock was a bloke who liked to be liked and would know everyone who were regulars by their first names or nicknames so calling someone 'fella' would indicate that there were strangers in there, people staying for a night or two, salesmen passing through, but strangers to the pub. Strangers who were welcomed and allowed to join in the party, even more so if they were willing to spend their money he guessed. Perfect for his needs.

The rattling of keys and door bolts brought Grant back to his current situation, he turned back to face the door as it swung open with a loud creak and the young girl stood in the doorway wearing a big friendly smile. Putting all his effort to keep his eyes away from the girl's enormous rack he immediately noticed the extremely short and clingy black skirt, the sort of skirt that if his daughter had been wearing he would say, "nice belt darling, you gonna pair that up with a pair of jeans?" The girl was pleasantly curvy, carrying a few extra pounds that would put off plenty of men but just what Grant liked. He couldn't imagine the other side of this girl's bed being cold on many nights!

"Are you going to stand there all day just looking or do you want to book a room?"

"Well looking is free," replied Grant.

"Maybe so duck, but the rooms are still cheaper than me," the girl said once again winking at him.

Inwardly Grant smiled, it had been years since anyone had called him duck. It was an endearment that he was familiar with, having been dragged up in Staffordshire every woman for the first sixteen years of his life had called him duck... well when he wasn't being bad they did. On those occasions, he had been called plenty of other names; the women of his youth were no wallflowers!

Leaving the door ajar the girl walked back inside calling out, "come on through and let's get your details." Grant walked through the door and started to close it behind him but stopped doing so when he was instructed to "leave the door open; the locals won't get here until midday and if they do they will think all their birthdays have arrived all at once."

He followed the girl into the bar, by the time he got there she was stood behind the beer-stained sticky bar holding a pen and a key attached to a large wooden block with the number 4 carved into it, on the bar in front of her was a book, obviously the guest booking in book. "I'm Emma by the way," she said as she offered the pen to him, "My friends call me Ems."

Grant took the pen saying, "Well Ems, nice to meet you, looks like I get room four."

Her finger through the key ring Emma jiggled the key about holding it up in front of Grant's face, "you sure have honey, best room the house has to offer with a view over our towns beautiful high street," she said in a bad attempt of a Texan drawl but a very clear hint of sarcasm.

"Anything else going for it?" asked Grant with an even clearer amount of sarcasm.

"Well not sure if it's a bonus but it is right next to room three which is my room," said Ems laughing awkwardly at her own forwardness.

Her laughing stopped and was replaced with a look of genuine hurt and reject as Grant, straight-faced asked, "Do you have a room at the back?"

Emma, clearly still stinging from Grant's response grabbed the guest book and spun it round to face Grant, unfortunately, it only spun halfway because of the sticky residue of last night's beers spills that overlaid years of previous beer spills. Angrily she grabbed the book and turned it the rest of the way, pointing at the page she said sharply, "Fill in your details."

Grant had genuinely not meant for his comment to attract this response and could almost taste Emma's feeling of rejection. He quickly went on the charm offensive.

"Ems," she didn't react her eyes remained locked onto the guest book. "Emma," he said again, this time placing a hand under her chin and gently lifting up her head so that she was looking straight into his dark brown eyes. "I'm sorry hun, you've clearly taken my request the wrong way, the thought of sleeping safely knowing that you are in the room next door ready to jump to my rescue should anything nasty happen fills me with joy. The only reason I asked about a room at the back is because I am a very light sleeper and I imagine that a market town like this has delivery lorries using this high street through the night."

Emma gazed into his eyes, almost hypnotised. This stranger must be twice her age at least but his soft voice and deep eyes kept her attention. It also helped that Emma was a sucker for any attention, anything that distracted her away from her boring Milton Dryton life that she was neither clever nor skilled enough to get away from.

One thumb now gently stroking her chin Grant continued with the charm, "I just want to give myself the best chance of getting a few nights of good sleep to recover from being on the road for days." Actually, the last thing

Grant had on his mind was a good night's sleep but feeling the smile developing on Emma's face before he saw it he knew that he had managed to rescue the situation.

"I understand," said a once again smiley Emma, "and I wasn't offended, I'm just a bit tired, late night last night. Didn't get rid of the drunks until one in the morning, sorry." She spun around deftly hanging up key number four on a brass hook and picking up key number one. As she spun back to face Grant her breasts swayed further to the left than the rest of her body, once again showing off their size and firmness. Taking the key with a smile, he knew those things were going to be an unwanted distraction.

He completed the guest book, name: easy. Leaving the surname box empty he moved the pen and hovered it over the box that wanted the guest's home address, he paused giving this some thought.

Emma looked down at the book "forgotten your address Grant?" she asked him.

"No darling, it's just I am doing a bit of travelling around the country so I don't really know which address I am going to be at from one day to the next. It's going to be a mixture of hotels, B&B's and dossing down at a few friends' places," he lied.

"Just put your home address, it's only in case you leaving anything here so we can send it to you," Emma said helpfully and also telling a bit of a lie. Grant knew that it was a lie, if he left anything here they would contact him by phone and ask him to collect it... if they bothered to contact him at all, he knew it was for marketing purposes and so that they could send him brochures and special offers.

"Well you see, therein lies the problem, I was renting but as I intend to be travelling around the country for several months I didn't sign the rental agreement when it came up for renewal, so effectively I am homeless," another lie.

"Just put down one of your mate's addresses," suggested Emma.

"Good idea girl," happy that she had come up with something that would allow him to further shroud his movements.

He wrote down an address from his childhood that he knew hadn't existed since 1973 when it was knocked down. Number 5, Queen Street, Fenton. What stood there now was a complex of maintained bungalows that housed the elderly. It would have to do.

He skipped the contact number box and signed and dated where indicated at the bottom of the page.

"You haven't said how many nights you want to stay and we definitely need a contact number, your mobile will do," said Emma.

"I don't own a mobile phone Ems," he said wondering how many lies he would eventually tell during this conversation. "Can't stand the things," quickly moving on he wrote the number 3 in the box asking 'How many nights stay'. "Let's say three nights for now but that may change, if that's ok?"

He looked up and saw a wide-eyed Emma looking at him, "you don't have a mobile? How do you cope? I'm never off mine!"

"Old school darling, I use public payphones" he lied again. The cheap twenty-pound phone he described as his untraceable throwaway sat snugly inside a secret sewn-in pocket inside his bike jacket, switched off so that a random text or phone call didn't give away his deceit.

"A man of mystery eh?" enquired Emma. "I'll be keeping my eye on you, now let me show you to your room.

The last thing that Grant wanted was anyone keeping an eye on him, especially a lonely horny young barmaid. *He would deal with that problem if it arose*, he thought to himself.

Emma walked from behind the bar and headed towards a door above which a wooden sign stated 'Bedrooms'. "Follow me mystery man," she said, "let me take you upstairs," a cheeky smile on her face. Grant just knew that it wasn't the first time that the young girl had said that to a man.

He followed her, feeling slightly sorry for this girl. She was slightly older than his daughter but that didn't stop him from admiring her firm arse tightly wrapped in that clingy skirt as she wiggled her way up a narrow set of stairs.

Making an Impact

The narrow stairs were covered with an extremely old and well-worn carpet. The patterning was similar to the 1960s and 1970s grotesque carpet patterns he had seen as a child. Mainly brown and emblazoned with large teardrop patterning that had once been a mixture of bright red and mustard colours but was now heavily faded and dulled with use and grime. The wallpaper matched the same era, big pattern, faded and dirty with the occasional tear. What a dump, this place must sell a large amount of beer to survive - it was perfect for his needs.

At the top of the stairs, Emma turned to her right and walked down a dingy badly-lit corridor. They walked past three doors numbered consecutively 5 to 3, obviously, the first three bedrooms thought Grant, his thoughts confirmed as they walked past door number three and Emma nodded her head in its direction saying "my room."

She continued walking towards the end of the corridor and up three small steps. Grant duly followed still snatching the occasional admiring glance of Emma's sexy bum. No VPL thought Grant, either a g-string or more likely commando.

Emma disappeared from his view as she turned left having negotiated the small rise in the corridors level.

They passed by door number two and ahead of them was the last door of their short journey. It stood at the end of the corridor - room number 1 - the furthest from the bar

28

area, at the back of the building, so far so good but he wouldn't know how perfect it was until he could take a look from inside the room.

Emma put the key into the lock, turning it to the left and deftly swinging open the door, it swung about a foot before coming to a stop, she pushed it further open. A backward glance over her shoulder in the direction of Grant was accompanied by another cheeky wink as she said, "It's a bit stiff!"

Another phrase he imagined she was no stranger to.

She waved her arm extravagantly towards the room, "your room awaits you sir," she said laughing at her own humour.

Grant decided to join in and bowing in Emma's' direction said, "Why thank you, kind lady."

"Would you like the grand tour while I'm here?" enquired Emma.

Not wanting to once again upset her but at the same time now getting a bit bored with the blatant flirting he said, "I am certain I can find the bed and the bathroom as well as you can but rest assured that if I need anything I know who to call."

Thankfully it worked, Emma smiled and began her journey back to the bar but not before saying, "well you know where I am, if there is *anything* I can do for you just let me know."

The emphasis she placed on the word 'anything' didn't go unnoticed by Grant.

"Thank you," he replied, "I will but you be on your way now and prepare that bar for your early punters."

"Oh they will arrive at twelve on the dot and stay until beyond closing. It's a Friday so it will be a busy night."

Perfect he thought, just what he wanted.

"Hopefully see you later," said Emma as she virtually skipped down the corridor and disappeared out of sight.

Oh, you will that alright, Grant quietly thought.

He walked into room number one and was not surprised at all to see that just like the rest of the place it was in much need of a good clean and a face lift, nothing much, just enough to bring it out of the 1970s!

Grant closed the door behind making a mental note to make this initial recce of the room a quick one having just remembered he had left his throw over saddle bags on the bike. He knew that Emma's tits would be a distraction. If those lads he had come across earlier were anything to go by, leaving his few belongings alone for too long was bound to end in trouble.

It took him five minutes to work out that the bed looked old and uncomfortable, the shower over the bath dripped rather than showered and the one window in the room opened outwards on to an old gated courtyard which was probably used for the delivery of beer barrels. It could prove useful as a more secure area to park his bike if he could persuade Emma or the establishment owner to let him have use of it. There was a chest of drawers on which sat a dated television and an alarm clock. One bedside table sat to the left of the bed, which wasn't quite a full double. Opening the drawer of the bedside table confirmed that the Gideon's had no standards when it came to where they left their bibles.

Grant decided it was time to retrieve his belongings. Leaving the room he noticed that unlike modern hotels which had self-locking doors this one required it to be manually locked with the key, another mental note to himself to make sure he did this every time he left the room. The last thing he wanted was uninvited guests freely wandering into his room and searching through his stuff.

He made his way back down to the bar, entering through the door marked above with the 'Bedrooms' sign he saw Emma behind the bar pulling a pint of bitter for a man sat at the bar on one of the red faux leather padded stools. The pint must have been for him as, so far, he was the only occupant of the bar. He didn't see Emma being a pint of bitter drinker but nothing in this place would have surprised him too much.

Emma looked over, "Hi, leaving already? It isn't that bad is it?" she asked.

"No, not at all, it's perfect. Just need to get my stuff off the bike," replied Grant nodding in the direction of the man sat at the bar.

The man raised his hand moving it left then right in a waving gesture, "Y'alright there sor," he said in a questionable Irish accent.

Must be Shamrock thought Grant and replied with a cheery "Top 'o' the morning fella."

"Well, well a fellow Celt to be sure, come have a drink and let's salute the tricolour," said Shamrock, his Irish accent becoming dodgier with every word he spoke.

"Not quite my friend, but let me get my stuff stashed away and I will happily join you for that drink."

He made his way outside, thankfully his bike and the saddlebags were still where he had left them, there was no sign of the group of lads he had encountered earlier but the high street was now a bit busier. Grant assumed they were all Milton Dryton residents as he didn't see this as a tourist destination.

He removed the saddlebag from the back seat of his bike and threw it over his right shoulder, a burst of pain shot through the shoulder and Grant winced slightly. Damn shoulder injury never let him down, he transferred the bags over to this left shoulder and gently rubbed the right one with his left hand. He had lived with the effects of this old injury for over 15 years but still managed to occasionally forget about it. He always carried a pack of Naproxen with him but couldn't afford to take any today, he didn't want the mix of a few beers and strong anti-inflammatories to cloud his mind. He needed to be focussed for the rest of the day and night to come.

He made his way back into the hotel, Emma was still stood behind the bar, this time, filing her nails, she smiled. "Ah, the mystery man returns and this time with belongings. Before you go up, can I have a quick word?"

She walked to the end of the bar leaning over it towards him showing off an ample amount of cleavage. This girl knew exactly what she was doing.

"Yes Emma, what can I do for you?" he asked maintaining eye contact on this occasion.

"A question like that could get a girl like me into trouble," she said cheekily, "and please call me Ems, we are friends aren't we?"

"Of course Ems, I forgot," said Grant already bored again with her flirtatious ways.

Whether he hid it well or she genuinely didn't notice, his boredom went unnoticed, continuing Emma said, "When you booked in you didn't write your surname."

Ah, here we go again with the familiar surname conversation he thought.

"Well, Emm......Ems, I don't have a surname."

She looked at him with a disbelieving look, "Of course you do, everyone has a surname."

Grant smiled, "Madonna doesn't and nobody questions her about it."

Emma looked bemused, "Come on don't fuck me about Grant, my boss will have a right go at me if the guest book isn't filled in correctly."

He looked directly at her and said simply and with no humour, "Ems, I really don't have a surname, my name is just Grant. It's all legal I promise you so if your boss starts to have a go at you about it point him in my direction and I give you my word that once I have spoken to him the first thing he will do is apologise to you."

Clearly still not believing him but having no choice to accept what he said she shook her head saying, "You better be for real Grant, I need this job."

He headed towards the door that led to the stairs to the bedrooms, looking back at the disbelieving girl he blew a kiss in her direction, "Trust me Ems, we are friends remember? Now pull me a pint of bitter and make sure Shamrock pays for it."

Shamrock raised his head upon hearing his name, "To be sure, put it on the tab Ems, a drink for my new found friend."

Grant left the bar laughing as he heard Emma tell Shamrock to fuck off and pay up in cash. *New found friend indeed* thought Grant, *more than you will ever know Shamrock, my fake Irish fella.*

Back in his room, Grant began to unpack his scant belongings. Three pairs of jeans, one blue, one grey and the third black, one plain black hoodie and four t-shirts - his most treasured of which was a Black Star Riders shirt he had bought at the launch party of their first album. His underwear comprised of five pairs of socks and five pairs of underpants, he wasn't an enemy of the wash in a sink method. A pair of battered old Nike Classic trainers was the only footwear he had other than the brown leather boots he was currently wearing, his favoured footwear when on the bike.

One saddlebag empty he turned his attention to the other, he thought about the contents of this and wondered whether to unpack them or not. He knew exactly what was in there and also knew he wouldn't be needing them for a few days yet. He decided to leave them in the saddlebag and place the leather Harley-style luggage carrier under the bed. His mind lingered on the contents, an odd and eclectic collection of items by anybody's standards.

One book entitled *The History of Death by a Thousand Cuts* written by Dr. Alexander 'Two Paws' Walters who claimed to be a historian, psychologist and 5th generation Native American. Grant didn't believe he was any of these and very much doubted the title of doctor also but it was a well-written book and contained the details he most desired.

A second book entitled "*How to Correctly Use a Tourniquet.*" This had no name to indicate who had written it and, to be honest, was more of a manual than a book but once again the contents were more important to Grant than anything else.

A black zipped soft shell bag with a small side handle contained the tools he didn't want to actually use but… well he didn't really know what situations he might end up in.

There was a large hunting knife, the blade of which was approximately 6 inches long and as sharp a blade as you would ever want. The first four inches were a fine sharp edged blade with the last two inches having a serrated edge. The handle was made from animal bone, precisely carved and smooth to the touch. It was very old but in immaculate condition and a real collector's piece. He had paid a pretty price for it.

A photograph of his wife and daughter looking so happy (and slightly drunk), his daughter's boyfriend had taken the photo on a night out at a Mexican restaurant.

At the bottom of the bag, wrapped in a soft cloth, was the one item Grant hoped he would never have a reason to use but he wanted all contingencies covered.

The Glock 17 was a dull black/grey in colour. Its polymer frame made it lightweight and resistant to weather, corrosion and impact. Its double stack magazine provided a capacity for seventeen rounds. It was a simple but very effective and reliable piece of equipment by all accounts. The serial number was, of course, scratched off.

The last item was a small box full of ammunition for the Glock. The magazine was already fully loaded and Grant seriously hoped that the seventeen rounds it contained were seventeen rounds too many!

He placed the saddlebags under the bed, went to the bathroom and doused his face with cold water. Drying his wet face and hands on the coarse towel that had been hanging on the back of the bathroom door Grant thought it was now a real good time to go and have a drink, meet some locals and make an impact.

Grant made his way once again down to the bar having had to return to his room as he had forgotten to lock the door behind him. Focus, he thought to himself, one stupid mistake could bring his plan crashing down.

He entered the bar to find his two new 'friends' Emma and Shamrock in exactly the same place they had been approximately twenty-five minutes earlier. He looked at his watch, black faced, limited edition from the Red Arrows collection; it had been a gift to himself about 3 years ago, he had never paid so much for a watch. 12.56, a little bit earlier than he had planned to be in the bar but thinking about the contents of the left saddlebag had put him in the mood for a drink.

As he walked over to Shamrock he noticed four other people now in the bar. All four were sat at the table that was in front of the large window at the front of the hotel. Two sat on chairs facing the window while their other two companions were sat on the red felt covered bench that ran the length of the front wall. They all had a pint of beer sat in front of them on the table; in addition, one of them had a shot of what could have been whiskey sat adjacent to his pint glass. At that moment he was the one talking as the other three listened with interest, Grant couldn't make out what the conversation was about not that it was important to him but he was human so naturally curious.

He sat on the stool next to Shamrock, a pint of bitter was sat at the bar waiting for him, he took a large swig. It tasted good and was so refreshing, he stopped drinking and held up the glass, which was now about a third emptier than it had been just seconds beforehand, in the direction of Shamrock saying, "Cheers my friend, may the fear of God make the demons stay away."

The old fake Irishman smiled at him and raising his own glass in a similar demonstration of good health replied "May the cockles of your heart be forever warm," which was the least Irish salutation that Grant had ever heard, and he had heard a few.

"So whereabouts in Ireland are you from Shamrock?" asked Grant, genuinely interested in hearing his answer, an answer that pleasantly surprised him.

Shamrock gave him a big grin showing all of his teeth which were stained brown except for the three that were missing, "Oh I ain't Irish, never even visited the place. They call me Shamrock because I've been known to have the luck of the Irish, I'm a gambling man you see."

An honest answer, Grant hadn't seen that coming. "So why the Irish accent?" he asked.

"Ah well, the locals seem to like it and I am pretty good at it even if I say so myself, fools most of the strangers I meet, yourself included by the looks of it."

Grant didn't bother replying, it was clear that Shamrock had never been to Ireland - North or South - as that fake Irish accent would have got him shot. Instead, he just took another gulp of the refreshing cool beer.

Over the next two hours, Shamrock regaled Grant with stories of his gambling successes, of how well known and liked he was right throughout Milton Dryton and the surrounding areas, bits and bobs about his family all of which were born and raised in Milton Dryton but who all now seemed to live elsewhere. How much the influence of Shamrock was a deciding factor in their decision-making process to move away, Grant could only hazard a guess. Not once did he ask anything about Grant, this was a man who loved himself and everything about himself, however, he was happy with it to continue this way. The fewer questions asked the less that Grant would have to lie. Occasionally he would look and watch Emma working behind the bar enjoying a delicious view of a bum when she bent forward facing away from him (definitely commando) and an even clearer view of her cleavage when she leaned forward over the bar to talk to the occasional customer.

Between ogling Emma's more than bountiful attributes and listening to Shamrock's tales of life Grant used his observation skills to take in his surroundings and more importantly the members of the 'dingiest hotel in the world drinking club'.

The old man who had been doing most of the initial talking in the group of four people when Grant had first walked in the bar was, as far as he could make out, either named Glyn or Glenn, his three comrades were Kieran,

Kelvin and Joe. All were aged between 55 and late 60's roughly and were all members of the Milton Dryton bowling club, they obviously had a game coming up, an important game by the sounds of things as they had been discussing bowling tactics for the entire time that Grant had been listening to them. It had been a very tedious conversation and took all of his concentration to stay focused.

The bar itself curved into a blind corner where Grant had worked out were a number of other drinkers, how many he wasn't too sure at this time but at least two, maybe three. They had been a bit louder and were definitely younger than the bowling club fraternity.

Grant was brought back to real time when Shamrock said, "You still with me boy, looks like you wandered off to a better place?"

Grant shook his head, "No, I'm still listening Shamrock, very interesting tale you have to tell, sounds like you are the man to know around here."

Shamrock smiled, liking the fact that he had kept the interest of this stranger. Grant smiled inwardly, wondering how much longer he would get away with blowing smoke up this old idiot's arse.

"Shamrock, you must have the bladder of a whale, I need to point Percy at the porcelain my friend, so please excuse me."

"I'll get another couple of pints in while you're away," said Shamrock tapping on the bar to get Emma's attention.

Emma walked towards them saying, "The gents are just round the corner past the pool table." She had obviously been listening to their conversation.

"Thanks, Ems," he followed the bar round to the left, immediately seeing the pool table which fitted in well with the rest of the décor, badly maintained, and for the first time also saw the other three drinkers in the bar.

Officer Ferguson couldn't believe his eyes, walking past him was the very man he had seen earlier that day. His police training kicked in and he prepared himself for some trouble but the man just kept walking towards the toilets as if he hadn't spotted him. Grant, of course, had spotted the young copper but pretended he hadn't, he had a spot of business to take care of first. Entering the gents Grant took a few seconds to ensure all the cubicles were empty, thankfully they were. He entered the last one, pushing the door slightly closed but not bothering to lock it, leaning over the toilet bowl he immediately stuck two fingers down his throat and threw up the majority of the beer he had consumed over the past couple of hours.

Warm, light brown liquid hit the clear water in the bowl of the toilet, bits of sticky organic particles splashed back up the bowl sticking to the porcelain. Grant gagged and threw up again, another throat full of yeasty liquid joining its predecessor turning the toilet water a darker shade of brown. He rested himself by placing one hand on the cistern block attached to the back wall of the cubicle, spittle-producing itself at an alarming rate causing Grant to spit generously over and over again into the toilet.

Eventually the feeling of wanting to vomit again subsided enough for Grant to think it was safe to flush the toilet, he didn't want to leave any evidence of this self-inflicted emptying of his stomach. His face was covered with a fine film of cold sweat; he walked out of the cubicle and made his way to the opposite wall where three grimy sinks were attached. He rotated the four armed handle of the tap and cold refreshing water poured out, cupping both hands beneath the flow he splashed his face with the water instantly feeling better. He repeated this process three times ending the cleansing process by checking the front of his shirt and jeans to ensure there were no tell-tale watermarks. Drying his face and hands on the rotating blue towel system that didn't look like it had been changed in years he walked over to the mirror and inspected himself. His face a little bit flushed and his eyes slightly glazed over with a protective liquid he leaned forward and pressed his forehead against the mirrored glass. The coldness gave a feeling of revival; he stood upright again and once again looked at his own reflection.

"Remind me again why I am doing this?" he asked himself but he didn't need reminding, the reason was very clear in his mind. He was determined to do what was necessary to achieve his end goal or die trying.

Grant walked out of the toilet returning to the bar area, the pretence of being drunk while staying sober was going to be more difficult than he had first thought. He looked in the direction of the three guys sat in the corner just the other side of the battered pool table. Once again the young cop he had encountered earlier that day was looking at him only this time Grant acknowledged his existence by raising the first finger of his right hand to his temple in the style of a salute.

Grant had a quick idea that would give him a bit of a respite "Hi there Officer Ferguson, nice to see you again," he said hoping that Ferguson would offer him a chance to join them. It came in the reply.

"In here my name is Pete or Fergie,"

Grant nodded his head and said.

"Ok Pete, I'm not looking for trouble, let me buy you a drink."

Pete declined stating that he had a drink already.

"That's ok" said Grant, "Well at least let me join you and prove there's no bad feeling about earlier."

One of the other two men sat with Pete used a foot to push out a chair away from the table, "take a pew, pal" he said, "and I don't mind taking you up on that offer for a drink."

As Grant sat he shouted "Ems, a drink for..." looking at the man who had offered him the seat, "sorry I didn't catch your name."

"Alan."

"A drink for Alan please, Ems. And one for your friend?" said Grant looking at the silent member of the trio, this individual shook his head to indicate that he didn't want a drink.

Emma's shrill shout came from around the corner, "One for you too, Grant?"

"No thanks Ems. I have one on the bar, but pour another for Shamrock and tell him I'll join him soon." Grant sat and filled the awkward silence by assessing this new group of acquaintances.

Officer Ferguson/Pete/Fergie looked no different other than he was no longer wearing his uniform, still lacking in confidence and clearly fearful of any conflict. Alan, on the other hand, was definitely not lacking in confidence, shoulder length black hair, an old Ramones t-shirt, and torn blue jeans. Twenty years ago Grant would certainly have concluded that he was not a member of the police force but with the lowering of standards right across the public sector these days, anything was possible. He could of course be a detective but Grant very much doubted that a detective would be socialising with a rookie cop.

The third man was a mystery to Grant, he hadn't said a word and hadn't stopped looking at Grant since he had re-entered the bar. He felt that he was visually being stripped bare by this individual - this one could be a cop without a doubt.

It was Alan that broke the silence, "So how do you know Pete?" he asked.

Grant looked over to Pete asking him if he wanted to tell the story, Pete shook his head saying "No, go ahead, it will be interesting to hear your version."

Grant told the story on how he had become acquainted with Pete, he added nothing and took nothing away. When he had finished he looked at the three guys.

"So you had a run in with Muttley?" said Alan laughing, "Most of us have in this town."

"Muttley?" responded Grant, quizzically.

It was Pete that explained that one. "Sergeant Murphy, his nickname is Muttley, a nickname he isn't fond of may I add."

"Yeah, like the dog off the Dick Dastardly show, always looking for a medal opportunity," said Alan, laughing even louder.

The third man remained silent, still looking intently at Grant. He thought about engaging with the man but decided to give it a bit longer.

"He just wanted to fuck with you," said Pete, "he doesn't really like bikers, in fact, to be honest, he doesn't much like anyone. You hadn't done anything wrong, he was bored and it was coming to the end of a very quiet shift."

"Does he ever drink in here?" asked Grant, not really wanting to fall out again with this biker-hating bitter copper.

"Muttley, in here! You must be joking mate," said Alan, "he would probably get lynched, anyway, he never goes out unless he's got his uniform on, a real anti-social bastard that one."

Relieved at hearing that piece of information Grant decided it was now time to get everyone involved in this banter. "And what about you?" Grant looked at the quiet bloke sat between Pete and Alan, "Any opinion about the unpopular Sgt Murphy?"

The man leaned forward placing both hands on the table, his face didn't alter from the blank expression he had held for the last five minutes, "He's my fucking brother."

Grant had not seen that one coming but holding the man's gaze and trying his best to show no external reaction to the curve ball that had just been thrown his way he replied, "And do you call him Muttley?"

Alan leaned so far back as he laughed violently that he almost toppled over out of his chair, pulling himself back by grabbing the table he looked at Murphy's brother.

"Fuck me Dave, come on even you have to find that one funny."

Dave Murphy's face remained expressionless but slowly, very slowly a faint smile appeared. "I have much worse names when I refer to him, any man who arrests his own brother, plants additional evidence and then gives critical evidence to ensure that brother spends time in jail is no brother of mine. He's a fucking prick and I am being polite because I appear to be in friendly company."

Grant relaxed a bit, partly because the company he was currently in didn't appear to be a potential threat to his plans and partly because taking a break from drinking with Shamrock had allowed his head to clear a bit, obviously the self-induced multi-coloured yawn had also benefited him.

"What does bring you to Milton Dryton?" asked Pete.

Smiling Grant said, "You asking as a copper or a drinker?"

Immediately Pete became flustered again, the merest hint of potential conflict sent this man into a state of mild panic, how this bloke was a copper defied belief, thought Grant. "I'm just pulling your leg Fergie, I've got nothing to

43

hide. I'm just travelling around the country, I plan to cover as much of England, Scotland, Wales and maybe even Ireland as I possibly can before the money runs out."

Seeing an opportunity to briefly leave this little group before more, and potentially more awkward, questions were asked, he said, "Anyway, talking about travelling, excuse me for a few moments guys I need to see if Emma will let me secure my bike in the pubs back courtyard."

Having excused himself, Grant made his way back to the bar and following a brief and once again flirtatious conversation with Emma it transpired that it wasn't a problem at all. Emma handed him a small key explaining that it was for the padlock that locked up the gate to the courtyard. Grant thanked her, grabbed her hand and kissed the back of it and made his way to the door that led to the bedrooms, he had previously seen a short corridor heading off to a back door that he guessed would lead to the courtyard.

"Where ya going?" asked Emma, look slightly confused. "I thought you wanted to put your bike in the back?"

"Yeah," said Grant, "I'm going to unlock the gate and then bring the bike round."

"It's locked on the street side silly," said Emma.

Surprised and slightly disappointed at this news Grant headed to the bar's front door thinking that he needed to change that situation if he could. Unlocking the hard top box he removed his helmet and placed it over his head, even though he was only moving the bike a matter of a hundred yards he didn't want any kind of trouble, he rode it round to the front of the courtyard's double-fronted wooden gate. Kicking the side stand and leaning his bike over to the left he walked to the gate looking at the padlock, black standard Chubb lock. He unlocked it and pushed the gates open a loud screech accompanied their movement, *another bloody job* he thought.

Riding the bike slowly into the courtyard he did a u-turn so that the bike was pointed towards the gates and almost directly beneath the window of his room. He decided he would have to wait to have a good look around the yard as he now needed to do a couple of things and didn't want to be out of the pub long enough to raise any suspicions.

He locked up the gate and walked to the corner of the high street. Across the road, and thankfully out of view of any prying eyes from the pub window, stood an elderly lady at a bus stop. He crossed the road.

"Good morning ma'am, I was wondering if you know of a hardware shop around here?" he asked as he approached the old lady.

She nodded saying "Just round the corner, old man Johnson's place," and pointed down the road in the direction from which Grant had first entered Milton Dryton.

"Thank you very much and have a good day," he said walking in the direction indicated.

Just as the old lady had said the hardware store was literally just around the bend in the road, looking like it hadn't been altered since the 1950s with many of its wares on display around the shop front including a dozen of more doormats hanging in front of the main window. Grant walked into the store through the wedged open door. The smell of old metal and several different kinds of oils and solutions hit him like a toxic fog, the smell of hardware items having been on shelves for years.

Not seeing anyone Grant called out "Hello, anyone about?"

From behind the old wooden counter a bald-headed man who was easily eighty years old appeared. "Hello back at ya, and how can I help you today?" he cheerily responded.

"I'm guessing you must be old man Johnson," asked Grant at which the old man's smile grew even larger.

"Been talking to the locals have yer? Yep, I am the very same. Clive Johnson, to be exact."

"Nice to meet you Clive, I'm in a bit of a rush, to be honest with you," said Grant said, telling the truth for a change. "I need some WD40 and do you offer a key cutting service?"

"Yes to the first," said Clive, "but no to the second but I do sell locks of all kinds if that helps."

Even better thought Grant.

"I'll get you the WD40, padlocks and the like are halfway down the shop on the left-hand side," said Clive helpfully.

Grant made his way and easily found the padlocks and a whole range of other types of locks including sliding gate locks, chain locks, in fact, more types of locks than he ever thought existed. He scanned the range of padlocks available and was pleased to see the almost identical standard black Chubb lock that currently locked up the courtyard gate... and it came with two keys.

He grabbed one of the padlocks and hurried back to the counter where Clive was waiting for him with his can of WD40 which he had already rung up on his modern-style till which looked very much out of place.

"Add that to the bill please Clive," said Grant handing over the padlock.

"Sure will, only had the large can of WD40 hope that's ok with you," said Clive scanning the barcode on the packaging of the padlock.

"No problem at all, what's the damage my friend?" asked Grant.

"Eighteen pounds and twenty pence in total; DIY comes at a price these days," said Clive shrugging his shoulders.

"Always a price to pay for doing a job yourself Clive," replied Grant knowing that the old man wouldn't be able to understand the real meaning of what he had just said. He handed over twenty pounds in cash and waited for Clive to return him the change and place the two items into a brown paper bag.

Before leaving Grant dropped eighty pence of the change into the Help the Heroes charity rattler that stood on the counter. Clive nodded respectively saying, "very kind of you sir, I'm an old soldier myself."

"Me too, the world needs a few heroes" said Grant, as he walked out the store.

Taking large strides while being careful not to look like he was in too much of a hurry, Grant headed back to the courtyard and let himself, pushing the doors closed. He ripped open the packaging of the padlock, took the keys and threw the padlock onto the ground. He kicked the lock around the courtyard's rough concrete surface, jumped on it a few times and then wiped off the dust on his jeans. If the gates had been ajar any bypassers would have thought they were watching the actions of a mad man.

Grant examined the new lock which was now scuffed and scratched a bit. *Much better*, he thought, *looks a bit more like the lock it's going to replace.*

He walked to the gates, opening them slightly and popped his head through the gap just enough to look up and down the street. Nobody in sight, his run of good luck continued. He took the old lock of the clasp from where it hung and replaced it with the lock he had just purchased from old man Johnson's hardware store, taking the old lock and the key that Emma had given him not long ago he returned to his bike and threw them and the can of WD40, still in the brown paper bag, into the bike's top box.

Leaving the yard he locked the 'new' padlock and deposited one of the new keys into his left front pocket. He took one last look at the padlock - only with a really good inspection would anyone be able to tell the difference between that one and the old one.

He headed back to the bar, key in hand ready to hand back to Emma and continue the pretence of getting drunk.

Everyone's New Friend

Entering the bar he casually placed the key onto one of the beer towels that covered most of the bar saying, "Thanks Ems, all secured now."

Emma smiled and nodded in the direction of two pints of beer standing on the wooden bar, "For you Mister Popular, I've never known the locals in here to be so generous to a stranger, in fact to anyone to be honest."

Grant smiled back picking up one of the pint glasses, wishing the locals would go back to their old ways of not being so generous, he sipped a mouthful of beer, patting Shamrock on the back as he passed him making his way back to Fergie and his mates. "I'll be back in a few minutes Shamrock, if I'm not back by the time you've finished your drink, help yourself to that extra pint mate."

Giving a thumbs up and wiping a dribble of beer from his chin Shamrock looked up "T'be sure, consider it done."

The four 'bowling buddies' looked up in Grant's direction following his movement across the bar, he nodded in their direction "Afternoon fellas, I may come and join you a bit later if that's alright with ya, I don't mind a game of bowls myself?" The four looked at each surprised that this new arrival had even noticed them, it was Kelvin who responded, "Anyone who likes bowls and brings a few drinks with them is welcome to sit at our table, my friend." Continuing his progress he nodded his approval.

As he arrived back at the table he had left not that long ago he swung the chair around so that the back of it was nearest the table and sat astride it, placed his beer on the table and leaned forward leaning on the back of the chair with crossed arms. "So fellas, what counts as a good night out in Dryton?"

All three of the men laughed and surprisingly it was Dave who replied, saying "This is it mate, about as good and raucous as it gets."

That is how the rest of the afternoon and evening progressed, the beers flowed, interspersed with bags of crisps and peanuts (Grant needed something to soak up the alcohol), the conversation became more fluid and free and Grant occasionally excused himself from his present company to join Shamrock and the 'bowling buddies' as well as the, perhaps too frequent, visit to the gents, each one that would include another forced vomiting session and on one occasion the ingestion of a small tablet.

Grant had obtained a small amount of these tablets in a club in London one evening a few weeks earlier from a local small time drug dealer. Iomazenil was not available on the open market or by prescription as yet as it was still undergoing tests, but tests on rats and mice had shown results that it negated some of the effects of alcohol, largely reducing the possibility of becoming blind drunk and preventing a hangover the next morning. Grant knew that using an untested drug was a risky move but with his new 'needs must' approach to things he bought half a dozen of the pills without further question.

His moving around from table to table also allowed him to leave unfinished drinks on the table he vacated knowing that these fleecers would be happy to finish off his drink in his absence thinking that Grant wouldn't notice, a game that he was more than happy to play.

He allowed himself one moment of solace and self-company during the evening when he sat at the end of the bar and enjoyed a bar snack of a cheeseburger and chips. He ate it slowly for two reasons, firstly to allow the food to more effectively soak up some of the alcohol he had consumed and to spend a while actually not drinking as he observed the goings on and listened in to the conversations. A few people entered the bar, had a drink and then left again but largely the population of the bar that evening didn't change at all.

He learned that Milton Dryton was effectively a dead market town, a victim of a lack of investment and a steady flow of its youth leaving the place as soon as they could to find accommodation and work elsewhere in the surrounding towns and cities.

A few teenagers were responsible for the graffiti and small-time crime in the area but Muttley seemed to be on top of most of this, probably more capable of dealing with troublesome kids than he was at actually managing real crime and real criminals. *A lazy copper's way of enhancing his reputation with the locals by dealing with the problems that they probably complained about, on a daily basis*, thought Grant.

As the evening progressed Grant found himself enjoying the beer less and less - a side effect of the Iomazenil he recalled, the actual purpose of the drug according to scientists who were looking for a drug to help alcoholics. Increasingly each mouthful of beer became more tasteless and unenjoyable but most importantly he wasn't feeling as drunk as he should be by now. A slight fuzziness of the head reminded him to slow down which, he thought, was a better option to taking another tablet.

By now Shamrock was leaning on the bar, swaying occasionally and on two occasions actually laying his head on the bar. His brief conversations with Emma became more lewd with each sentence and so, not needing this intoxicated fake Irish fool kicked out of the pub right now, Grant slid around the bar and once again sat next to him.

"How's it going Shammers, my old mate?"

Shamrock looked up in his direction, his eyes trying to focus on Grant's face "Ha-ha, it's the fucking biker boy, where'd ya go you little fucker? Been sat her alone, being turned down by Ems and having to drink the pints I've been buying for ya."

"Just been getting to know the locals," replied Grant.

"Yeah, yeah been seeing that," said Shamrock, his head rocking and nodding forward as the huge amount of beer took effect. "Ask a lot of fucking questions don't ya biker boy?"

Grant noticed a more aggressive tone in Shamrock's question; this is something he didn't need, a drunk paddy starting a fight.

"Hey old fella, I'm just being friendly, getting to know folk, being sociable. Surely a good Irish fella like yourself would understand that?"

Shamrock looked at Grant, studying him as best he could and suddenly he smiled, winked and threw his arms around Grant's neck, embracing him with a tight and overpowering beer-stenched hug. "Just pullin' ya leg lad, that's all, thought ya'd gone off old Shamrock I had to b'sure"

Grant slowly leaned himself forward directing Shamrock back onto his stool and eased out of the 'man hug'.

"Ya daft old fool, how could I find anyone that was such good company as yerself?" and waving his arm in Ems direction he called, "Ems my darling another pint of the black stuff for Shamrock please,"

Shamrock tapped his knuckles twice on the bar saying "a dram too, don't forget the dram."

Sure thing thought Grant.

"And a double whiskey too Ems, that single malt that hasn't seen the light of day all evening would be nicer than that cheap shit you've been serving."

Emma looked over at Grant, "one for you too?" she asked.

"No I'm good thanks," nodding in the direction of the nearly empty pint glass sat next to the empty plate he had earlier left further down the bar.

"Are you sure he should have any more?" she said looking towards Shamrock.

Shamrock sat bolt upright and, pointing his finger in Emma's direction said, "jest pour the fucking drink young lady otherwise my friend here will get some of his biker mates to fuck up your bar," that aggressive tone returning to Shamrock quicker than a fox on a chicken.

Grant placed a calming hand on Shamrock's shoulder, "Hey old timer, no need for that tone, the girl is just watching out for you."

The old man's head was once again leaning onto the bar, he raised his right hand waving it feebly in the direction of Emma, "sorry girl, really sorry, Ya know what I'm like, can't control the Irish freedom fighter in me sometimes."

Emma shook her head and raised her eyes to the ceiling, looking at Grant she said, "This is his last, you understand?"

Grant nodded as Emma patted Shamrock on the head saying "It's alright Shamrock, I know you love me really."

Shamrock turned his head, which one again lay on the bar, towards Grant, and with a smile he said in a loudish whisper "Love her, I could fuck the holy b'Jesus out of her."

Walking away Emma laughed and said, "In your dreams Shamrock, in your dreams." *Yeah* thought Grant, *probably every night.*

He turned his attention back to Shamrock, "What was that comment about my biker mates all about Shamrock?"

The old man slowly lifted his head and Grant could almost hear the cogs in his head turning as he tried to remember what he had said. The light bulb suddenly flickered on inside Shamrock's head, "Ah yer know 'em. You lot are a brotherhood ain't ya. That biker crew that rides out of Whitechurch, bet ya know a few of 'em."

Grant shook his head, "You got me all wrong friend, I've no affiliation to any bike gang or MCC, I'm a lone wolf." That was the most truthful thing that Grant had said all day.

***

The 'bowling buddies' stood up as one and walked over the bar, kindly returning their glasses. "Goodnight Emma," each of them said.

Emma smiled at them, "Have a good evening and sleep well."

Grant always wondered why bar staff wished you a good evening as you left the bar late at night, surely you had just had a good evening and it was effectively almost over, *still, nothing wrong with good manners I suppose*, he thought to himself.

They all playfully slapped Shamrock on the back and said their goodbyes to Grant. "Nice to meet you fella, see you around town maybe," said Glen (it wasn't Glynn).

Grant simply nodded back and said, "Have a safe walk home."

The three or four other people who had increased the number of drinkers in the pub slowly drifted away one by one, most silently making their way out while one waved his goodbyes to nobody in particular.

At ten minutes past eleven Emma shouted out, "Come on gentleman let's be having you home, I have a cold empty bed to go to," and she rang the old brass bell that hung at the 'toilet end' of the bar.

Dave was the first of the trio to appear from around the corner of the bar, "I'll warm it up for you Ems."

"Go home Dave," she responded, "to your girlfriend and that little boy of yours."

Alan and Fergie quickly followed behind Dave, Alan with a quick "sweet dreams Emma" and "goodnight men" accompanied by a weak salute directed towards Shamrock and Grant.

Fergie left quietly but as Dave and Alan disappeared out of the door he stopped and turning back to face Grant he asked, "What do I say when Sgt Murphy asks about tonight?"

He once again studied this feeble weak excuse for a man still wondering how he managed to get into the police force, "Muttley always question you about your off-duty time does he?"

"Yeah, most days," said Fergie looking down at the floor to hide his obvious embarrassment.

"Hmmm, ok, I give you a choice Fergie," Grant replied, "you can either tell him the truth, that you went out with a couple of your mates, saw Shamrock and whoever else you knew in the bar tonight and that you saw me, had a quick chat and shared a few beers with me and all in all had a quiet but enjoyable night."

Pete Ferguson waited for the other option, an uncomfortable silence remained in place for a few seconds before he asked, "You said you would offer a choice so what else could I say?"

Grant picked up his nearly empty pint glass that Emma had earlier retrieved for him when she had cleared away his plate from the bar, the same nearly empty beer glass that had remained that way for the rest of the evening; he took the remaining mouthful and placed the empty glass on the bar with a hefty slam.

"You can tell the fat cunt to mind his own fucking business."

For the first time all evening Officer Ferguson handled a situation confidently, "I think I'll go with option one."

"Thought you would Fergie," replied Grant, "sleep well pal. I'll probably see you around tomorrow."

Grant and Shamrock watched as Pete Ferguson walked out of the bar into the cool evening air, once the door had closed behind him Shamrock roared with laughter, "Fuck me sideways with a hedgehog, you have a way with words there stranger."

In the background, stood behind the bar, Emma looked at Grant. *The new man in town has a bad side by the looks of things* she thought. "Murphy piss you off or something Grant?"

"Not at all Ems," he said once again with a smile on his face, "but he is fat and he should mind his own business."

Emma wasn't convinced but smiled back like the dutiful barmaid she was.

"Shamrock," said Grant holding out his hand to offer a handshake which Shamrock eagerly took hold of. "You have been great company, a teller of wondrous stories and the best drinking buddy I have encountered for many months. I bid you goodnight, my friend."

Shamrock let go of the handshake and for the second time that night hugged Grant. "You sure is a strange one Lone Wolf but you has given me an entertaining evening and for that I thank yea." He walked, well staggered and weaved his way to the front door holding up his hand and saying, "Goodnight Emma my sweet girl." He walked into the fresh air and the door slowly closed behind him.

"Well once again 'Lone Wolf' it looks like it's just you and me," said Emma.

Grant rubbed his eyes, he was tired, it had been a long exhausting day and he guessed that it would be followed by a restless night. He folded his arms on the bar and rested his chin on them, looking up at Emma.

"Ems, I am tired (the truth) and I have had too much beer (the truth again) and to be honest am just a little bit drunk (not the truth, the untested tablet seemed to be doing its job) but you do make a very flattered old man very happy." He took hold of her hand and kissed the back of it "but I am going to bed… and yes my bed before you ask."

He stood up and put in a fake stumble just for effect, "See I can hardly stand, trust me you will have more fun alone," he said with a cheeky wink.

He headed for the door that led to the guest bedrooms, "Goodnight Ems, you have been the perfect hostess."

"Perhaps another time eh?" Emma asked hopefully.

He turned his head, "Never say never Ems," and blew her a kiss. In his head, however, the thought was *never in a million years young lady*.

He made his way up the stairs towards his room, he pulled his wallet out and searched for the key card that would allow him access and then remembered the room key was in his pocket. How easy it was in this modern world to forget about old-fashioned things like keys, especially when you are tired and badly needed a good night's sleep. Something he hadn't experienced for months.

Entering his room, he made his way towards the bed and then remembering the locking system returned to the door and locked it from the inside, he didn't want any surprise visitors tonight. He once again made his way to the bed and fell face down onto it. The pillow felt soft against his cheek and he hugged it tightly to his face. He turned his face into the pillow and pressed it even tighter against himself. It became harder to breathe, the air felt thick as his body struggled to suck it in and so he held his breath. No idea how long this process went on for he suddenly let go of the pillow and sucked in the cold air of the room, *it was impossible to suffocate yourself*, he thought.

He lay on his back, resting the back of his head this time onto the pillow and stared at the ceiling. Death would give him the rest he so badly desired, but for now, he couldn't allow it to happen. Shit had to be done and he had a feeling it was going to be shitty.

He closed his eyes and his mind drifted away momentarily from death and shitty tasks, he allowed himself to think about his wife and daughter. How he missed them both, he missed them so much he felt actual pain. Still, he thought, he would see them again soon.

Sitting up he reached for his leather jacket, on the inside, the secret sewed pocket where his mobile was also contained his medication, prescribed medication this time. He pulled a strip of Zopiclone and popped one out of its foil casing, putting it into his mouth he swallowed it dry. He thought about popping a second one but then resisted - what was the point in wasting them? - he knew from experience that a second never made a difference to his sleep pattern. Placing the strip back into the hidden pocket he threw the jacket onto the floor and undressed. He caught his reflection in the dirty three quarter length mirror that was attached to the wardrobe door and turned to look at himself.

Forty-nine, tired and gaunt-looking, a bit of a shelf developing over the toy shop he thought as he looked at his midriff. *Not in the best of shape* he mentally told himself but the thought of putting all his effort into transforming that one pack into a six pack made him feel even more exhausted. He would save his efforts for other matters and he knew for that what he lacked in physique and strength would be more than made up for with adrenalin and pure hate.

He climbed into the bed and pulled the quilt over his naked body, reaching over to switch off the bedside lamp he paused and listened as he picked up a noise outside his door. He heard a bedroom door open and then close, the person didn't lock it as far as he could make out, just Emma going to bed he thought. Leaving her door unlocked, forever hopeful. For a split second, he thought about making her wishes come true but it was just a momentary weakness, he switched the lamp off and was plunged into darkness, the heavy curtains doing the job they were designed for, considering their age they were probably in use during the blackouts in the 1940s.

Painful Memories

He awoke in the usual cold sweat, his body covered in a fine mist of perspiration. He looked at his watch, something he never removed these days, the face glowing bright blue in the darkness. 02.10 a.m., he had done well, the mixture of Zopiclone and beer had obviously had some effect on him.

He spun to a sitting position, clawing the old carpet with his toes, his effort to re-engage with reality. Every night the same nightmare, the same memories, the same inability to do anything to change the result. He stood and made his way to the sink, turning the squeaky tap he looked at his reflection in the scratched mirror.

He had always been told that he looked young for his age, many mistaking him as being in his late thirties or early forties as opposed to the truth: that he was in his late forties and rapidly approaching fifty. His reflection told him that this morning he looked much older. He splashed his face with cold refreshing water.

His mind remained on the mental images of his recurring nightmare. Screams, neon ceiling lights, sad pitying faces, questions, accusations, and suspicion. As if it ever could have been him. Time wasted and the repeated boring response of "we are doing our best, sir."

He sat back down on the bed and thought about trying to get some more sleep but deep down knew that it would be a pointless exercise so began to get dressed. Black was the order of the day.

After slipping into his black jeans he smiled as he selected a t-shirt, Black Star Riders was emblazoned on the front of it. He remembered the night he had purchased it at the album launch party. At the end of the gig he had wanted to hang around to meet the band and maybe get an autograph or two but his wife's knee was playing up again and she needed some fresh air. Despite her protests and insistence that she would be alright and would sit in the car to wait for him he went with her and they drove home, that is what loving husbands did. He smiled but it quickly disappeared because even the happy memories brought with them some amount of pain.

Pulling on his boots he stood up and located his bike jacket that was on the floor where he had thrown it, putting it on he zipped it all the way up. His helmet was sitting in the top box of his bike and so were his gloves unfortunately they could have been of some use.

He had contemplated leaving through his hotel room door but the thought of the forever randy young girl in the nearby room brought him to his senses, the slightest creak of a floorboard would bring her onto the landing probably wearing nothing but a thong and an alluring smile. He would stick to his original plan and leave via the window.

He had opened the window slightly before going to sleep and was now very glad that he had, as the noise it had made would have sounded a hundred times louder in the silence of the early morning. He pushed it open, slowly, as wide as it would go, the slightest of creaks occurred during this process but nothing to worry him. Looking out of the window he knew that he could make the drop with ease, the most difficult bit would be getting out of the fairly narrow window and twisting his body around to be able to hang from the window ledge, from there he estimated it at about a five foot drop from his dangling feet to the ground below.

Negotiating himself into the desired dangling position he was glad that he had made the choice of thick jeans and the leather jacket as he firstly scraped his upper arm against the old wooden window frame and then scraped his knee against the brick wall as he allowed his body to drop. His body weight was now being held only by his fingers that painfully grabbed hold of the window ledge; this is the point when the bike gloves would have been useful.

Allowing very little time to think he let go and fell, his feet making contact with the courtyard floor very quickly, bending his knees as he landed he rolled over onto his left shoulder and deftly onto one knee. He remained still and looked up towards the bedroom windows waiting for about a minute in that position, no lights came on.

He walked past his bike towards the locked gates of the courtyard, stepping onto a discarded metal beer barrel he easily reached the top of the fence and hauled his body upwards and over the other side landing on the pavement on the other side and immediately looking to his left and then right. The street was silent, empty and quite badly lit, *perfect* he thought.

Unlocking the padlock that he had placed there just a few hours earlier he swung open one gate slowly and carefully, it began to squeak and he immediately stopped. A gap just wide enough for him to get through had been created and that is all he needed at this moment. Making his way back into the courtyard he made his way to the rear of his bike and opened the top box, removing from it the spray can of WD40. A few sprays of this wonder liquid later and a quick movement of the partially opened gate resulted in a silent movement of its hinges.

Leaving the gate open wide enough to get his bike through he returned the WD40 to the top box and lifted out the black helmet placing it on his head, leaving the visor in the open position. He closed and locked the top box and then placed the key into the bikes ignition leaving it, for the moment, in the 'off' position. Lifting the bike off its side stand he pushed it slowly through the open gate and onto the street. The bike was heavy, he knew this bit was going to be hard work. Closing and locking the gate behind him he carefully placed the padlock key into the small front pocket of his jacket and returned to his bike. He looked at the hill in front of him, not overly steep but still a steady incline for about 200 yards, he just hoped for a downwards slope on the other side.

After only about 100 yards Grant began to really feel the weight of his bike remembering the words of the salesman who had sold it to him, "don't run out of petrol on this bugger mate, you wouldn't want to push it more than 50 yards."

Constantly looking around him looking out for any evidence that he was being noticed he made slow progress up the hill eventually reaching the top where it levelled out for a short distance before transforming into a long downward gentle gradient. *Thank fuck for that* he thought resting the bike back onto its side stand to allow him a short breather, he looked at his watch; 02.56, not the time to hang about.

He sat astride the bike and flicked up the side stand with the heel of his left boot, the metallic clang it made as it hit its upright position made him clench his eyes shut like it had proved to be a painful experience. He once again looked around waiting for a bedroom light to turn on or a tired face to appear at one of the many windows around him. Nothing. He mentally slapped himself for being such an idiot and then pushing with both feet he moved the bike forward until it began to freewheel down the hill, placing his feet onto the foot pegs he steered the bike off the pavement and onto the road. His right hand hovered over the front brake which he immediately moved so as to grip the handle, the last thing he wanted know was a squeaky brake kicking into action.

The bike coasted down the hill silently but Grant still enjoyed the feeling he got from being on it, this was the one joy left in his life. Reaching the bottom of the slope he allowed the bike to coast as far as possible along the now level road until it came to a natural stop and he placed both feet back onto the ground. Leaning forward he reached for the ignition key and turned it forward into the 'on' position. His right hand returned to the hand grip and his thumb hovered over the electric start switch. This was the bit of his plan that he could not control, the 1300 Midnight Star was not designed for a silent journey.

The engine fired up, it was loud as he expected and it began to stutter. It had been a cold night so the engine was cold and needed a bit of help from the choke but Grant refused to pull out the choke knowing that the noise of the engine would only increase. He rotated the throttle a tiny amount just to maintain the engine ticking over and then engaged first gear. He released the clutch slowly and the bike began to move forward, not increasing the throttle at all and by using clutch control alone he managed to move the bike slowly but more importantly relatively quietly. Approaching a large roundabout he took the third exit heading right, no indicators used, no headlights on, not for a few more minutes. As he began to clear the last few buildings of the outer limits of Milton Dryton he increased the throttle and switched on his headlamp following the gentle winding road to his destination. The small chrome clock in the middle of his handlebars told him that it was approximately 03.25 a.m., he had to make up some time so opened up the throttle moving the gears up to fifth, the speedometer indicating a steady sixty-five miles per hour.

About six miles later Grant began to slow down as he approached Blackbrook Woods, a large wooded area, very thick and almost impenetrable in places.

Leaving the road he rode the bike onto a narrow rabbit track and through the grassland towards the wooded area. Within a few seconds, both he and the bike had disappeared from sight as he rode into the woods and brought the bike to a stop in a small area of ground covered in dry bracken and surrounded by large bushes and foliage that formed a horseshoe shape around it. He switched off the bikes ignition and was plunged into absolute silence and darkness.

Taking a few minutes he allowed his eyes to become accustomed to the darkness and then slowly made his way deeper into the woods following a path he knew well. Ten minutes later after slowly covering a distance of no more than roughly eight hundred metres he lowered himself down onto one knee behind a small tree and peered beyond it looking towards a small circular opening in the dense woodland. A small wooden derelict building stood in the middle of this clearing, it was easily more than one hundred and fifty years old, windows long gone, the roof still pretty much intact barring a few holes where slate tiles had slid away. A makeshift door stood in the centre of the front wall that was almost directly facing towards Grant. He looked around the area trying to spot any evidence of people having been here over the last three months but saw nothing obvious. He stood and entered the clearance, walking towards the makeshift door, he knew it was not the original door because he had built and placed it there during his first visit to this place. He had made a few other improvements during that visit too but they were all on the inside of the building.

He stood still immediately in front of 'his' door and checked for signs that it had been moved. Looking up towards the top right-hand corner he noted that the small strip of green electrical tape he had placed over the rotting wooden frame and the edge of the door remained undisturbed and undamaged. Anyone entering this building would have had to enter through this doorway and by doing so would have moved or ripped this small strip of tape, he knew this because he had boarded up all of the windows during the same visit to the door placing.

Opening the door, (he hadn't placed a lock on it as he thought it would just raise suspicion to any inquisitive passer-by) the dim light from outside created a cutting line of illumination inside the dark interior. The first thing that Grant noticed was the smell. The pungent stink of decomposing flesh hit his senses like a brick. He raised his hand to cover his mouth and nose, instinctively turning away from the odour. He knew that he should have expected this but everything on this journey was a new experience. He turned to face the room and walked inside, pulling the door closed behind him and plunging the room back into darkness, not total darkness thanks to the small amount of light that managed to creep through the wooden boards covering the windows, just enough to allow a glimpse of the boot covered foot sticking out from underneath the tarpaulin sheet. The rest of the body remained covered just as he had left it all those months ago, still in a sitting position in the chair it was secured to.

Trying hard to ignore the body which was difficult as the pungent smell was now even stronger, Grant made his way to the far wall where a large wooden bench stood, from the small front pocket of his jeans he removed a key and placed it into the small lock in the left hand drawer of the bench. The key turned with some effort inside the old lock but eventually clicked allowing Grant to slide the drawer open.

He stared at the two photographs that sat in the drawer, he wondered why he never cried when he looked at these pictures, *any ordinary man would cry* he thought. But he was no longer an ordinary man, he was now a killer, a man who was willing (and able as he discovered) to torture another human being, albeit torture of a very basic and crude type. He diverted his eyes away from the photos and looked at the items that sat around them, ordinary everyday tools in the hands of most men but instruments of pain given the right incentive and just a little bit of warped thought.

He must wash off that hammer, he thought, looking at the caked layer of blood covering both blunt ends of it and then looking at the bag of six-inch nails wished he had purchased some more when he had visited the hardware store the day before. The broken saw was a reminder that he should buy more robust tools, ones that were up to the tasks. He closed the drawer shut, maybe he wouldn't need such crude tools of the trade if his 'delivery man' didn't let him down, he hadn't so far so there was no reason to think that he would now.

He sat on the dirty wooden chair that stood adjacent to the bench, one leg reattached by a length of strong string. *Not a bad repair job* he thought to himself as he sat and felt the chair creak but hold his weight easily. He waited and as always when he waited his mind filled with thoughts.

He had not spoken with Ian for well over 30 years when he found him on Facebook and contacted him. That first message and more importantly, the reply, confirmed

Grants initial thoughts, when you need a favour an ex-military friend is the one you should always turn to.

"Hi Ian, don't know if you remember after all these years?"

"Hello mate, Christ it's been fucking yonks, how are you?"

"Not too good mate to be honest, I need a favour"

"Anything pal, what do you need?"

"Face-to-face if you don't mind Ian?"

"Even better, we can have a beer at the same time."

Grant knew that Ian was a handy man with his hands, an ex-Royal Engineer who could build almost anything; he also knew that he hadn't always stayed on the right side of the law since leaving the military. The perfect friend for the current situation.

He met Ian at a pub in a town roughly halfway between where they both lived. The first half hour was spent man hugging and back slapping each and remembering the two years they had spent together in military training. After finishing their first pint and ordering the second Grant looked seriously at Ian.

"Listen mate, what I am about to ask you is serious stuff so if you want no part of it just say so but I need your assurance that you will tell nobody about what I am about to tell you."

"Assurances given pal, and when you say serious you mean illegal?" replied Ian with a smile.

"No pal, I mean a life sentence with no chance of parole."

Ian had looked down at the floor of the pub and then, still smiling, looked Grant straight in the eyes and said,

"Where's the fucking street cred in fucking parole?"

Sat at a corner table in what was thankfully an almost empty pub Grant, for the first time since it had happened, *explained everything to his old military pal. For almost 15 minutes, in a hushed voice, he left out no detail of what had happened and what he planned to do about it. Throughout the whole story Ian remained silent, his face was emotionless as he listened. Grant finished speaking and leaned back into his chair.*

Ian leaned forward placing his chin onto both of his clenched hands, his elbows resting on the table. He once again smiled, slightly, and said, "How many of these cunts are you going to kill mate?"

"I want them to suffer," replied Grant.

"Yeah granted mate but they still gotta fucking die, not that I am doing any killing for you, I ain't got the guts for that."

"I would not ask you to do that mate but I do need some stuff building. I have pictures and drawings of what I need and I will pay for everything with a little bit on top for your troubles."

Ian laughed and then in a low voice said, "Forget the bit on top mate, just buy me a few beers. I love building shit, got me an old shack, shed, barn thing in a wood up in the midlands area where I go occasionally. Don't disturb people with my noise that way."

Grant looked at Ian, "Is it really off the beaten track, this shed of yours?"

"Been there dozens of times mate, never seen a living soul, not even a fucking rabbit. Which is a pity cuz I have a shotgun hidden under the floorboards, always wanted to do a bit of hunting but not had the opportunity yet."

"Don't suppose you have a van do you?" asked Grant.

"Sure do pal, what am I moving... the stuff I build for you or bodies?"

They both laughed, a couple of drinkers looked round at them at this point but all they saw was a pair of drinking friends having what appeared to be a good laugh.

"Probably both," whispered Grant.

Back in the derelict barn that Ian used as a workshop Grant was returned to reality by the ringing of his mobile.

"Hello," he said as he accepted the call.

"Ya'lright early bird," replied Ian, "am I shifting it or burying it?"

"Both if you don't mind mate?" asked Grant, "I hope you haven't had a big breakfast, it is slightly on the side of stinking."

"Did it sing before flying away?" asked Ian.

Grant thought about how to reply before saying, "Only a couple of verses, but enough to begin writing the next chapter."

"Well hopefully what I have for you will be more effective than a hammer and a few nails mate."

"I won't be here when you arrive, hope that's ok?" replied Grant.

"No worries brother, leave the meat, I will collect and dispose of it. Oh, I will leave the new toy where we agreed. Speak soon kemosabe," said Ian laughing heartily.

Grant ended the call, locked his phone and placed it back in his pocket.

This crazy fucker is enjoying this just a little bit too much Grant thought to himself.

As Grant walked towards the door to leave the shack his foot brushed against the boot belonging to, who Ian described as, it. He looked down at it, a black old style motorcycle boot, short on the ankle the metal ringed style buckle broken. Grant's mind flashed back…

One a Year sat in the wooden chair his wrists taped behind his back and ankles likewise to the front legs of the chair. More tape had also been wrapped around his upper legs and around the underside of the seat of the chair, securing him extremely well. He was gagged with an orange in his mouth and more tape ensuring there was no way he could remove it. He looked around the dark dirty room he now found himself. A small trickle of dried blood on his forehead led from the small fresh looking wound at the top left side of his temple. The last thing he could remember was bringing his bike to a stop down the side alley that ran alongside the high wall which enclosed the clubhouse.

He had removed his helmet while still sat astride his beloved Harley-Davidson ride and then… blackness briefly preceded by blinding pain.

In his unconscious state, he was oblivious to being dragged by his ankles towards a van and unceremoniously dumped into the back of it. His attacker decided to use the orange and tape around his mouth and head at this stage. *Don't want the filthy fucker screaming* his attacker had thought.

The last thing this individual did before jumping into the driver's seat of the van and driving calmly away was to kick One a Year's beloved bike, toppling it onto its side. Chrome and paint crunched against the rough brick alley surface. The biker would probably have been happy to have been knocked out before this indignity was performed. As the van drove quietly away the driver looked over his shoulder into the open rear of the vehicle, "I can see where you get your name from, you fucking smell worse than a shit covered skunk you filthy scum cunt" he said laughing loudly.

The biker looked around the room, his head still stinging from the blow received about an hour or so earlier.

He tried to focus his eyes which was difficult because of the darkness of the room.

From the corner of the room, in front and left of him, a voice said, "Hello."

One a Year looked in the direction from where the voice had come but could not see anyone there, he tried to speak but the fruity mouth gag did its job, nothing but a garbled collection of grunts came out of his mouth.

"Don't worry, your time to speak will come soon," the faceless voice said, it was monotone and devoid of emotion. "I hope you've had your yearly bath," said the voice referring to why the biker had been given this unusual road name, "because unless we get on it may be the last you ever have."

The biker's eyes were focussed intently on the corner of the building from where the voice spoke and suddenly he thought he saw some movement in the dark corner. Grant stood up from the crouched position he had adopted for the last thirty minutes and slowly walked towards the immobile biker.

He walked into the middle of the room and stood in front of One a Year.

"Do you recognise me?" he asked.

The biker shook his head to indicate no and tried to scream some obscenity at Grant but the orange remained steadfast in its desire to ensure the biker could not be understood. Grant pulled a small knife from his jeans pocket and the biker suddenly went quiet. He hooked the small point of the blade under the tape that was holding the orange in place and with a quick flick of his wrist cut through the tape. With his other hand, he grabbed the tape covered orange and ripped it all from the bikers mouth and face. Spittle sprayed from the biker's mouth as he began to scream in the direction of Grant.

"I have no idea who you fucking are pal but you are dead, I mean D... E... A... fucking... Dead, you have no idea who the fuck you are messing..."

One a Year's threats transformed into a scream of pain as, without any warning, Grant stuck the blade of the small knife into the biker's left thigh. The short three-inch blade embedded itself, through the denim jeans, into the meaty flesh of the leg stopping only when the knife's handle touched the fabric of the clothing.

"Ssshhhh," whispered Grant looking directly into the bikers eyes.

One a Year went to speak but only released another agonising scream of pain as Grant moved the handle of the knife from left to right making the blade cut through internal flesh. Once again Grant advised the biker to remain silent, "Shhh now, it's still not your time to talk. I want you to listen and before you are tempted to open your putrid mouth again remember this: you only need one ear to listen to me which means you have a spare which I am more than willing to separate from your ugly shitfuck of a head. Do we understand each other?"

The biker nodded indicating that he fully understood.

"Good, now just listen and reply to any question I ask you," said Grant. "Now, about a year ago you and at least two of your biker mates burgled a house and during that burglary you came across two occupants. Do you remember that night?"

"I didn't do fuck all, it was the other two," protested One a Year.

Grant shook his head as if disappointed, leaving the knife embedded in the biker's thigh he walked towards a drawer unit against the wall to his left and opening one of the draws removed a large hammer and a bag containing a number of six-inch nails. Carrying these items he made his way back to stand in front of his still defiant interviewee.

"What the fuck?" started the biker before being punched squarely in the nose by Grant using the hand that held the bag of nails.

"Shut the fuck up moron, you seem to have a problem understanding simple instructions so I am going to help you."

As he spoke he placed the bag of nails on the floor and removed one from the bag.

"Many years ago a teacher of mine had a unique way of instilling new knowledge into his pupils, if it appeared we didn't understand he fucking hit us."

Grant knelt down onto one knee in front of One a Year and held the point of the nail against the biker's thigh that didn't have a knife sticking out of it.

"Please, please fucking don't," pleaded the helpless biker.

Grant looked up at him, "This is going to fucking hurt," and at that point he brought the head of the hammer down onto the head of the nail. The nail slipped into the flesh with ease burying about 2 inches of itself into the fleshy leg as the biker screamed as though hell itself had just ripped through his soul. Grant held his free hand slightly over the mouth of the biker silencing the sound of the screams slightly.

As the screams turned into a pathetic sob he released his grip around the biker's mouth and asked, "Do you now understand the instructions?"

The biker, whose head had dropped forward said nothing.

Selecting another nail from the bag Grant said, "Clearly not," but before he could hammer another nail into flesh One a Year called out:

"Please no, I fucking understand ok. You ask I answer."

"Yes," responded Grant, "you answer the question that I ask, not the question you think I am asking. Looks like my teacher was right, who'd have fucking thought it. I just thought he liked hurting helpless victims." Grant had a wry smile on his face.

Once again standing in front of the pain-ravaged biker Grant placed the hammer and bag of nails on the floor in front of himself. Looking at the sorrowful man in front of him he felt no pity, in fact, he felt nothing but pure hatred.

"Right do I need to repeat my last question?" asked Grant.

The pitiful One a Year shook his head, "No, I remember the night you are referring to."

"That's good, this could be over very quickly if you continue that way."

The biker looked at him with fear in his eyes, "Please," he quietly said, "please can I ask a question?"

"As you have answered mine, on this one occasion I will let you ask a question," replied Grant.

"Are you going to kill me?" asked the biker, his voice now quivering.

Dropping to a squatting position Grant looked directly at the pathetic figure in front of him and said, "You answer my questions and don't tell any lies, you will walk or maybe limp away from here."

Grant continued with his questioning of One a Year.

Did you touch the occupants of the house?"

"No"

"Why did you just watch, why didn't you stop them?"

"There was two of 'em and they would have killed me."

"Did you join in with pissing on them?"

"No, I said I just stood and watched."

"Was it fun for you, did it turn you on?"

"No, I was disgusted honest but I'm just a prospect."

Grant picked up the hammer, "Don't fucking lie to me you little cunt!" he screamed at the biker, showing the first sign of any emotion since One a Year had regained consciousness. Grant dropped the hammer back to the floor.

"Are you HA?"

"No, we're just a nobody bike club."

"Who else knows what happened that night?"

"Just the club members who were there."

"What are the names of the others?"

"I can't tell you that, they will kill me."

Grant walked behind the stricken biker who turned his head to follow Grants movements but was met with a backhanded slap to the side of his head. "Don't look at me you fucking oxygen thief," snarled Grant and then grabbing a handful of greasy hair he pulled the biker's head back and looked down at him.

"Tell me their fucking names."

"I can't, I fucking can't please, believe me, they will do me over big style" pleaded the pathetic One a Year. "I've answered your questions; let me go like you said you would."

Once again in that monotone emotionless chilling voice, Grant simply said, "You can't answer a question by saying you can't give me the answer. That is not complying with the rules and instructions and we both know what is now going to happen."

Grant walked back to where the hammer sat on the floor, picking it up he slowly walked back towards the terrified MC prospect.

"Please," pleaded the biker, "please, look there was one other there, fuck him he's a fucking loser anyway, his name is Lump but I can't tell you the name of the other."

Standing now a foot or so in front of One a Year Grant looked at him and raised the hammer. "This will only hurt until you die," he hissed.

Horrified One a Year screamed like a baby, "You said you wouldn't kill me!"

"I lied you motherfucker," said Grant calmly as he brought the hammer down in an arc straight into the head of the biker who, just before impact happened, opened his bladder and pissed himself.

Grant opened his eyes and tried to push the graphic images of what followed next to the back of his mind. He bent over and covered the biker's foot with the tarpaulin. He just hoped that Ian had a strong stomach for what the rest of that tarpaulin sheet was hiding.

A Good Friend Will Help You Move a Body

Leaving the old wooden shack (and the memories) behind Grant made his way back through the wood to his bike. It was time to get away from this place and continue with his 'ordinary and mundane' pretence of a life he had started in Milton Dryton, also he didn't want to be here when Ian arrived. As he walked quietly and observantly through the wood he reflected on his decision to involve this old friend in his venture.

He had only known Ian for about two years, their time spent together during Army training. In the whole scheme of life, it wasn't a great deal of time to have known someone but Army training back in the early 1980s tended to bond young men together into a tight team who had each other's backs. Not like today where apparently you can report your trainers for bullying or show them a red card as a warning that their behaviour or language was offending you! No, back in the '80s, military training was a whole different ball game.

Grant and Ian had met almost immediately as after getting off different trains they both boarded the awaiting military coach, waiting for them directly outside of the train station, at the same time. A large staff sergeant carrying a highly polished pace stick under his arm politely, but firmly, directed each new arrival onto the coach. "Leave your suitcases at the side of the bus gentlemen and board the bus quietly and quickly, lots to do and not enough hours in the day to do it," he would repeat as each new lost looking young sixteen year old lad arrived.

Ian dumped his battered suitcase as instructed and stepped up onto the coach giving the young military driver a cheeky wink, saying, "Deliver my bags to my room when we arrive at the summer club, my good man."

The driver gave them a hint of what the next two years were going to be like when, not even turning his head to look at Ian he replied, "Fuck off you little prick and sit down before I kick your tiny little bollocks into orbit."

Grant, who was directly behind Ian and heard all of this, smiled and quietly laughed to himself. The driver didn't miss a thing. "What's your problem laughing boy? Your job will be to find his fucking bollocks and bring them back, juggling the little marbles all the fucking way, now sit the fuck down."

The next two years comprised mainly of running and shouting. Running to the guardroom, running to the mess, running to lessons, running to, during and from PE sessions, quick marching around the parade square (quick marching was just a walk transformed into a smart run) and of course the shouting. Everyone shouted at the training depot, trainers, junior NCO's, the Squadron Sergeant Major, the Regimental Sergeant Major and especially the Drill Sergeant, and they all seemed to hate Ian and Grant with a passion. Running and shouting was interspersed with mild torture and humiliation, normally handed out by the junior NCO's who were in training themselves but were mainly in their second year of training and had been specially selected for their skills in bullying and being twats.

Young recruits were selected to endure such acts as being dragged around the corridors and up and down the stairwells of the accommodation block in a thick army mattress cover or using said mattress cover being hung out of the third-floor window, the mattress cover simply being hooked over the windows' long locking arm. Many a young recruit's life was saved by the fantastic craftsmanship of the people who made those metal locking arms. Cleaning floors and toilets with your toothbrush was another humiliating pastime enjoyed by the bullying mentors whose job it was to guide them smoothly through their early training weeks and months, the humiliating climax being made to clean your teeth with the same toothbrush you have just been polishing toilets with for the past two hours.

Throughout all of this, and more, Grant and Ian had each other's back. They became good mates who both on and off duty would be there to watch out for the other one.

After two years they went their separate ways, Grant posted to Northern Ireland and Ian went off to discover the pleasures of alcohol and sunshine in Cyprus. They joined up later when Ian arrived in Northern Ireland and they worked together for a short period of time but until that fateful phone call many years later neither had spoken to each other nor had their paths crossed again for well over twenty years or more.

Grant had learned however, one vital thing about Ian during those training days, he was not scared of trouble, in fact, he loved it.

Over the next nine years, Grant learned something else about military men: they could, invariably, be trusted. There was an old saying that used to be bandied around – a mate will help you move house, an army mate will help you move a body – so when Grant knew that he was in a situation that would probably involve trouble and moving a body he knew there was only one bloke he could possibly ask, his old army buddy Private Ian Churchill.

Grant approached the horseshoe-shaped protective barrier of bushes which hid his bike from any passing glances. Helmet and gloves donned he started up the bike and gently guided into back towards the road, it was much lighter now and he wanted to make haste to get back to the pub before too many people began the chore of waking up to a new day. The purpose of this journey, to ensure that the results of his previous visit to the barn had not been discovered by anyone, had been achieved. He now needed to return, preferably undiscovered, and wait for his next delivery.

The journey back went without a hitch and he arrived at the back gates of the pub with nobody in sight. As the last stage of the road leading to the pub was downhill he was able to switch off the engine and coast down to the gates in silence. Still wary, he kept a keen eye out for twitching curtains or any other sign that he had been seen.

Taking the lock off the gates and opening just one of them he pushed his bike into the back yard positioning it, as best he could, as it was before he left earlier that morning. Returning to outside the gates he closed them and clamped the padlock shut, checking that he still had the key in his jacket pocket before doing so, he then had a quick look around to ensure the coast was clear before climbing over the gates back into the yard area. Climbing back up to his hotel room's open window was not as easy as the morning dew made the plastic drainpipe slippery and it was the third attempt before he managed to successfully climb up and slip back into the room without being detected.

He checked his watch, 06.05, almost four hours since he had left, longer than he had expected to be. He walked to his room door and placed his against the cool wood, he heard only silence. As quietly as he possibly could he slowly opened the door just enough to see down the corridor, nothing. Nobody had arisen yet. He thought of the young bar girl who was probably lying asleep in her bed in the room just a feet away, he just had to hope that she hadn't tried to pay him an early morning visit. Another brief thought entered his head, one that involved him knocking on her door knowing that she wouldn't turn him away. He was full of nervous energy and the adrenaline from his early morning activity was still surging through his body. A good shag would probably do him good right now but he had always treated women with respect and using young Emma as a spunk sponge didn't sit well with him, he closed his bedroom door.

He returned to his bed and sat down. It was pointless getting back into bed he knew wouldn't sleep so he undressed to have a shower.

The water took an age to get hot but eventually it was at the temperature he liked, hot enough to heat up his skin and turn it red. Steam filled the small bathroom as he stepped under the flowing water and let it wash away the stress of the past four hours, thoughts again filled his head. The swinging of the hammer, the thud as it connected with flesh and then bone, One a Year's head denting and splitting, chunks of bone and lumps of brain mixed with splashes of blood. The biker falling to the floor still taped to the chair, now unconscious possibly dead already. The rage and anger ripped through Grant's body and mind like a tornado tearing through buildings. Aiming at the lifeless body now, reigning down hammer blow after hammer blow hearing bones crack. Dropping the hammer to the floor and continuing to punish this putrid body with kicks, blood splattering all over Grant and the tarpaulin that he had laid on the floor beneath the chair. Kick after kick until he was spent and fell to the floor in a crumpled half sitting half laying down position.

He began to cry and reached for the bottle of complimentary shower gel that sat on the edge of the bath. He leaned his forehead against the cold tiled wall and continued to cry. "I'm sorry," he whispered, "I'm so so sorry, but this cannot go unpunished. I need justice. I know that you both know that."

He squeezed a large amount of the shower gel into one hand and began to cleanse himself, rough at first his hands and short nails rubbing violently against his own skin and then soft, almost caressing his chest and abdomen. His hands lowered to begin cleaning his groin area and once again, to himself, he whispered, "I miss your touch darling, I miss you, I want you back," and once again the tears flowed.

Leaving the bathroom Grant grabbed a towel and commenced drying himself off, he felt spent and sat on the bed the towel over his lap. He used a corner tip of it to dry his face, of both cleansing water and salty tears. He hated himself for this expelling of weakness but recognised and appreciated the anger and rage it recharged within him, it was these emotions he needed to complete the job ahead of him.

A light tapping on the door released him from his self-loathing thoughts.

"Yes," he said rather shortly.

"You ok?" asked the familiar voice of Emma.

"Morning Emma, yes thank you I am fine," he replied.

"Thought I heard crying," the young barmaid responded.

Bloody hell thought Grant, *this bitch misses nothing.*

"Sorry, just stubbed my toe on the bathroom door, really hurt, must have been my muffled cries of pain you heard," lied Grant.

"Oh ok, want me to rub it better?" asked the cheeky and rampantly horny young girl.

"It's all good Emma," replied Grant laughing, "be a good girl and go and fire up those ovens, I am starving and could destroy a full English."

"No problem, see you soon," and with that Emma walked back to her room. Standing totally naked outside Grant's door had got her juices flowing and her mind racing like a Formula One car. "You could destroy me anytime you wanted," she said very quietly as she entered her room and closed the door behind her.

Grant shook his head in disbelief as he finished off the drying process. *Maybe I should just fuck the girl and get her off my back?* he thought to himself. *Yep, bend the bitch over, pump her for thirty seconds, empty my load and wipe my dick on the curtains before walking out of her room; that should make her lose interest.*

He began to get dressed, a large smile on his face formed from the thought that had just popped into his head. Pulling on his jeans and pulling up the zipper he said, "no better not, wouldn't want to spoil her for every other man on the planet," and laughing like he hadn't laughed for many months he searched his room for his boots.

Fully dressed he turned to the bedside table to retrieve his phone, the screen showed him a message:

Churchill Logistics

Missed Call

His phone had been on silent for obvious reasons, although he invariably had his mobile in this state, a habit that had always infuriated his wife. The call must have come when he had been in the shower. He wondered why

Ian had called him. He activated his phone and checked his texts:

You have 1 voicemail

He accessed his phone pad and pressed 121 raising the phone to his hear. A robotic female voice informed him that he had one new message, he pressed 1 to listen as instructed and Ian's voice spoke to him.

'Your logistics company here sir, delivery of the new tool has been completed but the rest of your consignment could not be delivered. Please call us on the usual number or visit our office for a further explanation'.

These 'covert' messages had been Ian's idea, *too many James Bond movies* Grant had thought but he could see the sense behind them if it all went wrong it did offer a bit of cover for them both. *A bit*, thought Grant, *fucking flimsy at best*.

Tool delivered but the rest of your consignment could not be delivered…Grant listened to the message again, he understood the meaning behind the secretive wording but he couldn't understand why the complete delivery had failed.

He picked up his room key and walked out of his room, remembering to lock the door behind him. He didn't want his stalker popping in for a souvenir pair of his pants or anything. He made his way down the corridor and then the stairs, looking forward to getting some food consumed and then he would think about calling giving Ian a call.

Making his way into the bar, the stale smell of last night's ale hitting him hard, he sat at a table with his back to one of the windows looking out onto the street outside. He picked the table that gave him the best view of the door and the whole bar.

Emma's head and shoulders suddenly appeared through two small sliding doors at the back of the bar just to the left of the line of optics, he hadn't noticed this little serving hatch last night. "Full English," she asked in a jolly voice, "or are you one of those healthy types who wants two slices of tomato on lightly toasted brown bread with no butter?"

"Full English will be fine thanks, Emma and don't be stingy with the butter."

She smiled, winked and disappeared behind the sliding doors.

"Oh, and a newspaper if you have one!" he shouted after Emma as the doors slid closed.

They quickly opened again and Emma's beaming face appeared again, "Posh or tabloid?" she asked him.

"Tabloid will do ta, and a local one if there is such a thing."

"Good choice as we don't have the posh ones and I'll see if we have this week's *Dryton Echo* somewhere."

"Thank you darling," Grant replied and winked at her this time.

"Happy to serve," she said and slid the doors closed once again.

As Grant sat and waited for his breakfast to arrive he extracted his phone from his pocket and he thought about Ian's message again. What had gone wrong, he wondered. There didn't seem to be any sense of urgency or panic in the words, he was sure that Ian would have tried to ring him until he had answered if something had gone badly wrong.

Emma walked from behind the bar through a door that must have led to the kitchen; she was balancing a plate filled with an ample full English breakfast, a rack of toast and a mug. In addition, she had two newspapers tucked under one armpit. Carefully she laid it all on the table in front of Grant, as well as a set of cutlery that she had been holding between her fingers underneath the breakfast plate.

"I made the assumption you were a coffee drinker, hope I'm right," she said.

"Coffee's fine," he replied, locking his phone so the screen turned black and slipping it back into his pocket secretly and quickly before Emma saw that he actually did own a mobile.

Looking down at the breakfast he said, "Looks good," an honest appraisal, "my compliments to the chef."

Emma smiled and gave a little skip and she walked away, looking over her shoulder she replied, "Compliments accepted."

"Pours a good pint, can hold a conversation and cooks a mean breakfast. A girl of many skills," he said, meaning it as a genuine compliment but forgetting that this girl never missed an opportunity.

"They're not my only skills," came the slick and probably well-rehearsed response from Emma, her tongue sticking slightly out between her lips.

Grant decided not to respond and lowering his gaze back to his breakfast he picked up the knife and fork and began to eat. Emma returned to the kitchen, the spring in her step clearly less.

Grant ate heartily and as always quickly. His wife had always told him to slow down and enjoy his food but it was a habit he had never been able to shake after leaving the army. During army training, you never knew how long you were going to get to eat your meal so every trainee soldier ate like someone was about to snatch it away from them.

A gulp of coffee and a huge bite of toast and he was once again chowing down on his breakfast. The whole lot was demolished within ten minutes. His attention turned now to the newspapers that sat on the table, a copy of today's Daily Mirror and, spotting the publication date, last week's Dryton Echo.

After this length of time he didn't expect to find anything in a national newspaper so after quickly skimming each page he tossed it onto the seat next to him and made his way through the local rag in more detail.

He took about ten minutes to scan each page of the newspaper looking for anything associated with a missing person, the police looking for a missing local biker or any incidents involving bikers or motorcycle clubs. There was nothing. Internally he let out a sigh of relief, not the first he had released over the past three months.

It would seem like he had expected, that nobody had missed or reported the disappearance of One a Year. It was most likely that anyone who had missed him had been told to keep their mouths shut and the MCC were never going to speak with the police about the disappearance of one of their own,

The Crippens were behaving just as he expected and needed them to.

He closed the paper and folded it in half just as Emma walked back into the bar to clear the table. She performed this task unusually quietly, stacking all the empty breakfast stuff on top of the plate and then walking away. Grant was surprised but not overly disappointed by her silence, however in typical Emma style, it didn't last long.

Having made it just a few feet away from the table she turned around and speaking with a 'little innocent coy girl' voice she brazenly asked, "When are you going to take me to bed?"

Grant had to bring this to an end, he didn't need the attention of a young horny girl following his every movement in the hope that she would be held against the pub wall and given a quickie.

Standing up and not even looking at the girl Grant replied in that emotionless voice that had become so familiar to One a Year.

"The only bike I ride is parked out the back darling."

Grant did not see the pain on Emma's face or the tear form in her eye and slide down her cheek as he slid the internal slide bar locks at the top and bottom of the pub's front door and walked out into the Milton Dryton street.

Research and Reconnaissance

The pub door closed behind him as he looked to his left and right, the town was still quiet and largely empty of people. He checked his watch, nearly a quarter to eight, too early to go to his next destination as he knew the local library wouldn't be open until nine that morning.

As he turned to his left to walk to the newsagents he had spotted when he first rode around the town he thought he heard a noise from inside the pub, someone shouting, but he couldn't make out what was said. He didn't give it another thought as he continued to walk.

Inside the pub Emma was the source of the noise heard by Grant as she had shouted, "you fucking bastard, I wouldn't fuck your old dick if my life depended on it!" She threw the breakfast dishes towards the table where Grant had been sat just moments earlier and then began to cry in earnest. It was hard to work out if she was crying because of the insult just delivered to her or the fact that she would be the one cleaning up the mess she had just created.

Grant reached the newsagent encountering nobody along the way and was pleased to see fresh editions of this week's local newspaper stacked up in a display stand just inside the door. He picked up a copy and a tin of his favourite small cigars. Paying the old newsagent with a ten pound note he pocketed the change and placed the tin of cigars into the angled pocket on the left side of his bike jacket. Just before walking away he noticed a charity collection tin on the counter, he retrieved a few coins from his pocket and dropped them into the 'Help for Heroes' charity coin collector.

"The world needs a few heroes," he said to the shopkeeper, who replied, without looking up from the paper he was reading, "It does that sir."

Leaving the shop Grant continued to walk down the street until he came upon a public bench, sitting down he reached back into his jacket pocket pulling out the tin of cigars and his lighter. He lit the cigar and inhaled rolling the tasty smoke around his mouth and then slowly exhaling.

Crossing one leg over the other he settled back into the bench and began to read the current copy of the Dryton Echo. 'Read' was a loose description of what Grant actually did, 'carefully scanning' would be a better description. He was looking, as earlier that morning, for any report referring to a missing person, one particular missing biker, a member of a local ragtag and unwanted MCC, a bike club responsible for about sixty-five percent of local crime if the police figures were to be believed.

Once again he found nothing, he remained slightly surprised that someone could just disappear off the face of the planet and nobody would seemingly give a shit. After spending about fifteen minutes perusing this thicker copy of the local paper he closed it, folded it in half and placed it on the bench. As he lit a second cigar he tasted the smoke swirling around the inside of his mouth with the satisfaction that the disappearance of One a Year had passed without any reporting of it taking place and convinced that after three months it was now unlikely to happen.

He was, however, neither stupid nor naïve enough to believe that nothing was being done about it. Just because the police weren't looking didn't mean others weren't or at least hadn't been at some time.

Finishing his second cigar he stubbed it out with the heel of his boot. There was a bit of a cold bite in the air and he thought about returning to his room at the pub but he didn't really want to come face-to-face with Emma. He knew that his last remarks would have hurt her badly and didn't really know what welcome was waiting for him when he eventually returned. He had regretted saying what he had said the moment the words had left his mouth but he needed Emma off his back and the delivery of that message had been well and truly made clear. His regret was born not so much out of the hurt he had caused but more by the concern that Emma might decide to clear his stuff out of his room and dump them outside. He really didn't need her rifling through his belongings.

He decided that allowing the young girl to have some space and cool down (he just hoped she didn't use the time to become more infuriated) was probably the best course of action (and also the most cowardly). He just wasn't in the right frame of mind for conflict right now and besides that he had a few matters to sort out.

It would be a while before the library would be open so now would be a good time to speak with Ian.

Not for the first (or last) time this day he took his phone out of his pocket and opened up his contacts page. Searching for and finding the entry that read 'Churchill's Logistics' he pressed the green phone symbol and waited for his call to be connected.

It rang about half a dozen times before a voice at the other end answered with "Churchill's Logistics, how can we help you?"

Grant smiled at this response.

"Fucking quit it Ian, you know it's me, how you doing?"

"Now, what if this call is being listened into eh? Can't you just for once keep up the pretence?" replied Ian, annoyed but in a humorous fashion.

"Who the hell do you think is tagging our phones mate? We are not on the radar of the fucking CIA" retorted Grant.

"The term is *tapping* not tagging you moron and those fuckers listen in to everybody's calls, don't you watch the news?" snapped Ian, not annoyed at Grant per say, more because of the early morning awakening. Ian was not a natural morning person.

"Yes, I do watch the news, I don't, however, get all of my espionage knowledge from reading 'Conspiracy Monthly' you grumpy fucker."

Ian laughed, "Am I that predictable?"

"Yes, now what is the issue? I got your message, anything I need to be worried about?" asked Grant.

Ian scratched his balls through his pants and sat more upright in his bed. He began to bring Grant up to date.

Following Grant's little *chat* with One a Year, he had passed on the information to Ian. Over the following few weeks, Ian had carefully followed Lump in order to obtain information about his movements, habits, rituals, looking for a regular occurrence that would find him alone and enable Ian to effectively kidnap him. He had immediately observed that Lump deserved his road name, he was a large muscular man, very much a stereotypical biker. Bald on top, what hair he did have had been grown long and tied at the back in a loose ponytail, his arms were covered in tattoos; many of them clearly 'prison tats'. A long goatee-style beard finished off the look and he was rarely seen without his fake blue lens Oakley wraparound sunglasses.

He spent much of his time in and around the Crippens' clubhouse and the other club members who frequented the place. He was clearly keen to earn his back patch and top and bottom rockers and be rid of his 'prospect' tag, doing all of the running around and 'gopher' type tasks that the full patched members told him to do.

His beloved ride was a self-built 'chop' built around a Suzuki GS1100 engine block, a real rough looking bike finished off with everything in powder coated black paint.

He more often than not slept at the clubhouse except for on the odd occasion when he would spend the night humping the hell out of a local slapper at her flat which was located about 3 miles from the bikers hangout.

It had been almost two weeks of watching this guy before Ian spotted a potential opportunity to grab the guy. One Sunday morning Ian had been sat in his van around the corner from the clubhouse, he had been sat there for about two hours and the boredom was causing him to fall asleep when the roar of a bike passing by made him open his eyes. It was Lump and he was alone. Although he couldn't see the biker's face Ian knew it was the biker he was following. The bike for a start was a dead giveaway, in addition to that was Lumps' favourite sunglasses, his clearly identifiable and illegal German storm trooper style helmet and the face scarf that when worn gave the effect that the bottom half of the bikers face was that of a screaming red demon.

While it was not unusual for Ian to find himself following Lump, what was out of the ordinary was that he was firstly alone and secondly this was very early for Lump to be out and about. Keeping his distance he carefully followed the lone biker, the fact that the wing mirrors (once again, illegal) on the bike were so small they were pointless, made it much easier to follow without being noticed. At first, Ian had thought he was following Lump to the flat of his casual shag but it became obvious this was not the case when the biker steered his bike west and out of town in the opposite direction to where his human ride resided.

After only a few minutes Lump brought his bike to a stop and kicking out the side stand, leaned it over at the side of the road outside a care home.

The biker dismounted and taking off his gloves and helmet, the gloves were then placed inside the helmet, and then removing his face scarf and sunglasses which he put into one of the large pockets of his leather cut, Lump made his way to the front entrance of the care home.

Ian drove his van past where the bike had been parked and turned left into a side road. Parking the van quickly, Ian moved himself across to the front passenger seat and looking out of the passenger window he watched the biker spit into one hand and run it through his beard, doing his best to straighten it out a touch and make himself more presentable and then push the care home door open and enter the building.

Obviously visiting someone who matters to him, thought Ian, *why else the pathetic attempt to make himself look presentable.*

Ian thought about what to do next. He had to find out who was being visited but casually walking into the care home and announcing himself as a kind hearted bloke who just wanted to chat with an old person would probably look a bit weird and raise some suspicion.

He spotted the sign on the grass frontage of the care home, *Green Firs Care Home for the Elderly*, but damned if he could make out the phone number which was in smaller print below the name of the building.

Picking up his phone from the centre plastic tray of the van he placed his finger against the bottom indented button and the phone screen came to life. Ian shook his head, fingerprint technology on phones made him nervous as the conspiracy theorist part of him was convinced that because of this modern piece of technical advancement somehow he was on an intelligence database somewhere in the world.

The 4G could be seen at the top left of his phone screen and quickly he opened his search engine and typed in the name of the care home.

A list of businesses appeared on his screen and third on that list was the business he was looking for. The phone number was highlighted blue and lightly pressing his finger onto the number he activated the hidden hyperlink that automatically rang the number.

A mature female voice answered his call.

"Good morning, Green Firs Care Home, how can I be of assistance?"

Ian put himself into biker mode and replied in the best version of what he thought a biker would talk.

"Yeah, d'you work there love?" he said gruffly.

"Yes, I am a member of the care home staff. You have come through to reception, how may I help you?" came back the polite response.

"Good stuff, I'm trying to get hold of Lump, is he there or what?" asked Ian thinking how pathetically fake and stupid he must sound.

"Lump?" said the receptionist, "I'm sorry I have no idea who you are referring to."

"Biker geezer innit?" said Ian sounding more and more like a middle-aged white man trying to sound black with each word he uttered.

"Biker," said the receptionist sounding confused at first but then adding, "Oh, do you mean Christopher?"

For a brief moment Ian was stunned, he never imagined Lump to be a Christopher. Almost forgetting to speak in his fake 'gruff biker come street rapper' voice he replied, "Yeah, yeah, that's him, rides a black bike, got a beard."

"Yes that's Christopher, he has just arrived actually. Come to visit his mum like he does every month. Shall I get him for you?"

"Nah it's ok darling," replied Ian now stuck as to what to say next, "err it's just a mate, I'll catch him later. Don't wanna disturb his visit with his old dear. Cheers, bye."

Ian pressed the red phone symbol on his phone. "Got ya," he said out loud.

Slipping back into the driver's seat he reversed the van out of the side street and made his way back in the direction from which he had originally driven, passing by Lump's bike he smiled happy that he had at last discovered a possible opportunity for nabbing this bastard. "I wonder if your little dear old mother knows what you like doing you piece of shit?" Ian said in a hushed voice as he drove away from the care home.

Still sat on the bench, Grant broke his silence.

"So what's the hitch? You must have had at least two opportunities to get hold of him by now listening to what you have just said and working out the timeline."

"Mate, you're right but since that visit he has been back once and, that wasn't alone. The month after that time I followed him to the care home he never visited, in fact the whole club are spending the majority of their time inside the clubhouse compound. Has been that way since One a Year left the club, if you know what I mean?"

Grant remained silent; he didn't know how to respond to this update. *Had the Crippens been spooked by the disappearance of one of their own? Maybe leaving One a Year's bike parked outside the club had been a mistake? Had somebody witnessed the snatching of the ex-Crippen?*

"Grant you still there mate?" Ian's voice broke the silence and brought Grant back from his concerns.

"Yes I'm still here," obvious concern in his voice. "So what now, do I stop, do I give up?"

"No mate, I have an idea but if you are still seeking the justice you initially wanted you are going to have to get your hands dirty on this one. I will need your help bro," answered Ian.

"My hands are already dirty! And I don't WANT justice Ian, I fucking NEED it. Let's meet at the factory and you can run your plan past me. Can you be there around midday?"

"No problem dude," responded Ian, smiling at the fact that his friend had used the code word 'factory' to refer to the wooden building in the woods. The code word he had suggested.

The phone call was ended simultaneously by both the men. Ian was only about 10 miles from the agreed meeting place. Sleeping in the van had become much more bearable since he had placed a mattress in the back of it!

Grant stood up and began to walk back in the direction of the pub but turned left down a narrow side street before reaching it. The town was waking up and coming to life. Ahead of him an elderly smartly-dressed gentleman was placing items of all descriptions on trestle tables outside of an antiques shop. Brass kettle, a few figurines, plates, and cups of differing sizes, ages and origin were all presented on the tables in a very organised manner. The man placing the items looked up as Grant approached looking at him warily but his demeanour changed as Grant wished him a good morning.

"Good morning to you too sir, interested in an antique or two courtesy of the best antique shop you will find in the

98

whole county?" said the man who Grant assumed was the shop owner.

Grant looked up at the shops wooden boarding just below the eaves of the roof. Allerton's Antiques was the name of the establishment.

"Mr. Allerton by any chance?" asked Grant.

"At your service; the antiques are for sale and the service is free sir," responded Rodney Allerton.

"Maybe another time Mr. Allerton," Grant replied politely. "Need to visit the library this morning."

"Got plenty of old books in here sir if that's what you are looking for, can do you a good price," said Allerton eagerly.

"Like I said Mr. Allerton, another time maybe," said Grant with a little more purpose in his voice on this occasion and having no intention of visiting the store at any time in the future.

"Well have a good day," Allerton said waving a goodbye in Grant's direction as he walked on by in the general direction of the town library.

It wasn't books he wanted, he required internet access and privacy, both of which he was sure he could find at the library. The town hall building, where the library was located, was open when Grant arrived at ten minutes past nine and following a short conversation with the librarian, a middle-aged woman with her grey hair tied back into a severe bun, Grant found an internet booth at the far end of the research area of the small room. There were only two other people in the library: one reading a newspaper and the other perusing the bookshelves containing books about travel.

Grant grasped the mouse and moved it, the PC screen lit up requesting a password when he duly entered having obtained it from the librarian during their brief chat.

Access gained and search bar found Grant typed in the words 'Crippens MCC'.

The search results appeared within a few seconds and Grant began to scroll down the page scanning the list. The first page was mainly results linked to Doctor Crippen, he clicked on the next page button and once again scrolled down through page two. About half way down was the result he had been hoping for. He clicked on the hyperlink that read 'Crippens Motorcycle Club' and waited. The page took a few moments to load but before long Grant was looking at the homepage of the Crippens MCC web page.

It was as expected very amateur, probably created via one of the many free website hosts that existed these days. The homepage gave a brief resume of the club's history. It was created in 2004 by three founding members - two now deceased - they had grown over the years to now have twenty-six members (assuming the site was kept up to date). The original surviving member, a character known as 'Doom', had in 2013 been granted lifetime member status. The current president, the incumbent since 2013, was The Priest who had joined the Crippens in 2006 after leaving an outfit named the 'Spirit Stalkers MCC'.

Grant decided to return to this information later, what he really wanted to see was the people themselves and clicked on the page entitled 'Gallery'.

The page loaded slowly as photographs gradually blended together to form a collection of twenty-two faces, the page title read – Patched Members – a collection of faces, some of whom you would automatically assume were bikers while a couple could have easily been anything from a refuse collector to a solicitor.

The top picture, sitting above all the others, was of Doom himself. Below his photograph were the words:

'Lifetime Member'

Original Founder

Twenty-one other pictures appeared below in three rows of seven photographs. None was your typical 'stand still and pose for me' photographs. They had all been taken randomly, some clearly at parties others outside, maybe while out riding. All had a title of some sort beneath the photo. Most titles simply read member but along the first row beneath the picture of Doom were different titles

The Priest – President
Panhead – Vice President
Pretty Boy – Sgt at Arms
Cowboy – Secretary
Tankslapper – Treasurer

The picture of Lump was on the third row amongst six other reprobates, below his picture was the word 'Member'. Grant was confused, One a Year had identified Lump because he was only a Prospect but here he was clearly identified as a full member. Either the tortured biker had lied, which Grant found hard to believe, or this website was being kept up to date and Lump had recently been patched.

Grant scrolled further down the page and what he found at the bottom was very interesting. Here were four photographs, or to be precise four squares three of which contained photographs of more bikers with the title 'Prospect' beneath their pictures. The fourth box was blank, blacked out or picture removed. Below this box read the words:

'One a Year'
'MIA'

So, thought Grant, this was how they were handling the situation of the loss of one of their own, listing him as missing in action. This was a badge of respect normally given to those that had died while representing the club is some kind of club activity (normally illegal) or who had been involved in some altercation with another bike gang or the police which had ended badly. Grant obviously knew that this wasn't the case, One a Year had been unceremoniously smacked around the side of the head with a baseball bat by Ian!

Grant spent the next thirty minutes researching the information published openly on the website. Events past and future, how to join the club, the ethos of the club (that one made Grant laugh – like these morons even knew the meaning of the word ethos!). The events pages mainly contained more pictures clearly taken at alcohol-fuelled parties and rallies. Many of the photos were of women and bikers with women, Grant thought they must be the biking fraternities' versions of groupies. Grant had done plenty of research over the past few months, most of his knowledge came from research based on the bikers scene of the USA where the bike gang culture was much bigger and more organised than that of the UK. He had learned that these women fell into three categories: 'Broads' were those who drifted in and out of the club scene, a general term for women who were used for casual sex when and where the bikers decided.

'Mamas' maintained an informal affiliation with the club but once again were involved with the social-sexual interactions.

'Ol' Ladies' were those that had established a long-standing personal relationship with an individual club member, be that a girlfriend or wife. This class of women were afforded respect as long-term personal companions and loved as active partners of club members and occasionally the club itself. Unlike the two previous classifications, Ol' Ladies were never used as passive objects of displays of machismo and sexual gratification; although some probably started off as either Broads, Mamas or both, working their way up through their own rank system.

Many of the photos Grant looked at suggested the women pictured were from the lower levels of Broad and possibly Mamas. Plenty of cleavage, ass crack and in two of the pictures bare breasts were happily being displayed.

Grant had also learned that while the bikers were happy to have these women around when they wanted to 'get their balls off' or 'get lots of head', generally most of them agreed that they tended to undermine the group's solidarity and could be the club's biggest downfall. Grant certainly hoped so.

He closed down the page and, before shutting down the PC (something the librarian had asked him not to do) he cleared the search history so that the next user would not inadvertently access it.

Happy with his research Grant decided that it was time to face the music and return to the pub. He had to go back anyway as he had a meeting to attend and he wanted to give his bike the once over to make sure it was 'ride ready'.

Poor Preparation – Piss Poor Performance

Pushing the pub door Grant found it locked and without evidence he just knew that this was a message to him. Emma had, quite rightly on reflection, taken his words in the way that they were intended to be taken at the time, with hurt and pain. He made his way round the side of the pub heading towards the back yard gates. Momentarily considering unlocking the replaced padlock, he changed his mind not wishing to disclose that he had replaced the padlock for his own secretive purposes and so instead, once again, climbed over the gate.

Once in the courtyard, he walked to the rear of it hoping that the rear door which he guessed led into the kitchen had not been locked to further prevent his entry. Turning the handle he found the door opened and as he thought he found himself walking into the pubs small but well-equipped kitchen. Emma was standing in front of a small industrial dishwasher loading it with breakfast dishes, probably his, and other food-encrusted dishes which had been left from the evening before.

Emma turned around and with no hesitation, making Grant think that this had been rehearsed in his absence, she said, "Pack your belongings and get out, you aren't welcome any longer."

Grant, himself less prepared having not expected to find Emma in the kitchen, nodded his head.

"Fair response I suppose. But maybe allowing me a moment to explain myself would lead to a small amount of generosity on your part in allowing me to stay for just one night," he replied.

"Doubtful," she said, still very clearly hurting, "but hey give it your best shot. Let's see how well that charm of yours can work when it really needs to." There was spite in her voice that Grant could almost feel physically.

Grant took a deep breath and started to speak. He initially apologised and added that he didn't expect it to be accepted but sorry he really was. The following few minutes comprised of a combination of truth and lies and if the real truth be known it was ninety percent lies.

Grants' story of woe explained how his family had been destroyed (truth) by his actions (lie) and that now he was basically running from his problems (a mixture of truth and lies) and was travelling around the UK (lie) which had been a dream of his many years (truth). Because of what had happened to him and his life he just didn't feel ready to enter into another relationship even if that was just for sex (absolute truth) and he didn't believe that he deserved the attention of any woman (truth) and he knew he would only bring trouble into any woman's life if they became involved with him (truth). He just needed one or two more night and then he would be on the move again and she (Emma) would never see him again (truth, sort of, another three or four nights would be better but he didn't want to push his luck too much).

Grant looked at Emma, her face had softened a little, and she appeared to be deep in thought.

"Please Emma," he said and then walking towards her, he held her and hugged her tight. "I really am sorry. I can be a real twat sometimes."

Reluctantly Emma pulled away from Grant's arms, it felt good to be hugged by him but it was clear that this man was a no go area and she saw no point in making it even more difficult for herself to resist this man by prolonging the hug that felt so very good.

"You are a complete and utter bastard and you really hurt me," said Emma.

Grant could almost predict the next line as being something along the lines of 'but I don't care so get out'. His prediction included the first word only.

Emma continued... "But I can see that you have been through some hurt yourself and you were just lashing out. You can stay for two nights, as you asked for, but then I need you out of my life. Clear?"

"Crystal," replied Grant and held his arms open offering another hug.

Emma shook her head negatively. Grant lowered his arms and decided it was time to go to his room. As he walked past Emma he quickly leaned into her and planted a light kiss on her cheek. "Thank you," he said.

Blushing, Emma responded quietly, "You're welcome, now get lost before I change my mind about trying to get you into my bed."

Grant smiled, "Never give up hope, I might pop by on my return journey, I could be really desperate by then."

Emma returned Grant's smile to indicate that she had recognised the joke but this time, she was going to have the last word and said, "Fuck off, I will never be that desperate."

Grant walked out of the kitchen, passed through the empty bar and made his way up to his room, content and relieved that he had got away with that one and bought himself a bit of much needed time.

***

After returning to his room just to take off his jacket and throw on a black hoodie Grant had made his way down to the courtyard and was giving his bike the once over.

Having removed the small tool roll from the middle of the bikes' handlebars he rolled it out and laid it on the ground. The tool roll held the basic tools he needed to 'tinker' with his bike to ensure it remained roadworthy and rideable. If anything major went wrong with it, he would have to rely on a garage, something he would rather avoid, he wanted to 'stay off the grid' as much as possible. He had checked the tyre pressures, brake fluid level and the condition of the brake pads and was working out how to maintain his bike upright and level to enable him to check the oil level when Emma appeared holding a refuse bag.

"Perfect timing," said Grant, "assuming you are in a mood to help me out for a moment."

Emma lifted the lid of the industrial rubbish bin and threw the refuse bag into it. "Stop begging," she said, "I've forgiven you. What do you want me to do?"

"I need the bike held upright; the oil level indicator is at the bottom of the bike and I can't hold it upright and check the level at the same time." This was a problem that Grant had not considered when he had purchased the bike, the problem of a bike that had no centre stand so always stood at an angle when on the side stand. "It's quite heavy though" he added.

"It can't be as heavy as some of the punters I have thrown out of the bar on a Saturday night," replied Emma laughing.

Hearing her laugh was a positive and, at the same time, a pleasant sound.

He stood Emma in front of the bike and placed her hands on the handlebars. Placing his hands on top of hers, he pulled the bike into an upright position. Standing behind her, as he was to enable him to do this, he groin pressed against Emma's bottom. Despite his not wanting or needing to sleep with this girl he was still a man and felt a slight amount of movement inside his jeans. He tried to ignore it and hoped that Emma had not noticed.

"Okay, I'm going to let go now, as I said it's heavy," he slowly released his hold from Emma's hands and at the same time the bike handles. "Can you feel it?" he asked, referring to the weight of the bike.

"Oh yes I can feel it," replied Emma putting on an innocent girly voice and then, back to her normal voice, "now stop grinding me you pervert and do what you need to do… with the bike of course!"

Feeling his face redden he quickly moved to the left side of the bike and getting down low to the ground checked the oil level indicator. "All fine," he said, he voice slightly strained because of his low body position and then placing his hands against the side of the bike he indicated to Emma that she could tilt the bike back onto its side stand.

"Right, can I now continue with my day without fear of being further violated?" asked Emma adding that familiar cheeky wink.

"Can't make any promises darling but you will be safe for the next few hours, I'm going out for a ride and a bit of sightseeing," he winked back at Emma, relieved that the damage his harsh hurtful words had caused seemed to have been repaired.

"Give me an hour and I could come with you," said Emma excitedly. "I've never been on the back of a bike."

"No spare helmet darling," Grant quickly responded, not needing a pillion on this journey.

"I can get my hands on one of those. Andy will be starting his shift behind the bar at eleven, he rides a bike, I can borrow his."

"Can I rain check that one?" asked Grant, choosing his words carefully so as not to open up old wounds with Emma. "How about tomorrow? I will use today to find some good riding roads, wouldn't want your first experience of a bike ride to be a bumpy one."

"No problem," replied Emma, "you get yourself ready for your ride out and I will get the key and unlock the gates for you."

Grant felt sick inside, the changed padlock was about to be discovered unless he thought quickly.

"You've done enough already, tell me where the key is and I will unlock the gates, that way when I return I can get back into the yard without having to find you again."

He was relieved to hear Emma say, "Always the gentleman, the key is at the back of the bar underneath the lemon slice bowl, see ya later."

She returned to the pub via the kitchen door and Grant released a huge sigh of relief. To think that such a simple thing as changing a padlock could have raised so many uncomfortable questions and possibly the involvement of the police. He had to switch on and be more careful from now on. He decided that the padlock would have to be changed back to the original as soon as possible and there were a few things that needed to be removed from his room and relocated elsewhere; he could no longer risk them being discovered by an uninvited visit to his room, be that for cleaning or other purposes.

Returning to his room he once again donned his bike jacket, picked up his bike luggage which contained the items that he didn't want to be discovered. After collecting the padlock key from where Emma had said it would be he left the bar, sliding back the bolts that had earlier prevented his entry through the front door he made his way around to the yard gates. Arriving back with his bike he started her up, she roared into action and he revved the engine a few times, enjoying the throbbing rumble that travelled through his body as he sat on the large comfortable Mustang leather seat. Putting it into gear he rode the bike out of the yard, stopping only to close and padlock the gates behind him, he used this opportunity to switch the padlocks back to their original status and then, mounting his bike once more, he roared her up the hill that only a few hours earlier he had pushed her up to avoid detection.

The repeat journey of earlier that morning felt different in the daylight and he let his mind relax so that he could enjoy the ride. As he rode he wondered if this bike knew how much enjoyment it had brought into his life, the only enjoyment in fact over the past year or so. Now out of the town and into the country lanes he relaxed his position and with his left hand he patted the tank of the bike. This simple action returned his mind to his present situation as he recollected the names of the members of The Crippins and Tank Slapper in particular wondering if this was how he became known by that road name.

He forced his mind to alter its path and returned to enjoying the winding country roads. After a few unplanned turns and having to stop once to get his bearings Grant looked at the small clock mounted on his bike and decided to head for Blackbrook Woods, getting there earlier than planned would give him time to prepare for the arrival of Ian, store away the few items that currently sat in his saddle bags and think over his future plans in an effort to discover any flaws. Since leaving the military many years ago the one thing he still stood by was the Law of the Five P's –

Poor Preparation normally resulted in Piss Poor Performance.

Having earlier lost his way slightly due to the many turns left and right he had done to further take in the scenery and prolong the enjoyment of the bike ride he found himself approaching Blackbrook Woods from the other side from which he had entered earlier that morning. He slowed down, looking around for the other entrance he was aware of from previous reconnaissance visits and eventually spotting the break in the wooded barrier he needed he came to a stop at the side of the road. Looking down the road ahead of him and then behind him he was happy that it was empty of walkers and other vehicles. With a small turn of the throttle, he steered his bike into the break and entered the large wooded area once again. On this occasion, he needed to go further into the wood before stopping at another hiding place for the silver shiny machine that took a fair amount of foliage to keep it from being spotted. He parked it up behind a collection of three large bushes and in front of a dense wall of trees and bracken.

Dismounting, he threw some of the loose bracken leaves that lay on the floor over the top of the bike and walked around to the other side of the large bushes. He looked at the hiding place and spotted no obvious sign of anything such as a glint of light bouncing off a layer of shiny metal, happy that it was well hidden he started to walk through the trees which became thicker, blocking the light out more and more the deeper into the woods he went.

Arriving at the edge of the small clearing where the barn/cabin/factory stood, he once again went through the ritual visual checks before leaving the cover of the trees.

He noticed immediately that something was wrong as he arrived at the door of the building; somebody had been here since he had left earlier that day. He slowly and quietly took his throw over saddle bags off his shoulders and unclipped one of them. Slipping his hand inside he felt around for the cold metal of the weapon that sat inside, now removed from its original smaller container.

His hand wrapped itself around the pistol's grip and he pulled it out of the bag. Leaving the bag on the floor he slowly pushed open the door with his empty hand to reveal the inside of the dark building. He pushed the door fully open and peered into the now much more illuminated room than it had been during his last visit. He could see about two-thirds of the room and didn't see anything of concern but his worry was what may be waiting for him behind the door, in the one-third of the room that remained unsighted.

He had, on many occasions throughout his life, been described as a man of little thought and too much reaction and he suddenly became that man once again as, without much thought at all, he rushed into the room and threw himself to the floor alongside the tarpaulin that covered One a Year's body. Rolling onto his side he aimed the Glock into the area room that had, up until a few seconds earlier, been unseen and hidden behind the door. He quickly picked up on two things: the room was empty of other people including dead people for the second thing he noticed that the body he had been aiming to use as cover was no longer there. One a Year had gone!

Grant's mind tried to search for answers to the disappearance of the biker's body.

One. He hadn't moved himself.

Two. Could the other members of the MCC somehow have found him?

Three. Had an innocent other stumbled across the grisly scene?

None of these thoughts made any sense especially the last one as there surely would be evidence of a police presence such as crime scene tape, police, and forensic people.

His mind cleared itself of panic and in the midst of this mental clarity came the answer. Grant had not made it to his meeting before the other member of that meeting. It had to be the work of Ian. As he got up to his feet, the pistol still in a 'ready to use if necessary' position he took another look around the room and spotted a cardboard box on the flat surface of the chest of drawers that had not been there hours earlier. Without needing to look at the contents of the box he instinctively knew that it was 'his new toy', as Ian had called it.

"Where are you, you fucker?" Grant whispered in the gloomy light.

In the rear corner of the room just to the right of Grant, through a broken pane of glass in amongst three other grubby window panes came a familiar voice.

"Who the fuck do you think you are, Jason fucking Bourne? You dived through that door like an old wounded warthog," said Ian emphasising on the word 'old'.

Grant did not need to turn to know that Ian would be looking at him with that stupid childish smile on his face.

"I thought we said midday?" and then Grant added as an afterthought, "and less of the old."

"You said midday old man," replied Ian, the smile he was renowned for remaining on his face. "I said I would be here."

Grant eventually turned around to face the window, he could just about see Ian but only because one eye was peering through the broken glass.

"Are you going to come in and explain to me what the fuck you have been up to?" asked Grant.

Less than thirty seconds later Ian walked in through the front door, covered in a layer of dirt and mud. Grant stared at him wondering how much longer he would be taken aback by this man, he opened his mouth to say something but literally words failed him. Ian looked down at himself.

"Oh," he said, "that biker was stinking out the place, I had to dispose of him. It had to be done at some stage and I didn't think you'd have the stomach for it."

The words came back to Grant.

"Don't have the stomach for it, are you fucking kidding me? It wasn't too long ago since I was caving the bloke's head in with a hammer and my boot."

"It's okay, you don't have to say thank you. I also got rid of his cut that you left hanging on the back of the chair over there too," said Ian sarcastically. "Any other evidence you need me to get rid of for you," this time a hint of seriousness in the question.

Grant walked over to the chest of drawers, sitting on the floor he leaned against it and lowered his face into his hands.

With a slightly muffled voice, it was difficult to work out if he spoke the next words to himself, to Ian or both.

"What the hell am I doing? I'm not cut out to do this. I'm making more mistakes than a four-year-old in a spelling competition. A blind man could find the evidence I keep leaving behind. I nearly got caught out by a hormonal undersexed young girl this morning all because I didn't fully think through the changing of a padlock."

Ian sat himself down in front of Grant.

"Ah, self-loathing and self-pity, two of my favourite emotions." He continued before Grant could speak. "Try asking yourself, what would my family want to me do? Am I doing the right thing? Can I stop now that I have started?"

Once again before Grant could respond he gave the answers to his questions.

"This, yes and no...they are the answers to those questions by the way."

"No they wouldn't Ian, and you know it," said Grant who having momentarily looked up now had his face back in the palms of his hands.

With no thought to his friend's feelings, Ian responded quietly.

"Well, we'll never know will we?" There was no response from Grant and as Ian hated periods of silence he continued speaking.

"How about I tell you a little about Lump and how I think we can turn this around. First off, the weekend that the entire club membership were stashed away in their clubhouse had nothing to do with the disappearance of One a Year. Our bloke only went and got himself fully patched up so they had a night of celebration and debauchery."

Grant interjected with, "Yeah but they still have him as MIA on their website."

"Something all these clubs do when one of their brethren goes missing without explanation. They wouldn't want to advertise that one of their own left the club under mysterious circumstances or because they didn't like the lifestyle anymore, now would they?"

Grant remained silent his face no longer in his hands although it remained in a downwards position.

Ian went on to explain to Grant that although there had been less movement from all the members of the club he did not think that this was in any way associated with the disappearance of One a Year. Further to this, while he couldn't fully explain the reasoning behind Lump having an escort when he last visited his mother in the care home he once again felt that it was an isolated incident.

"It might just be a tradition that a newly patched biker receives an escort when he next rides out as a mark of respect, I really don't know. But I do know that none of them appeared nervous or on high alert." Ian finished speaking and waited for a response, despite his dislike of periods of silence this was one he was not going to break.

"So, what now?" Grant eventually filled the silence with his question.

"The longer this goes the more chance of it failing or us getting caught," he added.

"Correct, but I have an idea," replied Ian, "however, you probably aren't going to like it and can I just clarify that it will be *you* getting caught not *us*."

Grant raised his head and followed this movement with his eyes further raising to look at the ceiling. He had lost count during training of how many times he had heard Ian say, *I have an idea but you aren't going to like it lads!* The worrying part is despite this warning he almost invariably managed to sell the idea to his fellow trainees.

"Sell it to me," said Grant looking at Ian, a narrow forced smile appeared on his face.

Ian laid out his plan which was quite basic in its structure. They needed to take control of the bikers' movements and it was Ian's gut instinct that the weak link was the obvious love that Lump had for his mother.

"We need to get him to go to the home outside of his normal monthly weekend visit, and what better way than make him believe that all is not okay with dear Momma," for some reason Ian used a really bad southern states accent for his last words.

Grant looked at his friend, a look of bewilderment on his face, "so you are suggesting we actually speak to him?"

"Don't be fucking stupid," retorted Ian, "there are no men working on the care home reception, that wouldn't work at all."

"Well thank fuck for some common sense!" exclaimed Grant.

"Exactly," said Ian pointing a wagging finger in the face of Grant, "we get that young bar girl to make the call!"

The Pear of Anguish

Grant could not believe what he had just heard from Ian and was now pacing around the inside of the wooden barn, his arms waving up and down through the dusty air.

"What the... are you... did you just hear what you... what the fuck Ian?" he said, exasperated and unable to find any words to express how he felt right now.

"I am open to alternative suggestions," Ian's sarcastic voice making another appearance, "but I think we both know the parts we play in this team. I am the ideas man and you are the one, who well... kills the fuck out of people... oh and leaves loads of evidence behind."

Ian stood with his hands on his hips, his face looking upwards and to the right in his best superhero pose. "I am the ideas and clean up man of this operation... fuck me I need a codename."

Grant stopped pacing around and looked at this man he had decided would be the best person to assist him in what was now very clearly becoming a total cluster fuck.

"Will you take a short break from being a complete prick and mentally go over, in your own little brain, what you have just suggested and unbelievably wrapped up and described as a fucking plan?" Grant could no longer even attempt to hide his frustration at this whole situation he now found himself in.

Ian dropped his hands from his hips but remained looking up at the roof, now adopting his best 'thinking man' pose. After a few seconds, he looked over towards Grant and spoke but no longer were his words delivered with any sarcasm, humour or any other inappropriate tone for the given situation. Now Grant listened hard, he had, at last, got the reaction he needed from Ian although he was still not totally comfortable with what he heard.

"Listen bro, the covert approach and watch, follow and react clearly isn't working anymore. We need to take control, we need to be calling the shots. Will it be risky? Of course it will, but let's face it, from the moment you called me, risk was involved. We are now in a situation where we don't have the skills required, namely a female voice and inadvertently you have produced the ideal candidate for this task."

Grant interjected with yet another question.

"How have I done that?"

"You found a girl that, for some unfathomable reason, desires your cock." Ian remained serious, not a hint of sarcasm could be detected.

"I am not going to fuck Emma to bring her into all this." Even as Grant said these words he could almost hear that a possible interpretation was that he was willing to bring a third party into their murky world of kidnap, torture and murder but he wasn't going to have sex with them to do that!

"No problem, I'll fuck her but I don't think that is going to have the desired outcome," replied Ian. The sarcasm had returned.

Grant paced again and thought. He did not want anybody else, least of all Emma, involved in what he was doing but he a) didn't have any plan of his own and b) despite his initial feelings he had to admit that Ian was right about one thing, it was time to take control.

Ian watched his friend pacing, he had seen this before and knew that Grant was simply digesting his plan and trying to add his own twist to it and by that he meant an element of safety. Ian remained quiet to allow his thoughtful companion to work out in his own time that the security of safety had become a distant cousin, something that you acknowledged was there but you were unlikely to see it again for a long time.

"I'll find a way to convince Emma to do this without her knowing what is really going on. I don't know how yet but that is my problem. It's either that or she is not involved at all and you, Mr. Ideas Man, will have to come up with something else."

Grant had found his element of safety, flimsy as it was, it clearly made him happier and Ian was willing to go with it.

"Okay," said Ian. "Can we look at my new toy now?"

The way that Ian could so rapidly accept an idea or suggestion without any apparent thought or consideration never ceased to amaze Grant.

***

Sgt Gus 'Muttley' Murphy sat in his office looking at the paperwork that was spread out over his desk. Even though it was over twenty-four hours after the event he was still smarting and angered by the confrontation he had experienced with the biker the day before.

It had been quite easy to find information on the guy; changing your name by deed poll was no way of hiding your identity, it was just another layer of paperwork to work through. The problem for Mahoney was that everything checked out and there was nothing he could find to suggest that Grant was trouble. He was a cocky bastard that was for sure, with an answer for everything but he was clean with the exception of one speeding offence back in 1998 for which he took a speeding awareness course and so no points were even added to his license.

Murphy had dug a little further after discovering Grants true birth identity through the deed poll records. Ex-military, ex-prison service, current employment unknown, a list of addresses going back to 1981, anything previous to that would prove more difficult as he was probably a minor prior to that year. There was nothing suspicious at all and this was the cause of Murphy's' further frustration, he had no official reason to enquire about more information. The two colleagues he had contacted had told him as much, no criminal offences past or present made this individual a person of no interest.

He shuffled once again through the papers, as much as he liked to believe he was a man of influence, a top cop as such, he was not a popular man with friends within the force. Furthermore, he had no contacts that he was aware of in the military or the civil service network, nobody who may be able to find out more about this man on his behalf.

Despite all of this, the many years he had spent in the police had taught him one thing, trust your gut feeling and Murphy's gut was telling him that there was more to this guy than first met the eye.

The police sergeant's frustration increased as he shuffled, sorted and flicked through the single sided pile of pages leading to most of them being swept off his desk and onto the floor.

Now even more angry, he looked down at the paperwork, scattered over the floor of his office. His eye caught one of the pages. It had landed face down and should have been, being a single side document, blank but half of the page had printed words on it. He leaned over and picked up the piece of paper containing the information that had been overlooked. Placing it back on his desk he studied this new information.

***

Ian pulled apart the two top flaps of the box sat on the chest of drawers, his foot tapped against the pistol which Grant had placed there when he had sat down.

"Are you going to put this away somewhere or is it more evidence I need to deal with?" Another flippant remark from Ian.

"Fuck off," said Grant equally as flippantly as he picked up the gun and placed it into one of the top drawers.

Ian watched him do this and raised his eyebrows.

"Wow, that will fuck over the forensic boys."

Grant squinted his eyes as he looked back at Ian's smiling face.

"I want it easily accessible, I may need to use it if you carry on being a sarcastic cunt," he said.

"Nice way to talk to your ideas man, evidence hider and now," Ian lifted the item from the box offering it to Grant, "inventor of the team."

Grant held the object observing it with a massive amount of admiration.

"Copying, recreating is not actually inventing," he said, his eyes still admiring the creation he was holding, "but this has convinced me not to shoot you right now."

The metal object was about ten inches long, the top end having a winding mechanism and the bottom end was pear shaped. Grant turned the screw at the top and watched as the four metal leaves that together made the pear shape separate and slowly open. He turned the screw in the opposite direction and the leaves closed to once again the shape of the fruit from which the object had gained its name. In a brutal and medieval fashion, the Pear of Anguish was a beautiful item.

Grant asked, "How wide does it open?"

Ian's tone was serious and his face held a look of worried concern as he saw the entranced look of admiration and pleasure on his friend's face.

"Wider than your needs require."

Grant could not take his eyes from the object of exquisite beauty that was designed to cause unimaginable pain and disfigurement. His faith and belief in his friend to create the objects he required grew with every second that his eyes admired this piece of work.

Reaching for the recreated item last used during the Middle Ages Ian cradled the Pear of Anguish as he lifted it from Grant's hold. He placed it back in the box, knowing how the object was used made him turn cold and placing it out of sight again made him feel easier again.

"Useless without the second required ingredient," said Ian. "So…?"

"I'll find a way of including her that will also protect her from the truth of what she will be involved in," said Grant, instinctively knowing what Ian was about to ask.

Ian walked towards the front door, without looking back he said, "I'll finish off giving One a Year the respect he doesn't deserve. Call me when you have sorted it."

He left the 'factory' and made his way back to the dense area of the woods to finish off digging the grave that would hopefully hide the remains of the dead biker for an eternity. He thought about the condition he had agreed with Grant way back when he had been asked to help out his old friend.

"I will not be involved in any killing," he demanded.

He now found himself wanting to witness the use of his creation, a warped desire to observe the tool of torture and human disfigurement working overwhelmed him. This need for a sort of self-admiration would ordinarily be absolutely unthinkable but ordinary did not come close to describing what his friend had been through.

By the time that Ian had arrived back at the grave digging site Grant was back on his bike. Before riding it clear of the wooded area he brought it to a standstill, dismounted it and walked to the side of the road. Once again happy that it was clear he returned to his bike and rode it out onto the country lane, turning right he headed back to the pub.

Back in the small Milton Dryton police station, Gus Murphy ended the conversation with the Herefordshire detective and replaced the phones receiver/transmitter back into its cradle. His gut feeling that there was more to this visitor to his town than first met the eye had been proven right.

The detective would only confirm that Grant had been involved in a criminal investigation as a witness and had never been a suspect. The details of the investigation, the crime or the depth of Grants involvement he would not discuss without Gus providing the relevant documentation required, that documentation would show that the Shropshire Constabulary had a reason to access this information because of an ongoing investigation of their own and Gus Murphy knew that he was never going to get that. He sat at his desk and smiled, this was enough to be getting on with, it was a way in to poke a stick in and stir it around. He didn't like drinking in the pub where Grant was staying, in fact, he didn't really like socialising at all but tonight he would force himself to enter that place and see where a few well thought out questions might take him. At the very least, thought Gus, it might just persuade this biker to move on and leave his town, he was a problem and Sgt Murphy did not like problems, they upset his easy life.

**

Grant was once again in his happy place as he steered his cruiser around the peaceful country roads. A few more vehicles now shared the road with him but not enough to spoil his ride or his thoughts.

The Pear of Anguish remained in the front of his mind, the device was fundamentally so simple in design and yet had the potential to be so effective and damaging beyond that which its image gave.

Shaped like the fruit which gave it the name it initially conjured up thoughts of pleasure and sweetness, the juices of a fresh pear dripping down your chin as you bit into it. Those thoughts were then taken to a dark place as the term 'anguish' entered your head.

Anguish – excruciating or acute distress, suffering or pain, to inflict with distress, suffering or pain, synonymous with agony, torment, and torture. Everything that Grant wanted to inflict on Lump with the added ingredient provided by this wonderfully evil article… disfigurement!

Grant pushed up his visor slightly to allow the wind to hit his face. Cold and fresh the air cleared his mind of the dark thoughts and brought him back to his next problem. How was he going to convince Emma to make the call to the care home without letting her know what she was getting herself involved in? Emma might think of herself as a bit of a bad girl, a maverick even, but this was way beyond her darkest nightmares.

Grant rode and thought and eventually a nucleus of an idea began to develop.

***

Ian shovelled the final pile of dirt over the already well-covered body of One a Year. He scattered a few leaves and bracken over the grave and rubbed his hands together satisfied with the job and to clear the dirt from his hands. He looked at the new addition now adorning the second finger of his right hand. A silver ring designed to look like two skeletal hands intertwined. He nodded his head down to the grave.

"Thanks, you prick, look on this as your payment for the ferryman," he said once again admiring the ring that he had taken from the finger of the now buried biker's hand.

The Girl, the Cop, and Lump

Grant arrived back in town and went through the ritual of parking his bike in the back courtyard. He once again entered the pub through the back door that led into the pubs kitchen hoping to find Emma alone but disappointedly found the kitchen empty. A quiet buzz of voices could be heard from the bar and not really wanting to make his way back to his room by going through the bar he looked around hoping to find another door that might lead directly to the staircase that climbed its way up to the guest's rooms. Once again he was left with a disappointed feeling as no door existed.

He entered the bar from the kitchen and looked around the bar area. He did not recognise any of the faces of the people enjoying a lunchtime beer and neither did he recognise the member of staff stood behind the bar.

The short and stocky young man was leaning against the bar talking to an elderly customer. He looked round as Grant appeared from the kitchen door, his long black hair was tied back into a ponytail and he was wearing dirty grey skinny jeans and a 'Sacrificed' t-shirt, a new band that Grant had heard of although he had never listened to any of their work.

He walked over to Grant and held out his hand offering it as a welcoming handshake. Grant grabbed his hand in the traditional handshake grip and then quickly transferred the grip to what is now recognised worldwide as the bikers or rockers handshake grip, two thumbs entwined, the hands raised upwards and forming a fist.

"You must be Andy," said Grant to the young barman.

"And you must be the biker guest that Emma mentioned, sorry I don't remember your name," replied Andy.

"It's Grant," said Grant, "where is Emma?"

"No idea mate, she's working the evening shift. Might be in her room, might be out with some of her mates."

Two lads, probably in their early twenties, entered the pub. Andy quickly acknowledged them by briefly turning his head to look in their direction and raising his right hand, holding up two fingers in the traditional 'peace' sign but on this occasion Grant guessed the barman was indicating that he would be with the new customers in a couple of minutes. One of the lads nodded his head to acknowledge that their arrival and custom had been noticed.

"So," said Andy turning his attention back to Grant, "I understand you ride an old timer's cruiser?"

"I prefer to describe her as slow comfortable ride, something you learn to appreciate with age," replied Grant, not really liking being described as an old timer

"Hey, no offence," the barman quickly replied, picking up on the subtle level of annoyance in Grant's voice, "am sure I'll grow into something similar myself one day."

This kid just couldn't stop thought Grant, he had the ability to offend without even realising he was doing it.

"Let me guess," said Grant, still smarting from the old timer's reference, "CBR, Ninja, Bandit."

The young barman laughed.

"You must be joking, one day maybe. I haven't even passed my test yet. I ride a Honda CBR125."

"Well I got the CBR bit right, no worries kid I'm sure you will grow into a big bike one day," replied Grant now happy to have been given the opportunity to get in a dig.

"Yep, sure will and when I do the Cripps are going to get a new member," replied Andy.

Grant tried his best not to react to this response from the young lad but it momentarily took him back. Not sure how well he had hidden his true reaction he quickly filled the silence, saying.

"The Cripps, not sure what you mean. What are Cripps?"

"Are you taking the piss mate?" said a genuinely surprised Andy, "The Crippens MCC, local bike gang. A cool bunch of muthers and nobody with a brain fucks with them."

"Sorry lad never heard of them but I'm not from around here and I'm a lone rider, not really into bike clubs," and quickly trying to get away from the subject he added, "anyway I'm going to my room. I'll catch up with you and hopefully Emma later."

Andy turned to make his way to serve the two lads who had entered the bar a few moments later and were now waiting impatiently at the bar. Without looking round he said to Grant.

"Yeah no problem, stay around long enough and you will probably meet some of the Crippens, they drink in here occasionally."

Grant made his way quietly to his room, his mind now distracted by the news that the Crippens were more local than he had imagined and maybe more notorious than he had thought. Once again the doubts began to invade his mind. He had come too far to stop now he tried to convince himself but the voice of doubt continued whispering, 'go home, you are out of your depth, you don't know what you are doing'.

Pills thought Grant, a couple (or three) sleepers would quieten the voice of doubt. Or maybe it was actually the voice of reason.

***

His room was dark as Grant woke from a deep sleep. His head felt heavy and he instantly regretted taking three sleeping pills and a Lorazepam. He looked at his wrist and was surprised to find that he wasn't wearing his watch. He rarely took this off, looking over towards the bedside table the neon lights of the watch face shone bright blue in the darkness; he couldn't even remember removing it from his wrist. Nearly ten minutes past six, Grant just hoped that it was PM and not the next morning. He sat himself up on the edge of the bed, he felt groggy but forced himself to stand up and walk towards the window that looked over the courtyard. He looked out into the darkening evening and beyond the double gates he could see the windows of two or three houses on the opposite side of the street. All had ground floor lights on, it must be the evening thought Grant.

After dousing his face for several minutes with freezing cold water and then cleaning his teeth he started to feel more human and awake. He hadn't slept that heavily for a very long time and to be honest he didn't want to do it again and more importantly could not afford to feel like this given his current position.

Taking off his sleep crumpled shirt he replaced it with a clean one. Opening the window he leaned out into the cold fresh air allowing it to add to the effects of feeling more awake that the cold water had started.

Taking his wallet from his jacket pocket and shoving it into the back pocket of his jeans and fastening the chain clip to his jeans he made his way down to the bar. He entered to find a few familiar faces, the bowling club were back and Emma was behind the bar and standing by the bar in front of a half pint of beer was Sergeant Gus Murphy.

"Good evening," said Murphy upon seeing Grant walk into the bar, "would you like a drink?"

"Very kind of you Officer," replied Grant hiding his surprise at seeing the police sergeant in the pub, "bitter please."

Murphy smiled and without breaking his eye contact with Grant said, "Emma, a pint of bitter for Mr. Richardson, please."

Grant didn't react, even though he had not been called by that name for almost a year. He pulled the empty bar stool away from the bar slightly and sat himself down next the cop.

"It is Mr. Richardson isn't it?" asked Murphy.

"It was, yes Sergeant Murphy, but hasn't been for a while now. Just call me Grant," he replied.

Murphy studied Grant's face looking for some kind of reaction to the disclosure of his newly acquired information about the man but saw nothing. He pressed on in the hope of pushing a button that would get a reaction from Grant.

"I'll stick with Mr. Richardson if you don't mind, Mr. John Richardson. After all, it is the name your mother gave you."

Grant had a deep desire to punch this interfering copper square in the throat but externally tried to remain calm and undisturbed by his persistence. Emma, having poured the pint of beer, placed it on the bar in front of Grant.

"That'll be three pounds twenty please Gus," her eyes flitted between the two men. She had enough experience of working in a pub to know that there was an uncomfortable standoff happening between them.

"Gus," she said trying to break the stare that the policeman still held with Grant, "you know your credit is shit here, pay up," she smiled to indicate that she was joking.

"Sorry Ems," he reached into the inside pocket of the dark blue blazer he was wearing and pulled out his wallet. Grant reached for the pint and took a sip, he would have preferred to take have taken a huge gulp of the cool beer to try and get rid of the lump that was currently stuck in his throat.

Murphy handed a five-pound note to Emma and reluctantly she turned away from the two men to go to the till to get his change.

"So, Mr. Richardson," Murphy continued to press but was interrupted by Grant.

"Sergeant Murphy, if you want to continue this conversation in this way I suggest you invite me to the station where a more formal setting will better suit the formality you are using, otherwise if you don't mind, thank you for the drink and please excuse me, I am in the mood for my own company tonight."

Grant picked up his drink and started to walk away having spotted an empty table in the far corner of the bar room, the furthest he could find from the bar and more importantly from Murphy. As he walked away he looked at Emma.

"Could I have a word later Emma?" he asked.

Before she could reply Murphy spoke again.

"Why were you interviewed by detectives about a year ago, Mr. Richardson?"

The continued use of his old name finally broke Grant's resolve. Stopping his progress towards the corner table he turned back and placing his beer on the bar he stood within inches of the annoying cop and spoke quietly into his ear.

"Murphy, stop calling me by that name and stop asking me fucking questions. I have not caused you any problems but if you want that to change I can arrange it. I will bring a level of hell into your life and drive Satan's stallions so far up your arse you won't be able to sit down for a fucking lifetime. Now back down you little prick."

Emma intervened immediately and, like Grant, she didn't raise her voice. Leaning slightly over the bar she said to both men, "gentlemen, I will not have trouble in my bar, now enjoy your drinks or," she nodded her head and looked downwards towards the large amount of cleavage she was displaying, "enjoy the view, but either way calm down or leave."

Murphy smiled at Grant, recovering his confidence slightly after initially been taken aback by the threat made by his target.

"No trouble Ems," he said to the bar girl and to Grant, "I never have any trouble sitting down." This time, he decided not to use the name that so troubled the biker who still stood uncomfortably within his personal space.

Collecting his drink from the bar and looking down at the police sergeant's huge frontage, Grant turned away but not without having the last word.

"Yeah I can see that," as he walked away, speaking now to Emma he said.

"That word please Emma."

Reaching the corner table he sat down, choosing the chair in the corner so that he could have a view of the whole bar and Gus Murphy. He was shook up by the conversation that had just taken place, he had not expected the police sergeant to look into his background, obviously there first meeting had niggled him more than Grant realised. He wondered how much more the copper knew about the police interview that had taken place and had yet to disclose or use against him, did he know about the crime that had taken place. Grant did not like not knowing, he did not like the fact that Murphy seemed to have the upper hand. He watched the cop sipping his half a pint of lager and was settled slightly when he saw that he wasn't receiving any more attention from him. He knew that this matter was not closed, it was obvious that Murphy would continue to pursue him until he left town and the one thing he didn't need was a copper breathing down his neck and watching his every move.

The arrival of Emma stopped his thoughts and concerns. She sat opposite him, no smile this time as she looked at him waiting for an explanation. He said nothing.

"Well?" she eventually asked. "Are you going to explain what just went on?"

"I don't think he likes me," replied Grant attempting to make light of the situation.

"Like you," replied the bar girl, her voice raised by an octave or two. "It sounded like he didn't even know you, who the hell is John Richardson?"

Grant thought for a few seconds and deciding that a total lie was not the way to continue this conversation he replied with a truthful but undetailed response.

"It was me, it's my past. I needed a new start; my life was a mess, socially and professionally. Believe me, I am not hiding anything, *(ok, maybe not a totally truthful explanation he thought to himself)*. I moved away from where I lived, changed my name by deed poll and started my life all over again."

Emma watched his face looking for some sign that he was lying to her, she saw nothing but still wouldn't want to play poker with this guy. She waited for a few seconds to see if there was anything else to be added but nothing came. While she didn't fully believe that Grant was being absolutely honest or at the very least was not telling her everything the increased mystery just made this man more attractive to her.

"You don't look like a John Richardson. It sounds like a name an accountant or a university lecturer would have," she said, the smile returning to her face.

"Neither I'm afraid," he said, "but he and that name are my past. Grant is my future, a future of freedom from complications." He now smiled, finding the fact that he had just described his life as lacking in complication both funny and ironic. In forty-odd years of being John Richardson, his life had never been as complicated as it had been over the past eighteen months and especially the last twelve.

"Okay, so what was the mysterious Mr. Richardson before he transformed himself into this troublemaking, moody but still mysterious biker?" asked Emma, now genuinely interested for personal reasons.

"He was a prison officer darling, a good one for over twenty years," replied Grant. Emma detected a hint of regret in Grants answer to her question.

The young barmaid was genuinely surprised.

"No way, *you* were a screw," and then before Grant could respond to the question/statement, she added, "yeah actually I can see that, you do look like a bit of a thug," laughing as she said it.

Grant didn't respond and Emma could see that he was now in deep thought, maybe the regret she had detected a few moments earlier was bigger than he was letting on.

"So why leave if you were so good at it?" she asked, still interested but the question was more used to break the uncomfortable silence and Grant's mood that had suddenly become darker.

Grant replied instinctively with one word.

"Complicated."

Emma knew that this conversation had just reached its conclusion. The man sat opposite to her now looked sad, an emotion she had not seen from him before. The sadness was mixed with anger and bitterness too. She didn't like seeing him like this.

"You said you wanted a word," she said changing the subject and hoping to change the heavy mood hanging over the corner table.

Grant looked up, the painful memories running around inside his head temporarily making him forget what he had initially wanted to speak to Emma about. He forced these memories back into the locked mental box he had placed them into a long time ago. He hadn't thought back to that part of his life for some time and the resurrected memories reminded him why. "Yeah, sorry," said Grant still struggling to put the bitterness back into the box where it belonged. He tried to think positively, the twenty odd years he had spent in the custodial world had left him with many contacts and skills that were now much better suited to his new life or at least this current part of his life which he just wanted to be sorted and out of the way so that he could continue to piece together a more settled normal life again.

"I need a favour. Need to pull a bit of a joke on a mate of mine and I could really do with your help to pull it off," said Grant putting into place the beginning of the story he had concocted on his bike ride earlier that afternoon.

Seeing the opportunity to finally be rid of the heavy mood Emma responded enthusiastically.

"Ooooh, I am always up for a bit of a joke," the smile on her face grew wider. "Tell me more," she said.

Grant explained what was (untruthfully) going on.

"I am up here because on old Army mate of mine, who I haven't seen for years, is getting married for the second time. He doesn't want a stag do and doesn't know I am here. Me and a few other mates of his want a stag do but we all know that he will not be up for it so basically we are going to snatch him and take him on a beer tour. The problem is that we need to take him unawares and that is where you come in. His mum is in an old peoples' home a few miles from here, so we thought if you called him and pretended to be one of the reception staff and somehow got him to come to the home. We thought that you could say that there had been some contract changes to the resident's care agreement that needed to be discussed and signed. We would then follow him when he goes there and we would grab the boring git and get the stag do started. It sounds bad but we all know that he would see the funny side of it and thoroughly enjoy himself."

"Grab him, snatch him," said Emma, "sounds more like a kidnapping!"

Emma had no idea that she had actually described the operation exactly for what it was.

"No, no," responded Grant slightly anxious that Emma would not agree to be involved.

"We don't intend to knock him out and throw him into the back of a van," which is of course exactly what he and Ian intended to do to their victim. Grant recalled the details of the conversation he and Ian had had earlier that day. Grant had suggested the use of chloroform to render Lump unconscious. Ian had explained the difficulty they would have trying to lay their hands on such a controlled substance and had opted for the baseball bat around the back of the head method. They had still not agreed on a solution to this part of their, or to be more correct, Ian's plan. Grant had no idea at that precise moment how relevant Ian's suggestion of a more direct and violent method would become. Emma thought about the request for a few seconds and then enthusiastically responded with a resounding "Yes."

Grant was seconds away from learning that even when you plan things out either in advance or on the hoof things don't always go as you thought they would.

The pub door swung open with a thud against the wall and in walked three large men, their leather jackets and cuts easily identified them as bikers.

Murphy and Emma were the first to look around on hearing the door bang, only slightly ahead of the rest of the inhabitants of the bar. As for Grant, he had no need to look round. He had a clear and unobstructed view of the three new 'clients'.

The two skulls and their skeletal spines that wrapped themselves around a sword made up the insignia of the back patch that clearly identified two of the bikers as members of The Crippens MCC, the third of the trio wore a denim cut on which no back patch was sewn. Grant assumed that he was a Prospect.

All three of the bikers looked around the bar as Murphy stood up from his bar stool and turned around to face them.

Pushing out his chest and unsuccessfully trying to suck in his belly, Sergeant Gus Murphy spoke with as much authority as he could muster.

"Get out. You know you are not welcome here."

The larger of the trio - a formidable character with long black hair and sporting a goatee beard that was tied and wrapped to form a 'chin ponytail' - looked directly at Murphy with utter scorn and hate all over his face.

"We aren't stopping Muttley, we're just looking for one of our own," he said.

Murphy visibly shook with anger at the sound of the nickname that he detested.

"The name is Sergeant Murphy and don't you forget it Christopher," he used the real name of the biker rather than his gang member name in a childish response to his nickname being used.

Grant didn't need to hear the road name of this individual; he just knew that when he heard Murphy call him by his given name that this was Lump.

The man was huge, his biceps almost ripping through the leather material of his jacket. His black jeans had the faded look of a pair that had been worn without being washed for way too long and his boots were large, bulky and scuffed, as unclean as the rest of him. Grant's first thought was, *how the fuck did he and Ian think they were going to take this guy out?* If ever a biker lived up to his road name Lump did it better than most.

Lump ignored Murphy's attempt to wind him up.

"Have you seen One a Year?" he demanded.

Murphy responded, "Not for months and believe me, I would remember seeing that filthy piece of scum." Lumps face almost blackened with anger, his eyes closed almost shut and his heavy broad forehead became a frown that forced his thick dark eyebrows over his eyes.

"I wasn't speaking to you, I was asking these cunts." The biker's voice so loud it almost resonated off the walls of the pub. He cast his arm and hand out in a large arc in the direction of the customers of the bar as he said it as if more emphasis was required to indicate that he meant the clientele.

Leaving his two comrades guarding the pub door he made his way through the bar. As he passed each group of drinkers he asked the same question.

"You seen him?"

Every time he asked he received the same response: the shaking of heads that indicated no.

He got closer and closer to where Emma and Grant were sat and came to a stop a couple of feet from the barmaid.

"Hello again slag, your snatch still as tight as I remember it?"

Emma's face turned bright red and she lowered her face to look at the floor.

"Please Lump just leave, nobody here has seen your friend," she said.

Lump ignored her and stared at Grant.

"And who the fuck are you?" he snarled.

Grant stood up, his six foot and a bit stature dwarfed by the frame of the biker.

"Nobody you need to be concerned about," he replied hoping that he didn't look as scared as he felt. The adrenaline was racing through his body and the fight or flight human response was kicking in just as Lump grabbed him by his shirt and took away the flight option.

"I don't get concerned by anyone," said Lump, the last thing he said before his face slammed into the table that Emma was still sat next to.

In an instinctive reaction borne from years of previous training, Grant had grabbed hold of Lump's clenched fist and wrist with both of his hands and while holding it into the centre of this chest where he had been grabbed he spun around, ending up standing alongside the surprised biker. He dropped his inside elbow onto the now straight biker's arm and forced it downwards against Lump's elbow and upper arm. Lump had no choice but to bend forward and this is how his face and head ended up slamming onto the table top, any reluctance on Lump's part to move in the direction he was being forced would have resulted in a broken arm and probably a dislocated shoulder.

The two bikers by the door made a move towards their restrained 'brother' but were stopped in their tracks as Grant applied more pressure to the armlock with which he was controlling Lump who released a scream of agony.

"One more step and this fucker will never wank again," and to emphasise his intent and ability he placed his thumbs behind Lumps clenched fist and bent it forward and inwards towards his wrist wrenching away the biker's grip from his shirt.

"I fucking mean it," he said as Lump gave out another yell of pain.

The bikers did not move. Murphy pushed his way past them and stood next to Grant. He didn't say a word and for the first time since meeting him, Grant felt gratitude towards the cop.

Turning his attention back to the biker who was still under his control he delivered a simple instruction.

"Now Christopher, I am going to let you go and step back a couple of paces. If you react in any way that suggests that you are going to be violent towards me again you will be leaving this pub in an ambulance. Once I let you go I want you to leave and take your puppy dogs with you. Understand?"

Lump grunted a response that Grant took as an indication that he understood. He released the biker and stepped away as he said he would do, Murphy stepped back also standing shoulder to shoulder with the man who not that long ago he had been provoking.

Lump stood up and backed away into the centre of the bar. He rotated his shoulder in the socket over and over again while rubbing his elbow, the pain of the arm lock still evident on his face.

Walking backwards towards his two fellow bikers he never took his eyes off Grant.

"Keep looking over your shoulder, friend, you have no idea what you have just done. You've just signed your own death certificate," he growled. "The next time we meet will not be pleasant."

Grant smiled, "Oh I have no doubt about that Lump," he said lingering over the biker's road name and ending with an emphasised 'pah' sound.

All three bikers left the bar still walking backwards, refusing and not wanting to turn their backs on this stranger. As he backed out of the door Lump gave one last indication of his intent by tracing an invisible 'cut' line with his thumb across his own throat.

The door closed much quieter than it had opened just minutes earlier and the silence was broken by the sobbing of Emma.

Grant was still tense and hyped up by the adrenalin so unfortunately for Emma sympathy was somewhat lacking as he said.

"Please tell me you didn't sleep with that turd?"

Through her tears and sobbing, Emma said quietly and with clear shame.

"You don't say no to Lump."

Grant felt the bile and anger simultaneously rise.

"Are you saying he raped you?"

Emma stopped sobbing and looked up at Grant and then moved her eyes towards Murphy as she said, "Apparently it's not rape if you don't say no and I just said you don't say no to Lump."

Grant glared at Murphy, "You fucking knew about this?"

Murphy ignored the question completely and with genuine concern said, "Grant, I suggest you leave right now."

A Change of Plan

Grant closed the door of his room behind him and placed his forehead against it.

"Fuck!" he exclaimed to the empty room.

He brought his right hand up to his face and rubbed both eyes at the same time with his thumb and first finger, moving these two digits away from each other and so stretching his eyelids wide across his face.

"Fuck," he repeated.

The process commonly referred to as 'the adrenalin dump' was kicking in and Grant's hands started to shake and his breathing rate increased.

He reached for his phone and with a still shaking hand unlocked it, his first attempt failed as somewhere in the process he pressed a wrong number. He slowed himself down and successfully unlocked it at the second attempt. Opening the 'recent numbers' page he pressed the screen for the number which would connect him with Ian.

It rang about five or six times before a tired sounding Ian answered the phone.

"What do you want me to invent now?"

"I've just met Lump and it didn't go well," said Grant. Silence.

"Say something," said Grant clearly worried because very little left Ian speechless.

"Fuck," was the initial response.

"Yeah you are about two minutes behind where I am right now. Suggestions?" asked Grant.

"Where is he now," Ian sounded concerned.

"I'm guessing he is somewhere between here and the clubhouse, nursing a sore arm and shoulder and almost certainly plotting his revenge," Grant answered the question even though he couldn't work out the relevance of it.

"What the fuck did you do?" Ian's voice was becoming more worried which each sentence.

"I defended myself," replied Grant.

The reply was typically Ian.

"For fuck's sake dude, could you not have just taken one for the team?"

With a high level of urgency, Grant asked, "Can you just stop with the fucking questions and come with some ideas?"

"Leave it with me, I will ring you, I have a plan. Stay put," Ian hung up the phone.

Grant hated it when his friend said he had a plan.

He sat on the bed and waited and as he waited he thought. He thought through the events in the bar, the revelation of Emma's words and the realisation that Murphy had known of it happening, had heard that young girl explain what had happened to her and advised her that what she thought had happened actually hadn't because she hadn't declined. His mind also dwelled on the last words that had been spoken to him before he left the bar and returned to his room, it wasn't so much the advice that he got to get away from here or the genuine concern in Murphy's voice that had made Grant realise that the cop was serious. It was the fact that for the first time since they had met Murphy had called him by his name.

Leaving was going to make his future plans awkward at the very least, staying could make remaining in one piece or even alive just as difficult. He had no doubt that sooner rather than later Lump and a few of his brothers in arms would arrive seeking him out to serve up a bit of justice and revenge.

He began to pack up the few belongings he had left in the room. On this occasion (and not for the first time in his life) Grant decided that running was a better option to staying. He would pack in anticipation of receiving that very same advice from his accomplice who was putting into motion his plan, whatever that may be. He didn't want to give that thought too much focus as he remembered the last time he had heard Ian use the words, 'I have a plan'. That had been over thirty years ago when they had both been young naïve soldiers in Northern Ireland. The stark days of the daily bombs and bullets had lessened somewhat by the early 1980s but the attacks still occurred on a fairly regular basis and the danger levels remained high. Soldiers were encouraged by the officers in charge to grow their hair slightly longer to blend in with the Irish youth but the squaddie fashion of bomber jackets, blue jeans and desert boots made it still quite easy to identify them.

The pair of them had finished a three-day covert observation exercise that had required them to remain out of sight for the whole of the three days in the confines of a small copse of bushes. It had been this period and situation that had forged their lifelong friendship, shitting into a plastic bag in front of another man could have that effect on you.

On the second day of the operation, a car had parked up just a matter of a few feet away from their hiding place making it very easy for them both to listen to the conversation that took place. The two occupants of the

146

vehicle, well-known members of a terrorist organisation were basically agreeing the final details of a plan to plant a bomb at the gates of a large and hugely important military camp, it would undoubtedly have been a massive coup for the terrorists. Grant had laid perfectly still and silent listening intently to every word so that he could deliver a comprehensive report back to base. The silence was broken by Ian's now famous catchphrase, this time, whispered into Grant's right ear, "I have a plan mate, watch my back."

Leaving his M16 rifle on the ground he had worked his way out of the copse by slowly shuffling backwards and once out had approached the vehicle from behind staying within the blind spots of the two occupants. He had crouched down at the back of the vehicle and retrieved a pistol with silencer already attached from under his jacket that had been tucked down the back of his belt or trousers. Before Grant had been able to bring his rifle up from his side and take aim in the prone position Ian had casually walked alongside the passenger side of the vehicle and through the open passenger window had fired two shots, both muffled of course by the silencer. Bullet holes were put into both men's heads.

Grant burst from the side of the clump of bushes, unarmed and shocked out of his mind. He could not believe that a simple observation mission had suddenly turned into murder without provocation. By the time he arrived at Ian's side, Ian had retrieved a square piece of card out of his pocket that was slightly bigger than a business card. In the top left corner was the red cross on a white background of the English flag, the bottom right corner contained the red hand of Ulster with the words U.V.F. For God and Ulster printed around it. Diagonally across the centre of the card was written U. V. F' d.

Grant watched as Ian tossed it into the lap of the dead passenger and then turning to Grant said, "let's get the fuck out of here mate."

They had called in their helivac and were waiting at the RV point when Ian said, "When we get back to base leave all the talking to me, you agree where you can and say you cannot remember if you feel you can't agree."

From that point forward, all the way through the chopper flight back to Bosnabrook and the onward drive back to base under Palace Barracks the pair never said a word to each other.

They were both questioned, together, by the unit commander a well experienced Captain. Questioned was actually a loose description of what actually happened.

The officer had simply asked, "Will what happened here be convincingly explained and believed?"

"Yes sir," had replied Ian.

"And you will both be saying the same thing?" the Captain asked while scanning his gaze towards both them.

"We both witnessed what happened, sir; it was clearly a UVF killing of IRA members. We both kept our position in covert mode as per orders sir," replied Ian like he was almost reading from a script.

"And what about you, son?" The officer was looking in Grant's direction.

Grant looked down towards the floor and quietly replied, "As he said, sir."

It was clear that this officer had no belief in Grant's ability to stand up to a hearing and one week later he was posted out of the province and over to Germany to a unit that spent nine months a year out on exercise in secret 'war' locations. Because of this Grant found that he was unable to attend the subsequent hearing which he found out years later had lasted no more than fifteen minutes. He also discovered that there had been an increased number of successful attacks upon the UVF and its supporters by the IRA during the months following the 'terrorist on terrorist hit' that had been witnessed by, as the hearing had described: two very brave and professional members of the British Army.

Grant's phone rang bringing him back to the reality of Ian's current plan.

"Shoot," said Grant as he answered his mobile, screwing his face up as the irony of his choice of word dawned on him.

"Not yet mate you trigger-happy bastard, but it may have to happen. Your failure and unwillingness to take a kicking have made all the little Crippens go running to their nest," Ian replied. Even though Grant couldn't see his face he just knew that Ian was smiling at this very moment.

"So, what is the plan?" he continued, "blow up the clubhouse while they are all together in one place?"

There was a moment of thought-filled silence before Ian replied, "Liking your thinking brother, liking it very much. End the mission quickly and get ourselves some well-earned R&R with some strong beer and dirty women, however, I couldn't make a bomb that quickly and I aren't climbing over that fucking wall and its gannet wire for no one."

"So it's over then," said Grant clearly disappointed that he was unable to finish what he had started.

"Far from it, me old mucka," came Ian's response. "We sit this one out and wait for them to make their move."

"But we know what their next move will be," said Grant. "hunt me down and fucking kill me"!

"Exactly mate, the only guaranteed way to flush them out of their little well defended den, you play bait." There was not even a hint of humour in his reply, Ian was being serious.

"So you expect me to sit here in this pub and wait for the kicking of my life to happen?" asked Grant.

"Of course not you twat," replied Ian. "In fact, why you are still there fucking amazes me. Leave, speak with nobody and go to the 'factory'. Usual drill: make sure no one follows you, use alternate routes and entry points and for fuck sake look out for ugly hairy bastards on bikes."

Grant didn't quite finish his next question of "Will you call me?" before Ian ended the call.

Grant put on his jacket, picked up his belongings and bike helmet and left the room. Leaving the key on the bed he did not bother locking the room. He made his way through a bar full of people watching him as he made his way to the kitchen door. Emma moved swiftly along the bar space meeting him at the kitchen door and as she began to speak Grant grabbed her and directed her through the door into the pub's kitchen.

"Leaving then?" she said the anger all over her face and in her voice. "Cause the trouble and fuck off like a coward leaving us to clear up the inevitable mess that will follow."

"They are looking for me, Emma so the further I am away from this place the better and safer for all of you," he said making his way through the small kitchen to the rear door that led outside to the courtyard.

"They will still come here first!" she screamed at him and then pleadingly, "Take me with you."

Grant stopped and turned looking at the frightened girl that stood in front of him. He walked back towards her and grabbed both her arms gently. "Here Emma, away from me you may just get a slap if you are really unlucky. With me, you are sure to get seriously hurt or worse. Tell them I have left and you have no idea where I went other than out of town heading north."

Emma looked at him and she put her lips together to say the word 'but', Grant kissed her and pulled her into his body. Slowly pulling away from her he winked and smiled. "They won't get away with what they did to you; that is the one promise I make. Now, any chance of unlocking those gates for me?"

Emma smiled. "Already done, I knew you couldn't stay," she said waving the small padlock key in his direction.

She walked over to the gates and pulled them open as Grant started up his bike gunning it loudly and putting his main headlights on, this time he wanted everyone to see him leaving. He revved the bike loudly again and rode it through the gates nodding at Emma as he passed. This time, he turned left back toward the town, helping Emma with the lie she would have to tell to the Crippens when they returned, the last thing she saw was him heading through town in a northerly direction.

***

The Crippens' clubhouse was full. The majority of the bikers were by and around the bar area, all drinking and all talking about what they heard had happened earlier that evening. Stories were swapped, pulled apart, embellished and questioned. The real business and the actual details of what had happened were being discussed in the smaller room that was separated from the main bar area with a large solid wooden door. 'Mass' had been called and the six 'titled' members of the MC were in heavy discussion in this room.

At the head of a heavy oak table sat the club president. He sat staring down the centre of the table engraved within it was the clubs emblem around which names had been crudely engraved into the wood, these were the names of the fallen soldiers of the Crippens MC, the freshest looking read One a Year.

The other five bikers were involved in something that could not even be loosely described as a conversation, it was a mix of questions, accusations, threats to kill and maim and angry outbursts about things not even connected with their current situation.

The Priest had heard enough and nodded at his vice president Panhead who in turn stood up and struck the table twice with the handle head of the large flick knife being held in his right hand.

"Quiet," he said, his gravelly voice making everyone in the room go silent immediately.

Panhead had a reputation of slamming people's heads into his bike engine or to use its other name 'the panhead', as was often used to describe a Harley Davidson's engine because of the distinct shape of the rocker covers. On his previous bike, these rocker covers were covered in dried splashes of victim's blood and were the only part of Panhead's bike that was never cleaned. Everyone in that room knew that many of Panheads victims had been fellow bikers and not one of them wanted to join the long and undistinguished list.

The Priest stood up and held up his left hand to show his requirement for the silence to continue. The little finger of his left hand was completely missing. He spoke to the motley crew of positioned club members.

"One of our brethren has gone missing, now presumed MIA," one of the gathered rubbed his hand across the freshly engraved name of One a Year. "Another of our brothers brings us together tonight to report on an attack of one of our own, the very man Lump himself." The Priest looked at Lump as he spoke these words who never noticed as he was still rubbing his still painful elbow.

"Now," continued the Cripps's president, "I am not suggesting that these two incidents are linked in any way but it does show that a certain amount of disrespect is being paid towards our little organisation and it would seem that it is coming from the very people that we protect with our love and concern for their very lives and livelihoods. Maybe we have been lacking in our duties, perhaps we have not been moving amongst our congregation to remind them of the love we have for them, maybe we have been focussed on the rewards of our work before putting the work in."

Cowboy, the Club Secretary had reached for his bottle of beer as his president said these last words and with second thoughts left it on the table untouched.

"It is my decree that we must be more in touch with our flock, move amongst once again and remind them of the good work that we do for them."

He paused and looked upwards to the roof of the room, the tattooed black band around his neck in which were white skulls with deathly grinning faces was his version of the priest's dog collar, a tribute to his poor dead father, a priest of many years before his son had killed him when he was aged just fifteen.

"But..." he said, "before the good work of our beloved master begins we have to educate a visitor to our parish, a visitor who believes it is alright to lay a hand on one of my brothers. And so within the next twenty-four hours, I would like one of this strangers hands laid before me so that I am satisfied that we have educated him correctly... do I make myself understood?"

The Priest cast his piercing gaze around the table at the bikers who sat at the very alter of badness. They all nodded.

"Ride in at least pairs," added the president, "and do not fail to bring the sacrifice I request."

Picking up a wooden gavel whose two ends were sculpted into the shapes of skulls he struck it with force against the top of a black wooden skull that sat on the table directly in front of his chair. The meeting was over.

***

Ian stood in the shadows of the buildings opposite to the entrance gate to the clubhouse complex and watched as three sets of paired riders rode out and headed out in the direction of Milton Dryton. The gate slid shut once they had left and he heard the heavy sliding locks clunk back into place.

Waiting for a few minutes to ensure no other bikers were going to come out of the compound he then made his way back to his van parked about a quarter mile down the street, as he walked he retrieved his phone from his pocket and called Grant.

He was glad that he received no reply assuming that Grant was already on the road and unable to take his call. The call went to a voicemail service, he left the simple message, "see you at the factory and dust down Bertha for me."

Into Second Gear

After leaving the pub Grant had ridden through Milton Dryton leaving the town behind him before doubling back on himself and heading back in the direction he needed to be going. He took a completely different route and took at least half a dozen pointless turnings along the way to ensure that nobody was following him.

He entered Blackbrook Woods from the west side which did allow him to ride his bike quite a way into the woods before having to stop and hide it as before. There then followed quite a walk before he reached the wooden shack, by the time he had reached it he had picked up Ian's voicemail.

Where there had been a tipped over chair and a piece of tarpaulin hiding a dead body now stood a more sturdy wooden chair with a heightened chair back. Unlike the other chair that had held One a Year in place this replacement was of a much better quality. Each joint was reinforced with metal fastening brackets and attached to the arms and two front legs were leather shackles with big heavy metal buckles. Another longer leather shackle was attached to the top of the heightened chair back with yet another about six inches below it. The chair itself was secured to the floor with strong metal brackets.

Clearly Ian had been busy after he last left this place.

On a small table, about two feet from the chair stood a small object covered with a piece of hessian cloth. Grant did not need to lift the cloth to know that the object was the Pear of Anguish.

He walked to the back of the room and placed his jacket in the corner next to a larger black bag which he then pulled out towards the centre of the room. Two straps fastened with buckles similar to those of a belt held the bag closed. Undoing the buckles he unrolled the bag rather like a tool roll which in fact was exactly what this bag was: an extremely large tool roll. A varying array of 'tools' were secured in place inside the roll with cloth loops, each measured and placed exactly to hold each tool in place ensuring that they would not move in transit and be damaged. The centre tool was Bertha. A heavy hardwood baseball bat with a polishing cloth tied around the handle. Grant removed the bat from the bag and after untying the polishing cloth he sat in the newly positioned chair and commenced to 'dust off' Bertha as Ian had asked. Grant knew that Bertha was only ever polished before being used, Grant also knew that this baseball bat had never been used in a game of baseball.

As he polished and waited for Ian to arrive Grant recalled the story that Ian had told him about Bertha and how he had first taken ownership. He had owned the bat from the age of thirteen - it had been given to him by his father, a violent drunk. One night no long after Ian's thirteenth birthday his father had a full on argument and slanging match with a neighbour. Nobody could recall the reason for the argument but Ian had no doubt it would probably have been about his father's behaviour following one of his many drunken nights out. Ian's father had been a violent man for much of his life spending a lot of his youth as a football hooligan, progressing to a skinhead gang and as he got older and a family was produced he became satisfied with a fight whenever it came along. A fight with Ian's father though was never a fair one, he fought with weapons and his preferred weapon of choice was the hardwood baseball bat.

The man though had become old and his body weakened through being put through so much violence and on the night of this particular neighbourhood argument Ian's father was both too drunk and too tired to dish out his own form of punishment. It would have to wait for a more convenient time, or so he had thought.

The following morning he had awoken to the sight of police cars and an ambulance into the back of which was being wheeled his neighbour, obviously in a bad way if his head and face were anything to go by. Walking into Ian's bedroom to tell him about the activity going on outside he found his son curled up in the corner of the room totally naked and clinging onto a blood-covered baseball bat.

Following the argument and after everyone had gone to bed Ian had taken his father's treasured bat and in an effort to prove his worth to his father had broken into the neighbour's house and battered him half to death as he lay in his bed. The man remained in a coma for nearly three months and following months of recovery and rehabilitation, he returned home to spend the rest of his days in a wheelchair and unable to ever speak properly again due to minor brain damage.

To return the favour, Ian's father had destroyed all of his son's clothing, cleaned and hidden the weapon and was Ian's alibi, stating to the police that his son had never left the house that night having had to undress him and stay with him throughout the night to look after him as he had been so ill. Despite their suspicions the police had no evidence to prove who did it and the crime remained unsolved.

A few months later his father presented him with a freshly and deeply polished Bertha along with a large tool roll style bag with, as his father put it, "enough room to add to your collection just like your father did over the years."

Ian burst through the door of the shack causing Grant to jump to his feet and brandish the bat in a traditional baseball game hitting style.

Ian at first smiled and then burst out laughing. "Couldn't hit a barn door you prick," and reaching for the bat added, "now give it here and never raise Bertha in anger again." Handing over the treasured baseball bat Grant enquired into how 'the plan' was progressing.

"Very well," responded Ian. "As we speak the Crippens are hunting you down with the intention of killing you - if you're lucky - the clubhouse is in a state of lockdown, they are riding in pairs…."

"How the fuck is that going very well?" said Grant.

"Because Lump could not resist leaving the safety of the clubhouse, he had to go out to find you again," said Ian raising his shoulder and then arms and palms of his hands to the ceiling in a 'it doesn't get better than this – you must be able to see that' kind of pose.

Grant still looked unconvinced and confused.

"Fuck me it's like working with a brain damaged ape. We lost control, our plans went out of the window, we should have been left in a position where Lump was unobtainable… he is out and about… we are now back in control… so to quote that little mouse thing, seemples"!!!

"How the fuck is this simples?" asked a now even more confused Grant.

"Jump in the van and I'll explain on the way," said Ian chucking the van keys towards Grant.

Five minutes later they both climbed into Ian's van as Grant started the engine Ian typed a road name into his sat nav. Grant was about to ask what was so important and where was Whitley Road when he noticed the ring on Ian's finger.

"Why in God's name are you wearing One a Year's ring?" he asked Ian.

"Firstly, I don't believe in God, secondly, it's payment for my services and the respect I showed towards his filthy corpse," replied Ian.

"It's fucking evidence Ian!" shouted Grant.

"It's only evidence if I get caught and having looked at my plan getting caught is not part of it, now bloody drive. Ozzy will tell you the way!" And right on cue, the voice of Ozzy Osbourne announced from the sat nav, "Take the next left man."

***

The five Crippens pulled up outside of the Old Tudor House Hotel and Pub. Lump dismounted his bike and spoke with one of the other bikers.

"I'm going in there just to take a look to see if that arsehole is still in there. If he isn't, I'll find out where he is. You and Bull take a ride around town and see if you can see him walking around."

Turning to another of the bikers he pulled a machete from inside his jacket and handed it to him. "You keep this ready but hidden away, understand me?"

The biker nodded his head.

He looked at the two remaining bikers, "You pair watch the doors and have my back just in case it kicks off inside."

Two bikers dismounted and followed Lump towards the pubs front doors, remaining outside as Lump entered the pub for the second time that night.

Lump stopped just inside the doorway, being more cautious this time he scanned the public bar for any sign of the stranger who had handled himself just a little bit too well for his liking. Comfortable that he was no longer around he walked towards the bar aware that everyone was watching him and the place had gone deathly quiet.

Murphy did not even look around as he said, "I'm assuming you came back looking for round two Lump?"

"Shut it pig," responded the pissed off biker and then directing his question towards Emma who was stood behind the bar he said, "Where's your latest shag, bitch?"

Emma tried to remain composed but her shaky voice did not help to hide her fear.

"He isn't my shag and I have no idea where he is. He rode out of town about half an hour after he shoved your arm halfway out of its socket."

"Rode you say, now that means he is either a cowboy or a biker and I don't smell no horse shit around here," said a smiling Lump.

"Yeah he's a biker, bit of a strange one though because he washes… every fucking day," replied Emma.

Sensing it was going to kick off yet again Murphy raised his bulky body from the bar stool and turned to face the troublesome biker.

"Lump just leave, your quarry is not here, You cause any trouble in here and I will arrest you and throw your sorry ass in a cell."

Lump ignored Sgt Murphy and made his way towards the bar and then climbed upon it. He walked up and down the bar kicking half filled and empty glasses alike smashing onto the bar floor. As he paced up and down he yelled at the clientele.

"The Priest wants you all to know that he is displeased, which for the uneducated amongst you means he is well and truly fucked off. So you will be seeing a lot more of me and my brothers again. However I give my word that anyone who tells me something that leads me to find the cunt I am looking for will be left alone."

He jumped off the bar landing on the side where Emma was stood. Picking up a bottle of whiskey he smashed it against the large mirror that was attached to the wall behind the bar, the bottle broke spraying a sweet smelling orange liquid all over the floor, bar, a few customers and Emma. He grabbed the latter by her hair and pushed her face up against the cracked mirror.

"How about I scrape your pretty little face up and down this cracked glass until you tell me the truth you fucking spunk sponge."

Emma screamed and pleaded with the biker.

"Please I've told you the truth, he left, headed north out of town, please don't hurt me Lump."

"Describe the bike before I put go faster stripes down your face," threatened Lump.

"Black, lots of chrome, cruiser style ride, think it was a Yammy."

Lump pressed her face against the mirror and with his other hand roughly squeezed her breasts. Then licking his tongue up and down the exposed half of her face he said, "See you later sweet cheeks and this time, we'll do the other hole."

Grabbing her hair again he forced her away from the mirror and threw her to the floor. Her hand slid across the glass-covered flooring and a large shard of broken bottle tore into the palm of the hand. She screamed in agony but Lump just ignored her. Murphy ran round to the other side of the bar grabbing a bar towel on the way and wrapped it around Emma's bleeding hand.

Gus Murphy stood up from behind the bar and yelled in the direction of the departing biker.

"I swear Lump that I will see you and your kind in hell first before I let you destroy my town!"

The biker stopped, turned and laughed.

"The boys will be glad to hear that news because hell is exactly what The Priest intends to bring to your shithole of a town." With that, he exited the bar leaving his bit of carnage behind him.

Outside, he instructed the awaiting bikers to ride around town to both find the riders who had gone before and see if they could spot Grant around the town and surrounding areas.

"I'll ride back to the clubhouse," he announced.

Battle warned against doing this.

"Remember what we were told," he told Lump.

"We are not to ride alone."

"Don't fucking tell me what I should or should not do," he retorted, grabbing Battle by the front of his jacket to emphasise his annoyance. "Now get fucking going, look around for about half an hour and then head back home. I'll see you all there."

With that Lump got onto his bike and started his ride back to the home of The Crippens to report back on what had happened, he wanted to take the full credit for the warning to the locals having been issued. He was desperate for a senior position in the club and he knew that The Priest rewarded men of action.

**

About a mile from the clubhouse Grant sat behind the wheel of the van which he had parked on the corner of a junction with the main road as instructed to do by Ian. Ian himself had jumped out of the van and made his way across the road and was now hiding in the shadows of a street corner, his trusty Bertha held loosely against the outside of one leg. Grant had decided not to ask any questions, not that he needed to, it was easy to work out what Ian's plan was. He had issued just one request to Ian before he had left the van.

"Don't damage his face."

The pair waited and waited, both having similar thoughts and worries; how were they going to go up against more than one of The Crippens; what if the bikers didn't return this way or didn't return at all?

They didn't have to worry for too long as about twenty minutes after parking the van a single headlight appeared in the distance at the top of Whitley Road. As the bike got closer Grant watched as Ian ran out into the middle of the road, the baseball bat raised ready to strike but the required swing never happened. Lump saw the figure run out from the side street and immediately recognised the outline of a bat being raised to strike. Panic forced him into making a big mistake, as he leaned the bike to the right in an attempt to swerve around the shadowy figure his right foot pressed down on the rear brake pedal. The rear tyre swerved and skidded one way then the other and the rider lost control resulting in a mixture of fortunes. As bike and rider slid down the road in amongst a blaze of sparks and the sound of scratching metal against asphalt it meant that Ian was not able to make contact with the biker and knock him from his bike but it also meant that Lump was now left vulnerable.

The bike came to a halt about twenty feet from Ian's position in the middle of the road. From behind the van windscreen, Grant watched as Ian slowly walked towards the stricken biker who was frantically trying to untrap himself from beneath the crashed bike. Ian stood at the head

163

end of Lump, his feet shoulder distance apart. Looking down he and the biker looked at each other.

Ian smiled and said, "Hello."

As the bat arced its way down towards Lump's head Grant screamed a plea, "Ian, not the face!"

The warning went unheard, but it did not matter for Ian had remembered his friend's request. Bertha slammed into the back of Lump's crash helmet-protected head and the biker fell unconscious.

Grant opened the driver's door and now stood next to the open door watching Ian struggle to move the bike away from Lump.

Ian looked over his shoulder.

"Are you going to fucking stand there all night like a gawping idiot or are you going to give me a hand?" he shouted at Grant.

Grant ran to his friend's aid and between them they managed to unhook the unconscious Crippen from what was a relatively undamaged bike considering the slide it had just completed.

"Grab a leg," Ian demanded as he grabbed a booted foot. Grant grabbed the other and between them they dragged the heavy body across the road towards the van. Opening the back doors the biker was then dumped unceremoniously into the back.

"There's rope in the back, tie his hands and feet," called out Ian as he made his way hurriedly back towards the bike.

It took Grant just a few minutes to tie up the hands and feet adding his own touch by looping the rope between the two sets of knots to leave Lump in a hogtied position. Proud of his work he jumped out of the back of the van and slammed the doors shut. Ian was still trying to get the bike upright and as he did so he glimpsed Grant watching him yet again.

Standing up he placed his hands on his hips.

"Watching me struggle is becoming a bit of an annoying habit. Help me you prick," said a pissed off Ian.

Even with the two of them lifting the bike it still took all their combined efforts to achieve it but eventually it stood upright and Grant flicked out the side stand with his foot.

"What now?" asked Grant.

"Will it start?" Ian replied.

Grant grabbed the clutch and squeezed it inwards, at the same time he tapped the gear peddle with his foot until the green neutral light on the tank centre panel illuminated in the dark. He sat on the bike. It was bigger than his own but felt comfortable although he doubted if it would be good for a long ride with its high handlebars. He pressed the electric ignition switch and the bike engine squealed and coughed but didn't catch. He turned the key switching off the ignition, left it a few seconds and turned it back on again. Green neutral light and yellow engine management light lit up, the latter disappearing after a second or two. He pressed the ignition switch again and this time the bike engine gunned into action and ticked over quite smoothly considering the treatment it had just received from the road.

"Looks like it does," confirmed Grant, looking at Ian his facial expression clearly asking 'what now'?

"Good," said Ian, "now dump it, I'll follow you and then we move on to dealing with our guest."

"Dump it?" asked Grant. "Where?"

"How do I know, do I look like a fucking search engine? I don't have all the answers, Grant." The stress in Ian's voice was clearly audible.

The bike ticked over, occasionally missing a beat, beneath Grant's frame. He thought for a few moments, smiled as the thoughts clarified themselves and began to form into an idea. He smiled at Ian and winked.

"Follow me, it's time to introduce myself," he said putting the bike into first gear and slowly releasing the clutch.

Ian ran to the van and started it up pulling out onto the main road, tucking in behind the moving bike. He just hoped there were no coppers in the area as he watched the bike drive into the darkness ahead of it telling Ian that the headlight had been damaged. To add to the law-breaking ride, one rear indicator was hanging by a wire and Grant was wearing no crash helmet. This was a rookie cop's dream come true.

Ian suddenly realised that Grant was not turning off the main road despite having a few opportunities to do so. He remained on the main road leading into the built up area and after travelling for nearly a mile Ian saw the familiar wall and gates that surrounded the MC's clubhouse.

"What the fuck are you doing?" Ian asked nobody in particular. He watched as Grant leaned the bike over to the right and come to a stop right outside the large metal gates of The Crippens' home.

As Grant saw the gates come into sight he pulled in the clutch of Lump's bike and coasted it quietly towards them. Quickly after coming to a stop he turned off the ignition, not bothering to put the bike into neutral gear.

Grant got off the bike and walked over to the now motionless van and opened the passenger door.

"Are you fucking crazy?" asked Ian.

Grant ignored the question saying, "Marker pen."

"In the tool box in the back," replied a confused Ian, adding, "I think you will need more than a marker pen if anyone inside spots us."

Grant made his way around to the back of the van and opened the doors. Lump was still face down, hogtied exactly as Grant had left him but he was now conscious. Groggy from the blow to the head he spoke slowly.

"You are going to fucking die motherfucker."

Ignoring him Grant opened the tool box and grabbed a stubby marker pen that sat on top of a variety of tools. He spotted a roll of silver 'gaffer' tape and removed that also from the tool box. Pulling a length of the tape from the roll and using his teeth to cut into an edge of it, he tore the length off the roll. Kneeling down next to the immobilised biker he roughly placed the tape over his mouth.

"Let's keep that mouth of yours shut for the minute," he said and climbed from the van closing the doors as quietly as he could.

He walked back to the bike with Ian watching him intently but at the same time keeping one eye on the gates of the compound. He watched as Grant used the marker pen to write something on the top of the bike's tank, throw the marker pen to the ground and return to the van. Climbing into the passenger seat he closed the door, slamming it shut with a loud bang.

"Let's go," he said.

Ian didn't have to be told twice, he floored the accelerator pedal and with a screech of rear tyres drove away from the clubhouse. In the wing mirror, Grant watched and saw the clubhouse gates begin to open.

The Crippens

Inside the compound The Priest stood silently and watched two of his crew open the compound gates and rush through them onto the road outside. One looked down the road and saw the van speeding away; it was too far away to make out the colour or the number plate. The second biker stood by the bike that had been abandoned outside of the gates looking down at the tank.

"What is it?" yelled the club president.

"There's a message written on the tank!" yelled back the biker.

"And what does it say?" This time The Priest's voice was quieter but in the clear night, it resonated with cruelty and anger.

The biker stood beside the bike once again looked down at the tank, reading the words silently. In fresh and still damp silver ink were the words:

LUMP
M.I.A.

The biker recited them back to his president.

The Priest walked back into the clubhouse without saying another word.

Sat at the clubhouse bar, a glass of Jack Daniels in his hand was the only surviving original founder of The Crippens. Doom took a mouthful of the drink and swilled it around his mouth before swallowing it allowing its warmth to fill his system. This worn looking biker no longer held a position of authority in the club and was bitter because of it. Over the last nine years, he had witnessed the rise in power of the current club president and felt the decline of his position at the same time. He did not like the direction in which the club had been taken but his body was too old and damaged to do anything about it anymore, plus he valued his life. Without having any proof he was certain that The Priest was responsible for the deaths of his fellow club founders.

From its humble beginnings, the three original founders had only one desire: to build up the club to a position where it would be recognised and welcomed into the family of either the Angels or the Outlaws, they didn't really care which. Two years after its formation a rider known at the time by the road name Ripper had joined the club. Within a relatively short time, this new addition had risen to the rank of Roadmaster, responsible for the planning and organisation of road trips, both for business and pleasure.

Following the unexplained disappearances and final acceptance of death of the other two original founders Doom watched on helplessly as he was passed over for the position of President, stripped of his position as Sgt at Arms and then removed totally from the top table as the newly appointed President cleverly bestowed upon him the honour of a lifetime membership. Ripper renamed himself The Priest and halted the original desire of acceptance into a larger and more powerful MCC family. It was the view of the new leader that being a one percenter was no honour to pursue, rather the new wish to be, as he put it, a nought point one percenter; a small number of men so far removed from both the law of the land and the laws of other bike clubs that they would eventually be hailed as the most feared bike club in modern history.

Doom knew that this was an unachievable dream or as he preferred to call it, a nightmare. This was the dream of a maniac, a social psychopath, a man so mentally screwed up that as a teenager he could murder both his parents. A man so warped and demented that he wore that crime like a badge of honour.

Doom tilted the glass in the direction of his President. "Problem?" he asked.

"Nothing you need to worry about and nothing I can't handle," The Priest replied, not really wanting to speak to his honorary member, the one original memory of this club that he had failed to get rid of.

"Of that I have no doubt. You are good at handling unwanted problems aren't you?" Doom looked at his adversary from the corner of one eye.

"Can I help?" he asked.

Yes you can fuck off and die, the words stayed in the club president's head rather than trickling off his tongue. Instead, he responded with words that he knew would really get under Dooms' skin.

"Nah, best leave this to those that can still ride a bike."

The old biker didn't respond. He knew that any response would only make his position even more difficult. Ever since having his pelvis crushed in an accident nearly two years ago he had been unable to ride a bike. He could remember being hit side on by the car while on a ride out to a bikers bash like it had happened yesterday and if he tried to forget it the colostomy bag strapped to the outside of his right leg was a daily reminder.

He slammed his glass onto the bar making the girl behind it jump.

"Another," he demanded of the girl. "In fact, just pass me the fucking bottle," he added.

The club president left Doom to drown his many sorrows at the bar and walked into the room he called The Church. He knew nearly all the club members were not fans of the title but hadn't put it up for a vote, many months of calling it The Church had resulted in a reluctant acceptance. He sat in his chair, something he would eventually replace with one more resembling a throne. He knew that would need to wait a while longer, one thing at a time to change this club into his own image.

None of the members knew about his religious experience, the miracle that had turned him to his God. It had happened a few months after being admitted to the secure mental hospital, a place that had taken years to get into, years that he spent languishing in prison. His God had come to him one evening and confirmed his personal belief that the 'murder' of his parents had in fact been a sacrificial killing, an unknown offering to, at the time, an unknown greater being. His God was a dark being who the uneducated would describe as evil but who he really knew was merely misunderstood by the masses, a bit like himself. This God had explained to him the work he needed to do and that he was to act as his priest in this world. For many years, this mysterious God had guided him and taught him how to play the game and achieve release from his imprisonment so that his work could begin.

He sat at the head of the table in deep thought. This meddlesome individual, as yet unidentified, had clearly been sent as a test. His God was testing him and his ability to do his work; he had been tested before and had passed those so he didn't see this one as being a problem.

He reached into the inside pocket of his leather cut and retrieved a small pocket knife, the sharp blade hidden inside a jet black handle. He pulled the blade out and ran it across the pad of his index finger. A small line appeared which within a few seconds turned into a fine line of blood. Placing the open knife on the table he proceeded to roll up the shirt sleeve of his left arm and admired the four crudely cut designs on the inside of his forearm. Four healed scars, each one the image of a small coffin. One coffin for each sacrifice he had offered so far. He smiled and licked his top lip relishing the thought of carving a fifth into his own flesh.

He drew the tip of his bleeding finger down his face from the top of his forehead to the tip of his nose leaving a line of blood, squeezing the finger to encourage more bleeding he bought it up to just below his left eye and drew another bloody line across the bridge of his nose to under his right eye. Leaning back into his chair and stretching his legs out under the table he crossed his arms over his chest resembling the old-fashioned placing of the arms of a corpse, closing his eyes he prayed to his God for guidance.

***

A short time after The Priest had started his prayers Ian was steering the van carefully into the wooded area, west of the shack. He drove deeper into the woods than he had done on his previous trips as he didn't really relish 'persuading' or, more likely, dragging the huge lump that was Lump further than he had to. During the journey, he had suggested to Grant that they knock out the biker again and drag his unconscious body to the building but Grant said no. He wanted him awake from the moment they arrived as he didn't want to wait a minute longer than necessary.

Ian eventually brought the van to a standstill about a hundred metres from the shack and only because he couldn't get it any closer.

Looking over to Grant he took a deep breath and said, "OK let's get the hard work done and move this clown but I don't think he is going to make it easy."

Grant's face was focussed, it was a look that Ian had seen before and had never been comfortable with.

"We move him like we used to move the rioters in Ireland, remember?" his gaze never moving from the dashboard the van.

"Yeah," replied Ian, "Hook and lift, but that only worked when they were handcuffed."

"Hogtied is good enough," said Grant getting out of the van.

The two men approached the back of the van and swung open the doors, Lump was still laying face down. Climbing slightly into the van they pulled the biker backwards by his belt until his centre of gravity was over the rear exit and his legs began to naturally drop towards the ground, as this happened Ian and Grant both hooked their inside arms under Lump's armpit and ended with their hands on the back of his shoulders. They lifted him to a standing position which the biker was unable to accomplish as the rope between his wrists and his ankles would not allow for his feet to touch the floor.

He let out a muffled cry of pain through the tape over his mouth as the weight of his body pulled on the rope tied around his wrists.

Half carrying, half dragging they moved him across the open area towards the wooden shacks front door and into the shady coolness of the interior. Lump raised his head to look around but Grant brought a stop to that by pushing down on the back of his head with his outside hand. They manoeuvred him towards the chair but as they attempted to place him a sitting position Ian pointed out one minor hitch in their plan.

"Being tied up like this won't allow us to sit him in the chair," he told Grant.

"Cut the middle rope," instructed Grant which produced a stream of muffled noises from Lump.

Releasing the biker's head Grant ripped off the tape.

"Cut the rope and see what happens, you bastard" Lump looked straight into Grant's eyes as he issued his warning.

Grant looked over towards Ian and nodded his head. Ian knew immediately what that meant and he released his hold at the same time as Grant and the biker hit the floor with a thud and grunt.

Grant walked over to the chest of drawers and once again told Ian to cut the rope.

"Erm did you listen to what this big fucker just said?" replied Ian.

"Just cut the rope," came the cool reply.

As instructed, Ian cut the rope with his trusty knife that he always had somewhere on his person and Lump stretched out his legs, bending them several times to return some blood into them. He rolled over onto his back but before he could say another word he found himself straddled by Grant who pressed the muzzle of the pistol against his forehead.

"Now what exactly is going to happen?" he asked the supine biker.

Lump didn't respond.

Grant stood himself up and indicated to Ian to assist the biker to his feet never moving the gun away from the direction of Lump's head. Once upon his feet Grant instructed him to back up and sit himself down on the chair.

Doing as he was told and never taking his eyes off Grant he sat down, saying;

"You the ones who took One a Year?"

Still ignoring any questions from the biker Grant told Ian to cut the ropes from his wrists and ankles. Ian looked at him with his best 'are you fucking serious' face.

"Just do it, this bastard doesn't want to die right now, he wants to find out if there is a way out of all this, don't you Lump?"

Feeling the bonds around his wrists loosen he brought them to the front of him and rubbed some life back into them.

"I'm not undoing his ankles until his arms are secured on the chair," said Ian.

Lump looked down at the arms of the chair he was sat in and first time noticed the leather straps.

"You a pair of perverts or something?" he said.

"You'd know Lump," replied Grant; the first of Lump's questions that he had acknowledged.

"Now lay both of your arms down so my good friend here can make you all secure," and as Grant gave the instruction he lowered the aim of his pistol to the area of the biker's groin. "Do it Christopher or I pull this trigger and turn you into a girl."

He did as he was told and Ian quickly secured the straps around the thick wrists and forearms just below the elbows.

Lump's only response was to say to Grant, "Never call me Christopher again or so help me I will break your head with this chair."

Happy that the biker's arms were now secure Ian cut the rope from around the ankles and started to move one of Lump's legs backwards to the chair's front legs.

The biker kicked out catching Ian off guard, the bikers boot caught him squarely in the chest knocking Ian from his squatted position onto his back. In a flash, Grant moved forward and with one hand slammed the bikers head into the high back/head rest of the chair and then brought the pistol up to the biker's face and forced its muzzle into his mouth. This time Lump both heard and saw the safety catch being moved into the off position.

"I will happily kill you now you fucking oxygen thief but I would rather give you the chance of leaving this place alive." Grant's voice was almost a whisper. "Now move your feet back so that they are touching the front legs of the chair."

As Lump once again did as he was told Ian moved forward and secured his legs with the leg straps that fastened around the shin areas. Ian stood and saw that Grant had not moved from his last position.

"Head strap?" he asked Grant.

"May as well while we have some level of cooperation."

Ian secured the wider leather strap around the temples and forehead of the biker and without asking decided to secure the chest strap into place while he was at it.

Grant slowly moved the gun from Lump's mouth.

"Nice having something hard and unwanted forced into your mouth was it... Christopher?"

"You a fucking gay boy eh? Wanna try shoving your cock into my mouth next do ya? Fucking try it queer and see what I do," spittle sprayed out of the biker's mouth as he virtually spat every word in Grant's direction.

"Not really my thing Lump but I do hear it's yours," replied Grant coldly.

"You tied me up to ask me about that slimy little slut from the bar? Ha, you could have asked me for those details freely. You into dirty stories old man, is that your game?"

"Why? Did One a Year watch you do her too?" asked Grant.

"What you going on about?" asked a confused Lump. "That dirty fucker wasn't there."

"No, but he was there on another occasion wasn't he? An occasion when he did watch you." Grant's voice remained calm and quiet even though inside he was feeling the beginnings of the angry bile bubbling in his stomach.

"You talking about them two bitches we robbed a while back? Lump asked. "One a Year been singing has he?"

He went silent for a few seconds and then looked once again directly at Grant and added,

"Something to you were they?"

Ian had stood in the background watching the developments between the two men and all the time he had been watching his friend's eyes which were by now almost glowing with an anger he had never seen before. He had not been present for Grant's 'chat' with the last biker to be sat in this building so wasn't really aware of how that one went, well except for seeing the end result.

Once again Grant ignored the Crippens's question, saying,

"If you had just robbed them you wouldn't be sat here right now, in fact, we would never have met. But you didn't just rob them did you?"

Lump smiled. "Nah, we had a little party too," he said.

Grant walked over to the small table that stood a foot or so to the side of the chair and placed the pistol upon it. Then he slowly removed the hessian cloth and revealed the Pear of Anguish.

Lump looked at the object but didn't react in any way.

"Tell me Lump, how did you manage to force your way into that girl's mouth and not risk her biting down so hard that she severed…?" but he could not finish the question.

177

"My cock," Lump happily finished it off for him. "Not difficult at all - her mother had a gun to her head. Persuaded the little tart to do me good, sucked me like a vacuum and swallowed me like I was pumping fine wine down her little throat."He smiled once again as if deriving some kind of warped pleasure from reliving the memory.

Grant turned away from the biker, he needed to compose himself. He rubbed his own eyes and swallowed a few times to keep the vomit down.

Turning back around to face the secured biker he placed his hand on top of the torture device.

"This," he explained, "is an ancient instrument designed to persuade people to talk. Now you decide if you want to talk or not but if you don't it will make sure you never talk again in your life." He waited for a reaction or response from Lump but got nothing.

"One question is all you have to answer," still nothing from the biker "who else was with you that night?"

Lump laughed.

"Santa," he said through his laughter.

"The Tooth Fairy."

"Batman."

"Mr. Go Fuck Yourself," this last made up name was screamed in the direction of Grant.

Grant picked up the Pear of Anguish and placed its tip on the lips of Lump's mouth. The biker forced his lips tightly together.

"You can try as hard as you like but this beautiful piece of design was shaped in such a way that no matter how hard you try, with very little effort from the inquisitor it will easily slip into the intended mouth," said Grant as he pushed just a little harder. As he had explained and predicted, the pear-shaped device forced the biker's lips and mouth open.

178

Placing his mouth close to Lump's right ear, Grant whispered, "Now feel it grow."

He turned the screw wheel at the top of the device and the leaves of the pear that were now securely in Lump's mouth began to open.

The biker tried to speak but what came out of his already filling mouth sounded something like, "Ooh uckin cun."

Grant turned the screw another full turn, as he heard the obvious cracking noise of teeth a spurt of blood squeezed its way out of Lump's mouth and all over one side of the torture device. The open-mouthed biker screamed in pain.

"Who else was with you?" repeated Grant.

The biker just glared back at him so Grant gave it another turn. A couple more teeth cracked inside the biker's mouth and then a small tear appeared at the corner of Lump's mouth, a small trail of blood trickled down to his chin.

He was doing his best to struggle but the leather straps and chair had been very well-designed and built by Ian and neither the biker nor the chair were going anywhere.

A mixture of gurgling, screaming and choking type noises filled the room. Grant turn the wheel another turn but this time in the opposite direction and the leaves of the pear moved back inwards slightly.

"Are you ready to tell me yet?" asked Grant.

"Kill ooh," said Lump and then repeated it again.

"Killooh or Kill you," said Grant, "what do you think Ian, is there a Crippen named Killooh?"

Ian, despite the gruesome actions that he was witnessing, smiled saying, "Don't think so mate."

"No didn't think so myself," replied Grant and turned the wheel again to reopen the leaves; this time, he turned twice. In an explosion of blood, both sides of the biker's mouth ripped open.

Grant didn't stop; he turned the screw again and once again. More breaking of teeth, more blood spurting and spitting from Lump's by now widened mouth and more tearing of the flesh around his mouth and cheeks and then a loud breaking of bones as Lump's jawbone cracked. The Crippen fell unconscious as his level of pain reached the point where his body's defence mechanism kicked in.

Grant stopped turning the screw and turned away from the mess.

"I need some fresh air," he said to Ian. "Unscrew it and clean it up a bit for me please mate."

Without another word he walked outside and threw up.

Minutes later Ian joined Grant outside, in his hand he held an old chipped mug filled with water and offered it to Grant who took it gratefully.

"You do know that this device was never meant to kill the victim?" Ian said to Grant.

Grant finished drinking the cup of water and then looked at his friend. Ian looked at a tired and drained face looking back at him and wondered if Grant was really up to finishing this job. Grant spoke, stopping any more of Ian's thoughts for the time being.

"This one is not about killing, this one is about suffering. To make him suffer like he made... Sha... her suffer. I don't care if he lives or dies."

Ian shook his head, "He has to die my friend, you know that, he HAS to die."

"Not until he has suffered so much that he begs me to kill him," Grant answered swiftly, the anger welling up inside him again.

A groaning noise from inside the shack said that Lump had regained consciousness. It was time to continue. Grant walked back in through the door followed closely by Ian.

Lump's face was a mess; three cracked teeth had fallen to the floor near to the front of his right boot. Blood was all over and around his mouth and down his chin and it was clear from the way his mouth remained in an open position that his jaw had either been broken or dislocated. The only reason that his head wasn't hanging down because of the treatment he had been through was because it remained securely fastened to the back of the chair.

Grant walked to the opposite end of the room from where Lump was sat. He stood in the shadows looking at his victim and had not one bit of sorrow towards him.

"Chrissie my boy just talk to me, give me one name. What is the worst that the Crippens would do to you for telling me? Kill you? Surely this is worse than dying?"

Doing his best to respond without being able to move his jaw the messed up biker remained defiant.

"Then kill me… I tell you nothing but," he paused and then, "but you die still. You die bad." The words were difficult for Lump to form correctly but he was determined that make it clear how it would end for Grant.

Grant thought a bit more, he needed a name, the name of that third attacker.

"Lump, I know how much you love your bike club, The Crippens, your family and then, of course, there is your beloved mother." The biker's eyes widened at the mention of his mum.

"You are doing them all a favour by just telling me the information I am after. If you don't I give you my word that I will wipe The Crippens off this face of this earth and then I will go and visit a certain care home. See how much your mother likes being fucked up the arse."

A tear rolled down Lump's face, his weak point had been found.

"Kill you, fuckin' kill you," he managed to get out, more blood flowing down his chin and dripping onto his chest.

"The name, that's all I want," said Grant.

An inaudible whisper escaped from Lump's broken mouth.

"Sorry didn't quite catch that." Grant walked closer to the biker.

Another whisper and Grant kneeled down in front of the broken Crippen.

"Say it again Lump," asked Grant without almost any kindness in his voice.

"Pretty.... Boy," said Lump he voice weakening with every word.

Grant walked to the back of the chair holding the biker in place. His hand went into one of the rear pockets of his jeans and he pulled out a small rectangle silver item.

"Thank you," he whispered, "and now, like any grass, you are going to die slowly."

Grant put the part rusty blunted razor blade next to Lump's throat.

"Be grateful you will be dead. It means you will have no knowledge of what I am going to do to your mother," and with that he began to make small sawing motions with the blade slowly cutting through the side of Lump's neck.

The biker's screams went on for about ten minutes as Grant sawed his way through his throat with the blunt blade. Grant thought that 'Lump' had died just moments before he reached his windpipe and then severed through that too.

Grant looked around the room looking for Ian but his friend had left as the throat cutting began. There was only so much torture his friend was willing to watch.

Grant made his way outside, his hands and arms were dripping with blood and his clothes were sodden in places and blood spattered in others. Ian was kneeling on the ground just to the right of the door, a pile of vomit was soaking into the grass in front of him.

Grant looked down at him and dropped the blood-coated razor blade into the puddle of vomit.

"Get rid of that when you clean up your puke," he said emotionlessly.

"What the fuck mate, what have you become?" his friend said, almost gagging again as he looked up and saw Grant dripping and covered in blood.

"I am what they forced me to be," replied Grant.

"Yeah, but Christ did you have to saw through his neck?" asked Ian.

"It was always going to end bloody my friend." Grant sat himself down on the ground and bringing his knees up to his chest and wrapping his arms around them he dropped his head so that his forehead rested on his kneecaps. "Bloody, just like they left my family," he continued quietly.

"Fine," replied Ian, "how the hell do I hide the evidence from this mess, do you mind telling me that?"

"Bury the body and burn the place," replied Grant without looking up and then added, "take his cut off him first, though."

"And what about you?" asked Ian looking once again at his blood-soaked friend. "Do I burn you too?"

"I'll wash up and strip down. You can burn my clothes too. I trust you have some spare stuff in that van of yours."

Grant looked up at last, his head raised to the sky, a look of sheer exhaustion on his face.

"Do you really think that we can hide a shit storm like this Grant?"

Grant looked over at his friend and shrugged his shoulders.

"If there is no crime reported there is no crime to investigate. Trust me The Crippens do not want the coppers involved, they would never turn to their enemy for help. They didn't report One a Year missing and they won't report the disappearance of Lump either," replied Grant in a cold matter-of-fact way.

Grant could see that Ian was weakening and he could sense that he was ready to back out.

"Just one more Ian and then it's all over and we can return to our boring mundane lives," said Grant doing his best to form a smile on his blood-spotted face.

"And if I burn this place where do we deal with this Pretty Boy?"

"Boring questions all the time," replied Grant, "just fucking sort it will you."

Ian smiled weakly back at his friend,

"I could fall in love with boring forever."

Leverage

The bikers who had been searching around Milton Dryton looking for Grant eventually returned to their clubhouse to find it almost full. The Priest had put a 'full recall' into action; every club member to be at the bikers' HQ immediately. The word had been passed around by phone call, text and the use of a couple of outriders. Within two hours every biker, patched or not, responded to the call, the newest and most notable absentee being, of course, Lump.

Upon their return Battle and Bull were summoned into The Church where The Priest, Panhead and Pretty Boy were sat at the top end of the table.

"Talk to me," whispered the club president. "Why was Lump riding alone?"

Between them, the two bikers told the club's higher echelon what had occurred the evening before. They were worn out and just wanted to get their heads down, understandable as it was the early hours of the morning but The Priest kept asking for details. A description of the mystery man who had taken on Lump was at the top of his wish list.

At the end of the questioning session Battle said, "We didn't bother arguing with Lump when he said he would return here on his own; he wasn't in the mood to be questioned."

"I will deal with the matter of ignoring my orders later, first we have to lure this rat out into the open. We need leverage and I know just the person to give us that."

Pretty Boy remained quiet throughout, having heard the description of this out-of-towner he was searching through his memories. He thought the man was familiar for some reason, not someone he remembered actually meeting face to face but nevertheless still familiar. A picture or photograph somewhere maybe, he wracked his brain but it wouldn't come. He kept his thoughts to himself as well as the nagging feeling in his gut that there were reasons that they should be worried.

He returned his focus back to the room just in time to hear his president giving Bull and Battle his instructions.

"Don't take your bikes, use the van and don't wear your colours," he heard the president tell the two bikers.

Panhead looked at The Priest with surprise.

"This is club business, they should wear the colours with pride," he said.

The Priest gave a look towards his vice president of pure hatred.

"Don't ever fucking question me again if you want to fucking live," he snarled at Panhead, spittle spraying from his tight-lipped mouth. "This man is not working against the club, this feels personal for some reason. We do this discreetly for now, do I make myself clear?" Panhead nodded before standing up and walking towards the door.

"I need a drink," he said, angry at the way he had just been spoken to in front of junior members of the club.

His president banged his skull-headed gavel furiously onto the table.

"Business concluded then!" he shouted and diverting his attention and gaze to the two bikers he said in a low voice, "Now go and don't fail me."

***

Emma sat in her room, alone at last. She and Murphy had decided to close the bar following the events of the evening and after locking up he had sat with her for hours, not wanting to leave her alone.

They had spoken at length about what had happened, at times it almost turned into a police interview as Gus asked her question after question about Grant.

"Tell me everything you know about him?"

"Where does he come from?"

"Why is he here? Where is he going?"

Emma told him nothing, not because she was trying to hide anything but just because her head was messed up by the visit of The Crippens and especially by the way that Grant had dealt with Lump.

"He knew what he was doing," she said to the police sergeant at one point during their lengthy conversation.

"That was instinctive not accidental," she said, "don't you think?"

Murphy hadn't answered the question but he knew from years of being a copper that the sort of reaction that he had witnessed came from years of training. He recalled the information he had received from his colleagues from across the county borders, ex-military and ex-prison service. This man had been more than a blanket stacker in his time.

Eventually, she had managed to persuade Gus that he should leave as she was tired and wanted to get some sleep. Reluctantly he had left and after returning down to the bar to lock the door behind him, she gave the bar area a quick glance and decided that she wasn't in the mood to put away the glasses or return dirty plates to the kitchen so returned to her room where she now sat, alone and tired but unable to sleep.

She decided to go through her normal night time routine hoping that it would put her body into sleep mode. Going to the bathroom she began to clean her teeth and having completed this twice daily task she pulled down her jeans and panties and sat herself down on the toilet to relieve herself. Seconds after beginning to pee she heard a noise outside coming from the back yard. She stopped peeing in mid-flow, the benefit of a young strong pelvic floor. Standing up she pushed open the small bathroom window and looked out onto the dark courtyard. The view from her window did not reach round to the courtyard gates as her room was located above the pub's kitchen. She saw nothing and without closing the window sat back down on the toilet. *Why is it always difficult to pee again after stopping?* she thought to herself, but before her thought could be given any more consideration she heard the smashing of glass.

Emma collected her panties and jeans together and pulled them at the same time quickly zipping and buttoning up her jeans before running to her bedroom door. She placed her ear against the door and listened intently, her heart beating at a pace that any cardiologist would be concerned about.

***

Bull and Battle had arrived at the back gates of the courtyard and parked the van right outside them. They had quickly climbed over the gates and made their way to the back door. It was clear that they were not bothered about alerting anyone inside of their arrival as Bull smashed the glass in the door with his elbow and then reaching inside to turn the key, unlocking the door.

Making their way quickly through the kitchen and bar they made their way upstairs heading straight to the room where they both knew Emma slept - most of the Crippens had visited that room.

They both placed their backs against the corridor wall opposite to Emma's room door, standing shoulder to shoulder and together they rushed to the door and hit it with one foot each. The door flew open smacking into the head of the young girl listening from inside the room.

***

Emma did not hear a thing until the final moment, seconds before the door struck her head and she flew backwards, hitting the floor. Her vision blurred and her head filled with intense pain as a trickle of blood ran down her right temple. She saw two figures approaching her and then manhandling her to her feet, she was aware that she was being dragged down the corridor and then roughly down the stairs, her feet banging against each step. She tried to regain some kind of foothold but couldn't make her lower limbs work properly.

The two bikers dragged her down into the bar and unlocked the front door, the fresh air rushed in and raised Emma's consciousness slightly, just enough to attempt to struggle against her abductors.

It wasn't enough and when Bull grabbed her by the throat and tightened his grip saying,

"Struggle bitch and you fucking die," she stopped the feeble attempts to get away and allowed herself to be taken and thrown into the back of a van. She lay dazed on the dirty floor of the van, her focus still fading in and out but aware enough to the see the back of black leather vest bearing the back patch of The Crippens.

The van skidded away as the driver floored the accelerator causing Emma to slide backwards towards the rear doors slamming the back of her head into them. She fell into a state of unconsciousness, her last conscious thought being deep fear.

She came round about an hour after been grabbed in her room, her head ached badly. She raised her hand to the side of her temple and felt dry caked blood. Looking around her new environment she immediately, despite her dazed and confused state, recognised where she was: in one of the clubhouse rooms that were often used by members to stay over for a night or more either for convenience or fun. Emma visually gave herself the once over and was relieved to find that she remained fully clothed and had not been used while unconscious.

The room was simply laid out and basically equipped. A small single bed that she had woken up on, a single door wardrobe, sink and toilet, bikers were easily pleased! She lowered her head in shame as she thought how ironic that statement was, maybe that is why so many had been with her… easily pleased.

She heard movement and voices outside, she knew the layout of the clubhouse so quickly worked out that whoever was talking were probably further up the corridor. She climbed off the bed and reaching the door pressed her ear against it remembering that the last time she did this the door had come flying in on her.

She couldn't recognise the individuals from their voices as they were quite faint as if some distance away but she managed to catch a few words:

"Nobody defiles her… tell them all."

"That one couldn't be defiled any more than she already has been boss."

"Just tell them." The voices went quieter and Emma could hardly hear what was being said. "I need her alive."

Those final words relaxed her a tiny bit, at least they weren't planning to kill her right now. She heard footsteps making their way down the corridor in her direction and she quickly returned to the bed.

The door opened and one of The Crippens walked in, she recognised him as one of the newer patched members, one that she hadn't slept with! Psyche looked at her but didn't say a word, in his hand he held a tin bowl which he placed on the floor and using his foot slid it across the wooden floor towards the bed.

He stepped backwards out of the room and relocked the door behind him. Emma looked down at the tin container, it was a dog bowl filled with a small amount of food, two slices of bread, a couple slices of meat and a lump of mashed potato. On the side of the dog bowl, someone had written in marker pen the word WHORE. Emma laid down on the bed and buried her face into the pillow and the tears began to pour.

***

Grant had washed up as best as possible, enough to ensure that he wouldn't get any strange looks from anyone who saw him but nowhere near enough to give a forensic science lab a difficult job. He had grabbed a pair of black trainers, a pair of jeans and an old 'The Damned' tour t-shirt from a pile of clothes in the back of the van, none of which really fitted but at least they weren't covered in blood. He would need to buy some cheap clothes from somewhere so he looked less like a refugee who had just visited a relief shop. He returned to where Ian still sat and placed his blood-soaked clothes on the ground next to him. He quickly went back into the shack and came out after less than a minute. He now wore his bike jacket, glad that he had taken it off prior to dealing with Lump and in his hand he carried the blood-splattered cut that used to belong to the now ex-member of The Crippens.

"Where are you going?" Ian asked him.

"Don't worry about that, I should be back soon. Just clean this place up," replied Grant adding the word, "Please."

Ian could see that his friend was tired, no exhausted was a better description.

"Why don't you get your head down in the van for a few hours first," said Ian genuinely worried.

"No time my friend, I need to return you to a boring life, remember," said Grant, smiling for the first time in a while.

Ian returned the smile; it felt good to hear a bit of banter from his friend.

"By the way," he said.

"What?" asked Grant, waiting for yet another problem to be announced.

With a now huge smile on Ian's face, he said, "You look like an aging punk hobo"

"Kiss my puckered hole," replied Grant and ruffled the hair of his friend as he walked away and made his way to his motorbike.

Arriving at his bike's location eventually, after losing his bearings in the forest on at least two occasions, he lifted the helmet from the handlebar where he had left it hanging. He cleaned off dirt and dew that had accumulated on the visor and helmet and then placed it on his head, finally donning his gloves that had been sat in his helmet. He fired the bike up smiling as it kicked into action on the first time of asking and rode it slowly down the narrow wide rabbit path that led back to the main road. About fifty metres from the road he heard a car approaching and brought his bike to a standstill, allowing the car to drive past the opening he was heading for, he waited for a minute or so before moving on and once again taking a cautious look in both directions before hitting the road he saw it was all clear and opened up the throttle.

He was heading in a direction that would take him away from the home of The Crippens and Milton Dryton, not absolutely sure where he was heading but hoping to find a small town where he could get a renewal of cheap clothes and one other item he thought might come in use later. As he rode he thought about the blood covered leather cut that now sat inside a plastic bag inside one of his saddle bags. He thought about the two options available to him with regards to how to use this item to best effect, return it home or return it to family. Best effect meant best impact and best impact meant causing the most pain and that thought process allowed Grant to arrive at the best option, returning it to family just seemed the most appropriate considering the impact, hurt, and destruction that Lump had contributed to in relationship to the lives of his own family.

Those dark memories once again returned, the days following the crime, returning to his home but not being able to stay there, numerous empty visits to the hospital. Conversations with over caring strangers who offered to 'take away the pain of making the arrangements himself', thoughts of ending his own life, illusions of going out with a bang. Committing a crime that would hit the headlines and give him a place in criminal history for generations to come and then, finally, weeks of pain and loneliness as he removed himself from everything and everyone that he had ever known. Pain and isolation that cleared his mind and allowed him to formulate a plan that had put him on the path he was currently travelling.

He forced the memories to the back of his brain as the images of the faces of his loved ones began to appear in his head, the beautiful long dark hair, a young girl starting off in life with a promising future ahead of her, a woman with a gorgeous soft round face and a heart of gold who loved him like she loved life itself. Grant lifted his visor and screamed out loud, a scream of pain and anguish that no man should ever feel, a scream of anger and vengeance. A scream that refocused him and reinforced his determination to complete the task he had set himself.

Feeling stronger he pulled his visor back to the closed position and opened up the bike increasing the speed and holding her at a steady sixty, he knew that he was heading in a southerly direction which after about twenty miles was confirmed by a road sign indicating that the town of Shrewsbury was a few miles ahead. *That would do* he thought to himself, a normal bloke on a bike looking for a bike shop and making a few purchases, it actually felt normal.

After stopping at a petrol station to fill up, paying cash as always (stay off the grid Ian had advised) he continued his journey eventually arriving in the outskirts of Shrewsbury. He had been riding for about forty-five minutes which left him feeling refreshed and full of life, the way bike riding always made him feel. The guy in the garage had given him some loose directions to a Honda dealer he knew about which Grant had sort of followed and eventually after doubling back on himself on a few occasions spotted the sign for the industrial estate that the garage attendant had mentioned. He rolled into the estate and saw the large red Honda sign on the front of quite a large bike outlet ahead of him on the left hand side. He guided the bike into the car park outside of the dealers, switched off the engine and sat on his bike for a few moments. He reached inside his jacket and located the secret pocket removing from inside it a roll of bank notes. His stash was getting a bit thin, maybe a couple of thousand pounds left. Taking a few twenties and tens from the roll totalling around three hundred pounds he returned the remaining cash into the pocket and made his way into the shop.

Grant spent very little time in the Honda dealers and engaged in very little small talk other than to say hi and ask for the location of certain items. He found a pair of leather jeans, old cruiser style, that fitted him perfectly and more importantly had been reduced in price down to seventy quid and then he couldn't resist buying himself a new pair of boots for just under a hundred pounds. He paid in cash and asked the assistant if he could use their small changing cubicle to put on the leather jeans and having done so he left the store.

He placed the jeans and trainers that belonged to Ian into the saddle bag containing Lump's cut and had a quick check that no blood had seeped from the plastic bag in which it was stored, glad to see that it hadn't and even more pleased with his new look he got back on his bike and headed back out on the road.

He needed to head back to Milton Dryton and check on Emma. He might have turned into a vengeful murdering maniac but he also remained a gentleman and anyway he quite liked the young girl.

***

195

That morning Gus had decided to head straight to the pub to see how Emma was before going to his office at the police station. He had not wanted to leave her alone the night before and had been quite willing to stay in one of the guest rooms. After getting dressed into his uniform he got into his police vehicle which he now always took home, one of the few benefits of being a police sergeant working in a small rural police station, and made his way into town. A few locals waved a good morning to him as he passed by them, Gus returned the gesture out of habit more than genuine interest.

The Old Tudor House looked inactive as he parked up outside. Gus banged on the front door and waiting for a few minutes he knocked it hard again with the side of his fist. Walking down the pavement he looked through each of the front windows but saw no movement whatsoever. Lights were out and he could see the remains of the previous nights custom, and damage, still uncleared, he knew Ems too well to know that she would not have left it in this state and would have been up early to sort it all out. Even though she wasn't the owner she ran the pub and hotel well and had pride in the way it was always ready for when the customers came in.

He walked back to the door knocking on each window as he passed and shouting Emma's name at the same time thinking that maybe she had slept in after last night's events. Once again he waited for a few minutes hoping to see Emma lean out of a top front window and shout some kind of abuse at him, but no such thing happened.

He made his way round to the side of the hotel towards the large gates of the rear courtyard and as expected, he found them closed and locked. There was no way he could scale those gates.

As he was trying to work out what action to take next he heard, in the distance, the familiar sound of an approaching motorbike. Looking up the road he fully expected to see one or more of The Crippens riding in his direction but was both surprised and relieved as he watched Grant appear over the brow of the hill and ride down it towards him.

Grant pulled over to the side of the road and stopped the bike adjacent to where Gus was stood. Lifting his visor Grant looked at the cop,

"What's going on?" he asked.

"Can't get a response from Emma. I left her quite late last night, at her request before you start having a go at me. Anyway I'm surprised to see you back here, don't value your life too much I'm guessing," said Gus.

"Nothing to value anymore," replied Grant; almost as a throwaway comment rather than a direct reply.

"If I climb over those gates are you going to get all 'I am the law' on me?" said Grant getting off his bike, removing his helmet and gloves and handing them to Murphy. He was halfway up the offending barriers before the policeman could even respond.

Jumping over the other side into the courtyard Grant immediately went to the kitchen entrance and saw the first signs of something amiss straight away. The broken glass and open back door were clues that even these local dumbfuck cops would be able to spot.

Throwing caution to the wind Grant made his way quickly through the kitchen and bar areas ignoring the banging on the front door that he knew would be Murphy. He raced up the stairs and before he was even halfway down the corridor he could see the damage to Emma's bedroom door.

The door hung loosely by its bottom hinge and a large crack could be clearly seen down the middle of the wooden door. He took a quick look around the room only expecting to find Emma in there if she had been left for dead. Before leaving to let Murphy in he spotted the blood on the carpet. His head began to spin as the memories of another bedroom containing blood and evidence of a crime came flooding back to him. He steadied himself against the broken door but his added weight forced it further off its one attached hinge, he quickly let go and sat himself down on the floor leaning his back against the wall. The images of the remains of the crime against his family swam in and out of focus, despite the police's best efforts to clean the place up it remained clear what had happened in that room, the only thing you couldn't sense was the suffering that had occurred.

He staggered out of the room struggling to regain focus as he battled against the horrendous memories slowly managing to push them back into the dark box where he always tried to keep them locked away. Making his way back down the corridor and down the stairs he concentrated on the problem, Emma was missing, there had been a forced entry… this had to be the work of The Crippens and this was directly connected to him and what he had done so far.

He found himself in the bar area totally unaware that he had managed to negotiate his way down the stairs. Gus was still banging on the door and was now shouting his name.

He quickly unbolted the door before the cop decided to kick it in and came face-to-face with a very worried looking Gus Murphy.

"What's happened; where's Emma?" he asked, his voice pitched higher than normal.

"Gus, calm down let's have a drink," responded Grant and guided the shaking police officer to the bar.

He made his way to the other side of the bar and poured two large brandies, taking a huge gulp of one as he handed the other to Gus.

"Just tell me what you've found. Is Emma dead?" asked Gus downing his drink in one.

"Well," replied Grant, taking a smaller mouthful of the warming and calming brandy, "if she is, she isn't dead here."

He went on telling Gus what he had discovered upstairs, the policeman listened intently, not saying a word until Grant had finished speaking. He remained quiet for a few seconds and then looking at Grant said, "This is all your fault, I don't know what your purpose is, why you are here or what you have been up to but I just know you are behind her disappearance. You need to start talking fella or I will haul your ass into the station and put you through so much hell the devil himself will give me a medal."

"Listen up Murphy," snapped Grant, "I have been to places that make hell look like paradise. This is the work of The Crippens, even you can work that out."

"Maybe but you are the cause of it all," responded Gus clearly becoming more agitated. "This girl means a lot to me."

Grant looked at the copper raising his eyebrows suggesting there was more going on between this man and the young bar girl.

"Not in that way you filthy bastard. I helped this girl to get away from the grip that The Crippens had on her. She was a hanger-on, a slut to these guys. They used and abused her, got her hooked on drugs, treated her like a sub-human. I helped her out, got her this job and have watched out for her ever since. She is like a daughter to me," Murphy's eyes became tear-filled as he said the words.

Grant felt for the guy but at the same time couldn't help thinking that despite the kindness that Murphy had shown towards Emma, she remained a 'daughter' he would like to fuck.

"I can't talk to you about what's going on Gus, you're a copper, the last person I need sticking his nose into this business," Grant explained.

"You need to tell me Grant, this is no longer official to me this is fucking personal," Murphy was calming slightly as the emotional exhaustion kicked in.

"Gus," said Grant quietly, "this has always been personal for me."

The Exchange

The door opened and instinctively Emma crouched into the far corner of the room. It was too soon to receive more food so she couldn't help thinking that something unpleasant was in store for her. She held on to the empty tin bowl tightly, the only thing in the room that she could use as a weapon to defend herself.

A tall figure stood in the doorway, he was alone and Emma did not recognise this Crippen.

"Calm child," he said in a voice that was softer than Emma expected, "I am not here to hurt you." He looked at the bowl in Emma's hands, clearly able to read the word written down its side.

"Put it down, please. I am sorry about what has been written on it, I will make sure that the guilty one will pay for that," said the stranger, his soft voice worryingly calming and trustworthy.

Emma placed the bowl on the floor, close enough to reach for it should she need to.

"Thank you, Emma," the tall man said and then he walked into the room and sat on the edge of the bed. He wore a long black leather coat, tight black jeans, and black heavy boots. Emma could now see his face which was in total contradiction to his voice. The dark goatee beard and piercing eyes gave him a menacing appearance. His eyes were empty, emotionless pits of nothingness. Emma reached for the bowl again.

The man stuck out his leg, his foot reaching the bowl before Emma could get her hand to it and flicked it away from her. It clattered across the wooden floor.

"Child, do not test me. I have come to you to talk, to explain. I have shown you no hostility, issued you no threat and yet you behave in a way that indicates you see me as your enemy," the stranger's soft voice had become more sinister.

Emma spoke, her voice trembling.

"What do you expect? I'm snatched from my home, knocked out... look," she pointed towards her head where the dried blood still remained, "and brought back to this fucking place. "Why? You say you are here to explain then answer me that. Fucking WHY?"

The man leaned forward and raised his hand towards Emma's face. Emma flinched backwards but the wall stopped her retreating any further. He gently stroked the area of her head which had been cut open, a crusty scab of blood had formed, performing its healing purpose. He lowered his hand and sat back on the bed allowing Emma to slightly relax again.

"In war young one, there are casualties, many are innocent and many are not. Now do not be fooled, WE are at war, a war we did not ask for or invite ourselves into. A war that confuses us, a war in which we do not know our enemy or his reasons. However, my child, you do know our enemy and maybe you know his purpose. Know I have been extremely rude and not introduced myself, I am the president of The Crippens, - you may call me The Priest."

Emma had spent too many hours of her past in many of the rooms at this clubhouse. Her memories were of self-disgust, humiliation, and regret but from all those visits and stays she had never felt fear like she did right at this very moment. This man was clearly deranged, mentally unstable and a clear threat to her life and yet despite all of these feelings her response was, "I have no idea what you are talking about."

The Priest threw back his head and laughed, it reminded Emma of a witches cackle.

"Oh dear child," he said, "you know plenty. You know the man who had the audacity to lay a hand on my brother Lump, you know his name and you probably know his story, the reason he is here, the reason why he seems to have a problem with my brotherhood."

"He was just staying at the hotel, checked in a few days ago, said he was travelling the country and just needed a few days rest from the road," replied Emma.

"His name, please child," the words were phrased as a demand more than a question.

"I can't remember," lied Emma.

The Priest shook his head in disappointment.

"You obviously need some time to think about my questions. I am a fair man and I can understand that you are confused, after all, you have been put through a shocking experience, so I will give you one hour. After that, my brothers who are sat not too far away will be released from their leashes. You see, they are very keen to revisit the intimate parts of your body that many have been to before. I assure you that by the time they have finished with you I will be able to drive a double decker bus up your cunt without touching the sides. One hour child, think hard, do the right thing. Give up this devil and save your soul," he leaned forward again, this time, forcing his face right in front of Emma's, "and your womanhood."

The Priest stood and without another word left the room, locking the door behind him.

***

Gus sat in silence and shock. He had listened to Grant for almost thirty minutes as he told his story, a story he had shared with only one other person. He had heard of and witnessed many crimes during his police career but this one was more horrific than any of them. No human, no woman deserved the kind of treatment he had just had described to him. While Grant had told Gus the details of the crime against his family in graphic detail he had only touched on his actions over the past few days simply explaining that revenge had taken place, neither had he included the involvement of his good friend Ian.

Eventually, Gus spoke, trying to choose his words carefully.

"Grant, I'm a member of this country's police force; I joined to uphold the law and protect people like yourself and your family against those that break the law and admittedly I have failed on many occasions. The law of this country does not allow for the kind of revenge you seek and I imagine have already handed out. I am guessing that this revenge was against One a Day and Lump?"

Grant nodded his head.

"I can only imagine the pain you have been through," Gus continued, "and part of me can both sympathise and empathise but the other part of me is the police officer that says we cannot allow vigilantes to take over the handing out of punishment."

"Then we have a problem Sgt Murphy," interrupted Grant.

"I hadn't finished," said Gus.

Grant was sat behind the bar directly opposite Murphy, his chin resting on one hand. He extended his fingers towards the officer indicating that he should continue.

"These people, this bunch of hell-bound scum has now involved a girl who has done nothing to deserve it. They have made it personal for both of us."

Grant considered the police officer's words carefully. The implied gesture, while appreciated, surely could not be accepted.

"I can't have you involved Gus, you are a cop," he said.

Gus responded without a second thought.

"Some coppers believe they are a copper 24/7, me... I have always lived by the rule that I'm not a copper when I'm on leave."

With that, he took his mobile from his pocket and after searching through his contacts list pressed the call button.

"Ferguson, it's Murphy. Listen lad, Emma has a bit of a family emergency and I said I would go with her, a bit of support kind of thing so I am taking a few days' leave."

Gus stopped speaking and listened to Ferguson speak words that Grant couldn't hear.

"Thanks lad," replied Gus to whatever Ferguson had said. "Oh, Emma is closing the pub for a few days while she is away, doesn't trust that moron to run the place for more than an hour by himself so be ready for a bit of flack from the locals, tell them to use The Star for a few days."

He ended the call and placed his phone back into his pocket. He looked at Grant, tilted his head to the left and raised one eyebrow.

"So, what next?" he asked

Grant was genuinely surprised by this man's reaction to everything he had seen and heard in the last forty to fifty minutes.

"Probably the end of your career and a life sentence for me," he said, "now I need to make a phone call."

"Go ahead," said Gus with a smile, "as long as it's you doing the life sentence. I need to get changed out of this."

He looked down at his uniform, "See you back here in an hour."

With his phone next to his ear Grant watched Gus walk towards the front door.

"Try not to look like an off duty cop," he said.

Gus's response floated back to me as the hotel front door closed. "Fuck off."

***

Ian was on his hands and knees scrubbing the wooden floor in the shack when his phone rang. Annoyed by the unwanted and unneeded interruption he grabbed his phone, placed it on the toolbox that sat on the floor next to him, pressed the green phone symbol to take the call and immediately put the phone into 'hands-free' mode.

"What?" he shouted

"Hi, is that Churchill Logistics?" asked Grant.

"Fuck off, thanks to you I don't have time for this shit," replied Ian who had returned to scrubbing the floor. Clearing up blood was hard work, clearing up this amount of blood was almost impossible.

"What happened to being careful, our phone calls being listened to, staying off the grid."

"What happened? I'll tell you what happened shall I?" replied Ian, increasing the intensity of his floor scrubbing, "You decided to saw through somebody's throat leaving more blood than you would find in an average slaughterhouse. Staying off the fucking grid has become a pointless objective."

"Glad to hear you say that," said Grant pursing his lips and squinting his eyes as he said, "because Gus is now part of the team!"

Ian stopped scrubbing the floor trying hard to make sense of what he had just heard his friend say.

"Sorry," he replied, "you have invited a fucking copper into our world of murder and mayhem? What new world of madness have you entered?"

"Emma's gone missing, The Crippens have taken her. He wants in; he says it's become personal. I believe and trust him Ian," replied Grant crossing his fingers of the hand not holding the phone.

"I couldn't give two flying fucks about what you believe or who you trust you dumb turd. He is a fucking policeman," Ian was incredulous.

Ignoring his friend's protests Grant continued.

"We need to meet, be here in the bar as soon as you can. Murphy will be here too."

Ian didn't reply, he ended the call and sat back in a kneeling position. He was covered in soil and blood, wet in several places from his attempts to scrub away the blood and the scent of burning remained on his clothes from the bonfire he had built comprising of a broken wooden chair and Lump's clothing.

He walked outside to where the bonfire was still burning and stripped off his clothing until he was stood in the clearing totally naked. He threw his clothes and the scrubbing brush and rags he had been using onto the burning remains of wood, denim and leather. He walked over to this van which he had earlier moved closer to the shack in an effort to reduce the walking distance between the two. Climbing into the back he rifled through the pile of clothes pulling out a pair of socks, underpants, jeans and a pair of boots, all of which had missed several washes between the occasions of wearing. Now with just the top half remaining naked he searched again through the pile of clothing and reluctantly pulled out an olive green t-shirt and pulled it on.

"All of this shit and he takes my favourite Damned t-shirt," he said out loud.

Grant knew that Ian was not pleased one bit but unfortunately he really had not had a choice. He would rather have the copper on the inside than outside of this murderous circle knowing what he now knew.

There was one thing, one risky thing, he now had to do and it needed to be done quickly. He looked around the back of the bar, the only thing he could find that was of any use was a box of crisps. He emptied the box of its contents and ripped it apart leaving himself one square side. Grabbing a pen from the back shelf of the bar he wrote the words:

SORRY
TEMPORARILY CLOSED
PLEASE ACCEPT OUR APOLOGIES

on the plain side of the cardboard square. He ripped off a smaller square from a piece of the box and wrote something else on that and tucked it into the back pocket of his new leather jeans. Looking around the bar again he was unable to find a roll of tape but did find a lump of old white sticky tack and pulled off four bits forming them into little balls. He stuck the sign on the inside of the front door window and retrieved the old fashioned large key from the door's keyhole. He picked up his helmet containing his gloves from the table where they had been dumped by Gus when he had entered the bar and walked outside into the cool air. He locked the door which took a bit of effort as the lock was stiff. He could easily believe that this door had not been locked from the outside for years. Testing the door was locked by placing his foot and shoulder against it and pushing slightly (old habits were hard to stop) he made his way back to the courtyard gates where his bike stood, parked almost like it had been abandoned by a thief eager to get away from the scene of his crime.

He got himself bike ready and following a quick u-turn he headed off on one of his riskiest journeys so far. He didn't hold back on the throttle either, this was not the time to be slow, careful or quiet.

Within a short time, he was once again at the top of the road that led down to The Crippen's clubhouse. He pulled his bike over to the side of the road and kicked out the side stand after putting it into neutral gear. He reached backwards undoing the saddlebag and retrieved the plastic bag that still sat under the clothing he had borrowed from Ian. He reached inside moving the leather cut around until he located the inside pocket and placed inside it the small piece of cardboard he had written on earlier in the bar. He rolled up the plastic bag as tightly has he could and tucked it under his right armpit. Side stand up and kicked into first gear he stormed the bike down the road towards the clubhouse performing another u-turn at the gates and skidded the bike to a halt. Allowing the hold on the bag to relax it dropped into his right hand and he quickly threw it upwards watching as it looped and arced over the clubhouse gates and disappeared out of site. Releasing the clutch, almost too quickly as to cause the bike to stall he revved the bike hard and came as close as he had ever been to pulling a wheelie on his heavy cruiser. He roared the bike back up the road heading back to the pub not looking back to see if anyone was watching him ride away. The time for anonymity had come to an end.

***

The lookout stood next to the entrance door to the clubhouse smoking a cigarette. He was glad to be out in the fresh air away from the dark angry atmosphere that existed inside. He heard the bike approaching the gates and knowing that every member of the club was inside the building made the safe assumption that this was not the sound of an approaching Crippen. He was just about to go inside to tell the others when he saw the object come flying over the gates and hit the floor, seconds later he heard the bike roaring away.

Not certain what the package was he approached with caution eyeing up the now visible plastic bag. He was loath to pick up the bag, the recent events had made every member nervous and he didn't want to be the next Crippen to appear on the M.I.A. list.

"What is it?" a voice from behind him asked. Pretty Boy had come out to take a turn on lookout, a job well below one of the top table members but he needed a break from listening to what the bikers were going to do to the bitch locked up in the back.

"No idea" the lookout called back.

"Well, pick it up and bring it here you fucking pussy," said Pretty Boy. He was pissed off with this breed of new members: cautious, always want to plan things out, never fucking willing to take risks. Risk taking was part and parcel of this way of life.

The lookout picked up the bag with an outstretched arm keeping the article at arm's length, well away from his head and face.

Pretty Boy shook his head in disbelief.

"If it's a bomb that won't save your ugly mug, now bring it here for fuck's sake."

The young biker willingly handed over the bag to his Sgt at Arms without bothering to look at the contents. Pretty Boy however was keen to see what the bag held and with one look he worked out what it was. He returned inside with the bag and walked straight towards the door of the meeting room calling out at the top of his voice, "Top table, meeting room now." He refused to call it 'The Church' like his President desired. All this religious shit was getting on his nerves.

The Priest was sat in his normal place at the head of the table.

"Come in Pretty Boy, take a pew," said the President with a wry smile knowing the religious term would nark his Sgt at Arms, a position he planned to relieve him of as soon as possible.

"He's reached out to us boss," said Pretty Boy ignoring the obvious attempt to wind him up.

"Call me Priest," replied the President.

Ignoring him again Pretty Boy reached inside the bag and pulled out the blood-splattered leather cut and laid it out on the table. The road name patch was covered in dried blood at one end and now read 'LUM', the P illegible beneath the dark browny red dried crust of blood. The other three members of the top table were now making their way into the room each looking at the leather cut that was not presented for everyone to see.

Pretty Boy looked at each of the bikers saying, "I think we can safely assume that Lump is one stage beyond MIA."

The Priest stood and using his right index finger traced out an invisible inverted cross in the air in front of him.

"May his journey on the road to hell be a warm one," he said reaching forward and pulling the waistcoat towards him.

He first placed his fingers into the two front pockets and found nothing; he pulled the waistcoat open to show the inside of the two front panels.

The other bikers watched him, all confused. Cowboy asked the question that they were all thinking.

"What you looking for Priest?"

The President continued to search and in one of the pockets found what he was looking for. He pulled out the small cardboard square and placed it on the table.

"Unlike the rest of you, I do not underestimate this individual. Whatever it is that he wants it is obvious to me that he has planned things, thought about things probably for many months. However you were right Pretty Boy, he has reached out to us," he held the piece of cardboard and waved it in the air for the four bikers to see.

"Is it a message?" asked Panhead.

'The Priest' nodded to indicate yes.

"What's it say?" asked Tankslapper.

The Priest initially read the note to himself and then looking up read out loud the message that Grant had written.

9pm tomorrow, the girl for me
Outside clubhouse gates
Take the offer or another dies
Pretty Boy does the exchange
Grant

Looking in the direction of his Sgt at Arms whose face was now slightly paler than a few seconds ago The Priest said, "Looks like you have a new friend"!

The club President picked up the note and left the room, leaving the others to discuss the new event by themselves.

He made his way to the back room where Emma was being held.

As she heard the door unlock she prepared herself for the worst and was strangely relieved when she saw it was only the one person at the door. She was less relieved when she recognised who it was.

The Priest held the cardboard note in her direction saying,

"Tell me about this knight in shining armour."

***

Gus stood on the pavement outside of the hotel front door waiting, for what he didn't really know. He had arrived well within the hour that he said he would only to find the pub locked up and a closed sign in the window. His first thought was that Grant had decided that the best course of action was not to include a copper, probably what he would have done if he was stood in Grant's shoes. His second thought was that he had locked up the front and was securing the back and couldn't hear him knocking on the door, he quickly excluded this one when there was no response to his shouting Grant's name from outside the courtyard gates. He never thought that a van would pull up outside of the pub and that a man he had never set eyes on lower the front passenger window and from his position behind the steering wheel say,

"I'm guessing you are the copper. I'm Ian, the better looking half of the vigilante crew, do you want to get in? Grant will be back soon."

Gus went to open the door when he heard the now all too familiar sound of Grant's motorbike. It appeared around the corner and pulled in behind the van, Grant positioned it an angle so that it was facing outwards.

Grant got off his bike and without removing his helmet went to the door and unlocked it. Pushing it open he turned to look at Gus and shouted, "Inside, we don't have much time. And bring that pillock with you."

Ian smiled as Gus looked in his direction,

"That'll be me then, he loves me really."

The three men made their way inside and all sat huddled together around a round table adjacent to the door that led to the stairs.

Grant explained to the other two what he had done. Murphy looked shocked adding only, "Wow, really?"

Ian just shrugged and said sarcastically, "Subtle."

"Yeah I thought so too," replied Grant, equally as sarcastic.

"And are you really going to exchange yourself for Emma?" asked Murphy.

"I hope not to," Grant answered, "it all depends on you pair doing your part." Then looking at Ian he said, "Once this is done mate, it's over."

Ian looked surprised.

"What about number three?" he asked.

"It's gone far enough, we've been lucky so far. I don't want anyone else to die." Ian could see the disappointment etched all over Grant's face as he said these words.

"I'm sort of relieved, the last one was bad enough; the next one would have been stomach churning. Sort of pissed off though that I won't see my last creation in action," said Ian trying his best to lift the mood.

"I could always try it out on you at a later date. But only because I count you as a friend," said Grant grateful for the opportunity for a bit of banter.

"Thanks for the offer 'friend' but my ass is a one-way system only outgoing," replied Ian and then added, "and by the way I am your only friend."

214

Murphy sat between the two men following the conversation like an eager tennis fan at Wimbledon, his head turning from left to right and back again several times. At last he got a word in, saying.

"Sorry excuse me, the last one? Ass? Would one of you crazy fuckers explain this shit to me?"

Ian looked at him and said, "Muttley you really don't want to know, trust me."

Murphy glared at him, deep furrows appearing on his forehead.

"You call me that again and I will put my boot so far up your arse you will be cleaning the heel of it with your tongue."

Ian laughed and looked at Grant.

"I fucking like him."

All three men began to laugh. Grant let the laughter subside naturally and then announced.

"Down to business gentleman, we have less than thirty-six hours."

Three Become Two

The conversation between the three men had been going on for about an hour when Ian asked the question that needed to be asked.

"This planning shit is all fine and stuff but what is the actual aim? Are we rescuing the girl and if so are you really going to give yourself up for her?" Ian looked at Grant and waited for an answer.

Grant responded with an empty stare.

"Or do you really still want that last one?" asked Ian.

Grant looked down at the table they were sat around, looking back up he glanced at each of the other two men in turn.

"Yes," he eventually said.

"Yes to what bro?" asked Ian, becoming irritated and impatient.

"Yes I want to get Emma out of there and yes I really want Pretty Boy. I came here to hand out the justice that the fucking law couldn't provide," Grant held his stare with Ian as he responded to his friend's questions.

The two men continued to stare each other out, years of friendship and experiences were being tested in this simple test of strength. The tense silence was broken by Gus.

"Will one of you tell me what the hell is going on? I thought we were just looking for a way to free Emma."

Ian looked at Gus, breaking his stare from Grant's and immediately regretting doing so. He felt he had lost the battle of strength with his friend. He clearly didn't trust this new member of their team.

"You are being told nothing copper; I still have no idea why you have become involved in our business. I don't know if you are shagging this fucking girl and I couldn't really care less but the one thing I do know is that you are still a copper and right now I still trust those scum fucking bikers more than I do you."

Gus's response silenced the two men and sent them into a stunned state of shock and surprise.

"She's my bloody daughter."

It was Grant that broke the silence. The tenseness between the three of them could almost be seen as a solid wall.

"Does she know?"

"No, she has no idea and it stays that way," answered Gus.

"But... well... how?" asked Ian.

"Do I really have to explain the birds and the bees right now?" responded Gus sarcastically.

Not willing to allow the police officer to gain the upper hand in any form whatsoever Ian struck back just as sarcastically.

"No, I meant how the hell did you find a woman who was willing to have sex with you?"

"Will you two boys put your rattles down and pick up your dummies," interrupted Grant.

Looking at Gus he asked, "Why didn't you say anything before now?"

"I swore on my life to her mother that I would never let anyone know," replied Gus, dropping his head as the sudden realisation that his promise to the only woman he had ever truly loved had finally been broken.

"Wow," said Ian and then like a schoolyard bully striking while his victim was on the ground he continued, "you are going to hell."

Even Gus had to laugh, a short and stifled laugh but still a show of humour. The other two smiled and Grant just shook his head. No matter what the situation you could always rely on Ian to say something that would break the tension.

Gus looked at Grant, his face became serious once again as he said, "This is why it has to be me that is used as an exchange for Emma."

"Won't work Gus," said Grant. "They aren't interested in you, it's me they want. If you want to see Emma alive again then only exchanging her for me will do."

He used the silence, allowing it build the suspense and also giving his two accomplices to come up with a better idea than the one in his head but nothing was forthcoming.

"However," he finally said, "I have no intention of putting myself into the hands of those bastards so listen up; this is how it is going to work."

***

Emma tried to work out how long had passed since her visitor had left the room. She was wasting even more time trying to work it out, her mind was in a state of fear, all she could hear were the threatening words of The Priest just before he had left the room.

Give up the stranger or be treated in such a way that should she actually survive the ordeal she wouldn't want to live anyway. She had been a survivor all her life, always made the decisions that suited her even if it caused pain or heartache to other people. She had been this way ever since her father had left their family home without any explanation, her mother would never speak about it and so from a very young age she rebelled against everything, especially if it was against adults and even more so if those adults were in a position of authority.

Her rebellious ways had led her into a life of drugs and abuse which had only ended because of the intervention of someone who represented everything that she hated: a policeman. Gus had found her on the streets one morning following a drug and alcohol fuelled bikers' party during which she had done things that would shame the filthiest of prostitutes. He had sheltered her in his home, used his contacts to get her the help she needed from professionals and eventually persuaded the owner of the pub to give her a job. All the hard work to keep her life clean and as straightforward as possible was now being threatened and all because of a man she hardly knew but still she didn't want to return to the decision-making process of her youth and take the option that best suited her and yet at the same time she knew that this time that decision was the correct and only decision she could make.

The door unlocked, shocking her out of her thoughts and focussing her eyes on the entrance way to the room. Fully expecting to be faced with a horde of filthy horny bikers she started to reach for the 'food' bowl again but lowered her arm as she saw a sole figure as the door was pushed inwards and fully open.

Her relief was short lived as she recognised who the lone figure was. Pretty Boy looked down at her and smiled.

"Hello gorgeous," he said as he rubbed his hand over the crotch of his jeans.

"You going to use that pretty mouth of yours to talk or to blow?"

It would appear that her one hour thinking time was up.

Pretty Boy grabbed her by her arm and pulled her up to her feet, he pushed her towards the door.

"After you ma'am," he said sniggering.

"Where am I going?" asked Emma, her voice trembling as she feared the worst.

"To the only room in this building where you haven't been fucked…to the Church," replied the biker.

Emma looked back at him, confusion all over her face.

"I have no idea where you are talking about."

"Oh yeah," responded Pretty Boy, "things have changed a bit since you were last here." He pushed his face up to the side of her neck and licked his tongue up her neck and over her ear, "We have missed you," he hissed, "now go to the old meeting room."

Emma made her way down the corridor closely followed by Pretty Boy. They followed the corridor to its end where it opened up into the bar area which was full with every member of the club now being virtually imprisoned inside the safety of its walls. She was met with a hail of hisses and abuse and a few words reminding her of the exploits of previous visits to this hell hole.

"Do you still drip like a tap girl?"

"Hmmm, I remember that smell."

"Pulling a train later Emma?"

"Choooo choooo!"

Raucous laughter followed and mingled with each call out.

She focussed on the floor and quickened her step as she made her way towards the door that led to the only room in the clubhouse that she had never been in as she had earlier been reminded of so subtly by Pretty Boy. As she raised her hand to push the door open she stopped and lowered the arm back to her side. The door was being opened from the inside, The Priest appeared and smiled.

220

"Welcome my child, to the only holy place in this house of lost souls." Then looking around the bar he raised his voice shouting, "Quiet you pack of dogs, keep your filthy words in your heads and your filthier dicks in your pants until I say otherwise."

He held his free arm out in a welcoming pose, swinging it backwards to invite Emma inside.

"Come, Emma, let us talk," he said.

From a back corner of the bar, a biker called out, "Oh don't worry boss, she will come for you."

Emma walked into the room and just before closing the door The Priest leaned towards his Sgt at Arms and whispered, "stripe that animal and bring me his ear."

He closed the door watching Pretty Boy making his way to the back of the bar.

Inside the room, he led Emma by the arm towards the head of the table and pulled out the chair where the Sgt at Arms would normally be seated.

"Take a seat Emma."

Emma sat down. She looked around the room, empty chairs around the large table, she was alone with this freak. On the wall behind the largest chair at the table where The Priest now began to sit himself hung a leather cut. It was hanging on a wire coat hanger which itself was hanging from a nail in the wall. The cut was splattered in blood and dirt but the name tag clearly identified as the one belonging to Lump.

He looked over his shoulder when he spotted Emma looking at the cut.

"As I said earlier, every war has its casualties," he placed his hands together in the position of prayer. "I am sure my brother is now in a much warmer place."

"What are you going to do with me?" asked Emma.

221

"Patience my child, your fate is not in my hands. That responsibility belongs to your friend. So tell me, are you ready to talk?"

If Emma had been in any doubt about talking to this individual that doubt had been removed the moment she walked through the clubhouse bar. The lustful hatred that she had heard in those few short seconds had convinced that once again she had to make the decision that was best for her… even if others were harmed because of it.

"His name is Grant," she blurted out. "He arrived a few days ago, said he was resting up like I told you earlier, had a run-in with the cops on the way into town I heard him tell one of the customers in the pub, I thinks he comes from London but I'm really not sure about th…"

The Priest raised his hand "Slow down," he said, his voice soft but still with that evil undertone. "I am glad that you have decided to enter into dialogue with me and it is comforting that you have started with some truth."

Emma looked at him surprised and confused about the sudden trust and belief in her.

"Oh I already knew his name young one," he responded to Emma's surprised look. "But it's a full name I would like."

"I've not idea, honest. He signed in as Grant, just Grant. I even questioned him about it but he said that he was called Grant, nothing else. Suppose it's like a road name, all you bikers have road names don't ya?"

"Ah, a fellow worshiper of the road, a lone wolf maybe, a troubled soul running away or maybe towards something."

Before anything else could be said between the club President and his captive, the door swung open and Pretty Boy walked in. His hands were covered in blood, in one hand he held a switchblade knife and in the other Emma couldn't see as he was clenching something inside his closed hand. She didn't have to wait long to find out what it was that he was holding as he threw a bloody ear onto the table in front of them both.

"Thank you Sgt," said The Priest without reacting in any way. "Is the dog being cared for?"

"Yes boss, got a new road name already. He looks like he's only got one handle so they're calling him Teapot. Get it, only one handle?" replied a laughing Pretty Boy.

"Yes, yes the humour of the brothers never ceases to amaze me," responded the president, no trace of humour in his voice.

"We have some business to take care of," The Priest continued.

"Send two of the younger brothers out, as civilians mind, no colours."

Looking at Emma he asked, "You mentioned our friend having a run in with our friends in blue, who in particular?"

"Gus and that young copper," replied Emma. "Think his name's Ferguson."

"Ah young Fergie, we know him well, quite a useful lad."

He returned his attention to Pretty Boy.

"Get our boys to pay a visit, find out what he knows and make it clear to them. They cause him no harm, understood?"

"Clear as a bell boss," replied Pretty Boy and turned to leave the room.

"Sgt," said The Priest.

Pretty Boy turned back around to face his president.

"Yes boss," he said.

"Call me Priest."

***

223

"So, can it be done?" Grant asked Ian.

Ian rubbed his eyes and shook his head.

"You're asking a lot mate and it's going to take time to get that stuff together," he replied.

"We have twenty-four hours, can it be done?" Grant once again asked Ian with a matter-of-fact tone.

"It's possible but I need to reach out to Ordnance. He lives in Wales somewhere, normally in a caravan so basically he could be anywhere."

Grant looked intently at his friend.

"Ian, I need to know, can you do this?"

"Yes I can fucking do it now lay off with all the serious shit, you are freaking me out," replied Ian playfully.

He stopped smiling when he saw the level of seriousness on Grant's face. The frown that appeared also helped him to appreciate how serious his friend was.

The two men stood and hugged each other. Ian tried to pull away but Grant held the clinch.

"Let go," said Ian, "you'll be squeezing my arse next."

Grant released his hold and Ian stepped back, he nodded his head towards his friend before walking away to leave the bar. As he reached the door he turned around smartly and slammed his left foot onto the floor, standing to attention he threw a salute towards Grant and said, "It's been a blast my friend."

He walked out into the street and Grant couldn't help but think if he would ever see his friend again. Looking at Gus he said, "So, just the two of us now, we'd best get busy."

Outside, Ian sat behind the wheel of his van looking through the contacts list on his mobile phone. Eventually, he found the name he was looking for and pressed the screen. The phone rang and rang, Ian didn't think he was

224

going to get a response when just as he was about to end the call a tired sounding voice spoke to him.

"Whoever you are you better have a good reason for waking me up and it this is one of you PPI people I will shove this phone down your fucking throat."

"I see you haven't lost your people skills Ordnance, said Ian.

"Who the fuck is this?" the voice asked.

"Its Ian, I know it's been a while but surely you remember your old mate Ian."

"Ian fucking who?" the voice on the other end of the call now becoming more irritated with every word spoken.

"Ian. You know… Northern Ireland Ian. Remember the officers' daughter's car you helped me to blow up and it got blamed on the Irish bastards?" Ian waited, the silence was torture.

"IAN" the voice yelled. "How the fuck are you pal?"

"I need a favour mate," replied Ian.

"Shit yeah, what we blowing up this time?" asked Ordnance.

Ian smiled, glad to hear that his old mate hadn't lost his sense of humour or regained his sanity.

"Just hold your firing devices mate and tell me where you are," he asked him.

"In me caravan," came back the most simple of replies.

"No, you fuck arse, where in the country?" asked Ian, already in his head questioning the reasoning behind involving this idiot, except for the obvious that he was great at making explosive devices, loved blowing stuff up and he needed his help.

"Oh sorry bud, Wales," responded Ordnance.

This could take a long fucking time thought Ian.

Ordnance

As Ian headed off to the middle of a moor in the middle of nowhere just over the English/Welsh border, Gus walked out of the pub and headed home to grab a bite to eat. There wasn't much he could do at this time and he got the impression that Grant needed to be alone. He was tired, too much sitting behind a desk and living alone eating greasy fast food was not the best preparation for becoming part of a small gang of vigilantes.

His head was down as the sound of approaching motorbikes could be heard but the situation he now found himself in forced him to look up. He caught a quick glimpse of the two bikers as they passed by, nothing out of the ordinary, no colours being displayed, *just two lads out enjoying a ride*, thought Gus.

The two bikers, being new prospects to The Crippens, didn't recognise the portly man as they rode past. Had he been in uniform they may well have taken more notice and may have even thought twice about continuing their journey. The Priest's message had been made very clear to them: keep it low profile. On this occasion, their ignorance and lack of knowledge about the local law enforcement had made no difference and Gus's tiredness had helped.

Grant had followed Gus to the door, told him that he would call round for him later and then locked the door. He returned to the same chair he had been seated for the last couple of hours and looked around the bar.

Up to a year or so ago he would never have walked into a place like this, his wife and daughter liked welcoming and, to put it bluntly, places a bit more upmarket.

He had spent his childhood and youth in places rougher than this however. As a child, he would often have been sent by his mother to look for his father in tatty, smoky working men's bars. Back then children were not allowed in such places but after spending a few minutes trying to look through grime and tobacco tar covered windows for his father he would chance it and run the gauntlet of the hands of the men who would try to smack him around the back of his head shouting at him to 'get the fuck out' as he shouted back, "Have you seen my Dad?"

Grant smiled as he remembered the mixture of banter from the hard working factory men.

"Go on with ya, you little fuckin' bleeder."

"Do ya want a beer lad?"

"Go home and take your little pencil dick with ya."

He learned to navigate the pubs frequented by his father, working out entrances, exits and clear (ish) pathways between them. These places and these men became familiar features in his life as he grew into a young teenager and began to integrate with them, consuming his first pint at the age of fourteen, his first cigarette two months later and his first real punch in the face a short time after that. He learned the art of street fighting with these men who had fought through every day of their existence and aged before their time because of it.

As the memories raced through his head Grant's smile disappeared. He recalled how his life had almost gone down the wrong road as this life in a tough Potteries town began to consume him. He had begun to hang out with the wrong crowd, his love of bikes which had been encouraged by his father, a bike rider of many years, steered him towards bikers and wannabe Hells Angels and he became part of a gang famous for carrying Stanley knives which they used to cut the faces, or striping as it was commonly known, of anyone who crossed them.

It was following a 'striping' that his life had taken a turn for the better when that evening he had been literally grabbed by the collar of the local beat 'bobbie' and told to meet him the next Saturday morning on the town high street.

Despite his wayward attitude and hatred for the law and the men who governed it, Grant had turned up as told and met up with the policeman. The man stood next to him in his smart civilian clothing and pointed in three directions saying,

"There's the Army recruitment office, there's the Navy recruitment office and just down the street there, is the police station. Now make your choice lad."

"I don't wanna join the fucking Army," said a young John Richardson to the copper who just smiled and looked down the street.

"Police station, court and prison it is then young man," said the copper and reached to grab the young lad by his arm.

"Fine," said the boy who was to become the man known as Grant, "I'll go and talk to the soldier boys." He walked away from the police officer and crossed over the road. He had no intention of joining the military but saw this as the only way to get away from this interfering man. He walked into the Army recruitment office coming to a standstill once inside and looked back through the glass paned door waiting for the off duty copper to walk away. Two or three minutes passed as the young lad watched the copper who just stood on the opposite pavement looking at the recruitment office door.

A booming voice from behind him broke the deadlock, "Good morning lad, come to join the Army have you? Good decision, it will make a man of you."

Grant, or John as he was then, turned around to see a tall, broad man stood in front of a desk, his uniform was spotless, the creases in the shirt sleeves and trousers looked as sharp as the Stanley knife secreted away in the young lad's jacket. On the wall behind the Army recruitment sergeant was a poster proclaiming 'Join the Army, see the world and get paid for doing it'.

"I'm Sergeant Bull," said the soldier, "come take a seat lad and let me tell you how I can change your life.

It was 1979 and little did he know but that local beat police officer who had seen something in young John Richardson other than the yob he was becoming had just become the single most influential man in his life thus far.

The memories faded and the disappearing smile had become a frown as Grant contemplated the irony of his life that had begun with the actions of a kind-hearted police officer that had taken him away from a life of trouble and which now stood in the midst of murder and mayhem with which he was being assisted by a kind-hearted police officer.

Grant stood up: it was time to journey back to the location of 'the factory'. He just hoped that Ian had remembered to hide his belongings somewhere in the woods before destroying the building and the terrible secrets it held within.

***

About three miles out of town two bikers steered their bikes through a modern housing estate and pulled up outside the small front garden of a one bedroom starter home.

The road was empty and quiet as the two men got off their bikes keeping their helmets on just in case anyone was peering at them from behind net curtains or wooden blinds. The taller of the two men led the way up the short pathway up to the front door of the small house and knocked on the door. A short while passed before the door was opened by a skinny ginger haired man dressed in a pair of dark blue jogging bottoms and a white t-shirt.

The tall biker placed his hand on the chest of the man at the door and gently pushed him backwards saying, "Hello ginge, we need a word."

All three men walked deeper into the narrow short hallway, the second biker closing the door behind him.

A nervous Pete Ferguson looked at the two men and addressing the one with his hand still placed on his chest said,

"What the hell are you doing here Alan?"

Both of the bikers removed their helmets, Alan, the same Alan who had been sat in the bar with Pete when Grant had sat with them a couple of nights before looked at the young copper.

"We need to talk about our mutual friend, the stranger who was in the bar the other night, the stranger that you were so friendly with," he said.

"I don't know any more than you do, you were there and you were being friendly too," replied Pete.

"No, my friend, I was being inquisitive. He only told us what he wanted us to know that evening and that wasn't much at all," said Alan.

The other biker who had been silent until now suddenly sprung into action and grabbed Pete by the neck of his t-shirt wrapping the material around his fist.

"Let's beat the info out of him, he's filth above anything else, he's only a friend of The Crippen's to keep himself safe," he said.

"Let him go Stig, let's sit and talk first," demanded Alan to the young stocky biker. Stig reluctantly let his grip relax, pissed off that an opportunity to make a name for himself had been snatched away from him. This young prospect would have you believe that his road name had been given to him because of his skill on the road and the speed he was capable of: the truth was that he was called Stig because he always smelled like he lived on a dump.

***

Crossing into Wales just west of Whittington, Ian continued to drive westwards making his way towards the area where Ordnance claimed to be. Leaving the main B-road the roads quickly became country lanes and narrower as each mile went by. After only about fifty minutes of driving in Wales, the road Ian was on came to an abrupt end. A metal gate stood between stone walls and as Ian got out of his vehicle he looked around the sparse open land around him. It was getting dark and seeing too far was difficult.

Ian waited but as it became darker it got colder and he decided to sit and wait back in his van hoping that his mad friend would come to find him. He sat behind the wheel and grabbed his mobile, only to find he had no phone signal. If he was in the right area and Ordnance was nearby then Ian guessed that as he had no signal but the caravan dwelling bomb maker had a signal when he had phoned him earlier then he must be on higher ground. Looking out of the van windows Ian scanned the slowly disappearing horizon of hill tops. As he looked to his left a light flashed on and then disappeared after a second, Ian kept looking and after about thirty seconds the light flashed on and off again.

Ian spent the next twenty or so minutes painstakingly making his way across the moors towards the light which flashed on and off just once more during his bog-soaked journey. By the time he arrived at the battered caravan he was soaked from feet to knees and covered in a layer of greyish mud. His hands and face were layered and flecked in the same stinking mud from falling over twice and he was not what you could describe as being in a good mood.

"This had better be worth the fucking effort!" he shouted.

The caravan door opened, a small candle flickered from inside but the light from it was quickly and almost entirely blocked by the shadowy figure of a huge man that appeared in the open doorway.

Ordnance was huge! It wasn't just the extra poundage that he had put on since leaving the Army, mainly caused by an unhealthy diet of fast food, beer, and his favourite meal, cold baked beans eaten directly from the tin. This man was big, easily six feet four inches, a round barrel of a chest and the arms of a champion weightlifter which matched his heavy thighs. An old faded grey tee shirt which at some stage during its life had had the sleeves ripped from it strained itself around the man's large chest and belly, on it could just about be seen the figure of a man running and the words in a circle around him say, 'If you see me running we are all fucked'. A pair of three-quarter length khaki shorts finished off the ensemble which could only be described as hippy/grunge meets military.

Ordnance sported a full facial beard which was as scruffy and unkempt as the rest of him but all of this was softened as the white teeth appeared through the huge smile that broke out on his face as he looked down at Ian.

"Come give me a hug little man, it's been too long."

He stepped out of the caravan and grabbed Ian, pulling him towards himself and embracing him in the most welcoming and painful 'man hug' Ian had ever encountered in his life. With what he thought might be the last ounce of oxygen in his body Ian gasped, "Let me go you big fucking ox, you're killing me."

The big gentle giant let go of Ian and took a step back, once again looking at Ian.

"It has been many years my old friend, are any of the old crew still alive?" he asked.

"Can we get inside first mate, I'm wet and cold and could do with a beer," said Ian, his mood not much improved by the warm welcome received.

"Oh yeah, sorry, for sure man," spluttered Ordnance. "Where are my manners? Got a heater inside you can hang your wet 'uns around that."

"If you think I am sitting in that turtle shell on wheels in just my undercrackers with you, you have another thing coming pal," replied Ian jokingly.

Ordnance placed his arm around Ian and guided him into the caravan saying, "You don't have to worry, unless you have four legs, a cute face and are covered in wool I'm not interested," the two men entered the caravan laughing together and closed the door behind them.

Inside the caravan was warm; an old four bar electric heater threw out heat that was more than adequate for the small caravan. The throb of the generator outside that provided the power for the few electrical items inside could be just about heard. The word ramshackle to describe the interior of the caravan didn't really do it justice, however, the word death trap did.

Bits of circuitry, wiring, explosive material, detonators, and homemade timing devices were all over the place. A small bench housed an array of tools, soldering irons and more bomb-making materials including what Ian was sure was a lump of plastic explosive. Ordnance was a one-man terrorist cell!

A retired member of a bomb disposal team, it was clear that the big gentle giant who now settled himself into an old sofa chair that had seen much better days had not lost his interest or skills in making anything that would cause an explosion. He had long been known as the go-to man for any type of IED that you needed to be constructed in ways other than the conventional military way. As well as being involved in the dangerous world of decommissioning, deactivating and disposing of explosive devices he had also become a student of the world's best bomb makers, studying the work of the IRA, Iraqi insurgents and reading all he could about such organisations as the Tamil Tigers and Basque separatists. His favourite weapons of mass destruction were explosively formed projectiles (EFPs), directionally focussed charges and basic satchel charges. Evidence of his love of cell phone trigger mechanisms were scattered over the bench, old broken up mobiles were all over the place.

"Is there anywhere safe to sit in this place?" asked Ian after casting his eyes around the interior of the wheeled shack.

"Nope," replied Ordnance, "but take those filthy jeans and shoes off first before you sit down, you'll get the place dirty"!

***

The two bikers left Ferguson's house and made their way back to the clubhouse. Having chatted and mildly roughed up the young police officer they were confident that he had told them all he knew, which to be honest wasn't much. Alan, aka Razor because of his favoured weapon of choice, was certain of a couple of things though. Firstly Emma was just an unfortunate victim of events, the lone biker had never intended for her to become involved and secondly he must be receiving help from someone. This second certainly was not based on evidence just a gut feeling, he could not believe that a brother such as Lump could have been taken out by one man alone.

They headed away from town, this time, taking the longer route back to the clubhouse and their club President, just two bikers enjoying the open road... and planning revenge on this lone (ish) wolf who had dared to cross them.

***

Ian allowed Ordnance a short while to reminisce and ask questions. It was clear that he did not get to talk to many people and his 'hobby' certainly ensured that company of any kind must have been rare, if any at all.

After about half an hour Ian had to bring his friend to a halt saying, "Ordnance it's great to catch up with you but I'm on the clock pal."

"Understood sir," the large bomb-maker promptly stood as straight as the caravan would allow him, his neck bent allowing his head to lean forward so as not to bang it on the ceiling. "Come with me."

The two men left the caravan and Ordnance led Ian around to the back of his 'temporary' accommodation. He walked an unclear but obvious path known only to this man and approximately twenty feet from the rear of the caravan he came to a step and bent forward, his hand reaching to the ground and felt around in the undergrowth. Grabbing

235

the round metal handle the large man lifted a wooden trap cover with ease and then when lifted to waist height he used both hands to firmly push it backwards. Ian watched as the trap door fell smoothly backwards hitting the ground and once again becoming hidden in the flora and fauna of the moor. From where he stood, he could not see a thing, his friend beckoned him forward.

Ian walked and stood next to Ordnance and looked down into a large hole, wooden boarding all around its walls and Ian guessed also on its floor. He only guessed this because he could not see the actual base of the hidden cache because of the amount of stuff that was contained inside, but Ian thought that the amateur bomb maker wouldn't want any of his creations getting damp.

"Ready for when Allah's wrong 'uns reach this shore," said Ordnance proudly, standing tall with his hands on his hips.

Ian looked down in absolute amazement, there were months if not years of work sat in a hole in the middle of a Welsh moor. IEDs of every description, homemade claymores, satchel bombs, pipe bombs, the list could go on forever.

"Jesus wept," said Ian.

"Fucking right he did pal, them nails must've hurt," replied Ordnance. "Now let's get your stuff out of here and get you back on the road."

"How much do I owe you pal?" asked Ian.

Ordnance looked at his friend and smiled. His response was typical of this man.

"A couple of pints, a few hours of your company and all the details of what damage my babies caused."

A Speck of Light
in a Cloud of Dust

Grant stood in the clearing staring at the building instead of a pile of burned ashes as he had expected. He walked inside and looked around, he was impressed with the clean up job that Ian had done, nothing that would test a forensic team obviously but more than enough to convince a group of kids looking for a secret place to do drugs that nothing too terrible had occurred. Bloodstains had been scrubbed and then it looked like Ian had spread and rubbed soil into the wooden floor to dirty it up even more.

This cleanliness check took Grant seconds to complete because the greatest level of his impressiveness was being held by the piece of carpentry wonderness that had been assembled in the area of the building that he now secretly called 'his torture room'. In almost the identical area that both One a Year and Lump had ceased to exist now stood a structure that even he did not think Ian was capable of creating, and yet here it was. He would never underestimate his friend again.

His gaze never left the wooden structure as he made his way to where he had left his stuff. Briefly tearing his eyes away from Ian's piece of artwork he checked that the knife, Glock, and ammunition were still there. Having done so his eyes once again returned to the latest device of pain that had been left for him.

Grant walked around it taking in every detail. Despite its simplicity, he could still appreciate the work that had been put into creating it.

A three-legged 'stool' made of sturdy hardwood sat beneath a hanging chair. The chair was hanging from a combination of ropes and pulleys, the weight taken by one of the buildings strong wooden beams. Two subtle designs made both the stool and the chair different from those that most people would imagine if asked to describe these two everyday objects. First, the chair had a wide hole in its seat and secondly the stool did not have a flat seat but instead a wooden pyramid. The Judas Cradle was beautifully designed and sublimely recreated by Ian.

Grant walked closer and ran his hand up one of the smooth pyramid walls to the pointed tip, he pressed a finger against this tip. It was sharp, covered by a tiny steel top, he placed his finger into his mouth and sucked the small droplet of blood that had appeared as the sharp metal tip pierced his fingertip.

***

Ian had carefully placed the two satchel bombs and the homemade nail bomb carefully into the back of his van making sure that they were secured and well hidden, which wasn't that difficult in his untidy vehicle. The two smoke grenades that Ordnance had thrown in for fun he put into a small bag and placed that under the driver's seat.

He began his journey back, this time driving a bit slower for two obvious reasons, he didn't want those explosive devices being thrown around the back of the van and blowing him to kingdom come and this was the one occasion he did not want to be stopped by the police. Explaining this cargo would test even his imaginative mind. As he drove back over the border into England he ran the basic details of Grant's plan through his head.

1. Pick up explosive stuff √
2. Meet up with Muttley on way
3. Leave Muttley in van
4. Get himself into place
5. At the agreed time blow shit up
6. Get the hell out of there

A plan on the same level as the capture of Bin Laden he laughingly thought to himself, what could possibly go wrong!

Once again thinking about his payload he concentrated on the road and mile by mile made his way to a situation for which he could not predict the outcome.

***

Gus sat at home considering his options. The problem with having time on your hands while you waited for a deadline or waited for a plan to start was that you began to doubt the decisions you had made.

His part in the plan was crucial to the escape of Emma, his daughter, a secret he had shared with nobody including the girl herself until just a few hours ago. If he pulled out now who was to know if the rescue would be a success but even if he played his part the outcome was still unknown. If you decide to take on the devil you play by his rules and those rules are unpredictable, to say the least. He could, of course, try to persuade the powers that be that his role up to now had been one of observation, almost undercover so to speak so that he could ascertain what was going on in order then to report it and stop the crime or crimes being committed but only a fool would believe that. His final option was to carry on with the plan, play his full part to the best of his ability and at least choosing this option allowed him to narrow the possible outcomes down to two, his career would be finished and he would end up serving time in prison or he would end up dead.

He sat and waited, waiting for contact to be made by Ian. Maybe at that point, he would finally decide what to do.

***

Razor and Stig sat at the main table in the chapel of the clubhouse. The club president and the Sgt at Arms sat at the decision-making end of the huge wooden table and listened as they recalled the content of their conversation with Constable Ferguson.

It became quickly apparent that the young police officer knew very little more than The Priest already knew. The one piece of information that did raise interest with the club president was the fact that their adversary was ex-military. Apparently Ferguson had overheard Murphy mention it, he knew that it would have been foolish to underestimate this stranger too much.

Pretty Boy sat and listened in silence. He had been deep in thought for some time now mentally putting into place all the pieces of the jigsaw that linked his two missing - and probably dead - brothers and himself and the same event kept coming up, the robbery that went badly wrong. It had been so long ago he had almost forgotten all about it, as bad as the average person would have viewed the outcome to Pretty Boy it had just been a party. Fair enough a twisted fucked up biker party but just a party none the less, the fact that two of the participants could hardly be described as

240

enthusiastic had, in his warped mind, made it more enjoyable.

He recalled the moment as he was forcibly buggering the mother that he looked up and saw the horror and fear on the daughter's face as Lump held a knife to her throat making her watch the whole event. At that moment, he had emptied himself inside the older woman. Just sitting here recalling the memory was turning him on again.

"Sgt," said The Priest, annoyed that he had had to say it twice to get the attention of Pretty Boy.

"Yeah, what?" asked the Sgt at Arms mentally returning to the meeting.

The club president repeated himself,

"I said, you aren't saying much, anything you'd like to share with us?"

He knew that the last person he needed to share these thoughts and that event with was his club leader.

"Just thinking Priest, wondering how best we can get our hands on this fella and keep the girl as well," he eventually said.

"You are right about one thing Pretty Boy we do need to ensure we, or shall I say you, don't let this man get away because as requested you will be doing the exchange." The Priest studied his Sgt at Arms as he spoke, "But the girl is nothing of importance, she will be released."

Panhead the Vice-President who hadn't said a word spoke up asking, "What if it goes totally pear-shaped?"

"Then what will be will be," replied the President in a matter-of-fact manner.

Panhead looked intensely at Pretty Boy. He knew that the Sgt at Arms was worried about something and knew more than he was letting on. It was time for a private word as soon as the opportunity presented itself.

The meeting ended and The Priest told them all to leave and prepare for the exchange. He sat alone, he knew hardly anything more about the Grant fella than he had before and this was a huge concern to him. Since taking over this club he had ruled by knowing everything but it was clear to him that this man had a vendetta against his organisation. A vendetta usually meant revenge and revenge was always the result of an action, an event... something personal. Whatever had happened had taken place without his knowledge and it hadn't been brought to his attention either. The fear he held over most if not all of the members had always resulted in somebody informing him of things that happened. Whatever had occurred must have been so bad that it had not been talked about and if bikers hadn't talked to at least some of their brothers about something then that something had to be unacceptable. Unacceptable in his life was unthinkable.

Panhead watched Pretty Boy walk out of the clubhouse and casually followed him. The Sgt at Arms walked around the corner of the building into a quiet area of the huge courtyard and lit up a cigarette.

"Wanna tell me what's going on?" asked Panhead.

Pretty Boy spun round taken by surprise, not aware that he had been followed outside.

"Nothing bro, just having me a smoke," he replied. He offered his cigarette pack to the VP who took one out of the pack and lit it up sucking in a deep lung full of smoke and holding it in for a few seconds before exhaling the smoke slowly.

"The one thing I have learned about our way of life is there is always something going on. Back in the day we talked about everything, we sorted problems, we handled discipline, if a brother needed help he got help, if a slap was required one was handed out and everyone accepted and lived by our internal laws." Panhead paused waiting for a reaction but got nothing.

"Of late," he continued, "too many brothers are trying to impress, make a name for themselves. They feel a need to get in the good books of a maniac, to share a place on a top table of a club that is slowly imploding. We have lost the respect and the fact that one stranger feels that he can take us on and win is proof of that."

"Can't say I've noticed," replied Pretty Boy taking one last drag on his smoke and stubbing it on the ground.

"That's not good bro," said Panhead, "but while you have been walking around with your eyes shut I've had mine open. You were always close with Lump and One a Year but there has been a distance developing between the three of you for months." He paused again but once again got nothing from his fellow biker.

"What happened on that ride out you all went on about a year ago?" The question was put bluntly and right of the blue.

The Sgt at Arms was clearly surprised by what had been asked, his eyes wandered all over the place but he didn't make eye contact with his VP. The question unsettled him and he had no immediate response.

"Ride out; can't say I recall it," he said trying to sound casual but failing massively.

"Yes you do brother and you need to start talking. Whoever this guy is he is serious, he has disappeared two of our members and I have a feeling that you are his next target." Panhead stepped towards Pretty Boy getting right into his personal space. "What the fuck went on?"

"It was just a drug deal, a chance to get a bit of personal money in our pockets," said a panicked Pretty Boy.

"Bollocks bro, a man doesn't kill because of some poxy small-time drug deal." Panhead was now angry and his face was just inches from the face of Pretty Boy.

The Sgt at Arms was shaking his head, looking down at the ground. It was clear that he was worried about something, knew more than he was letting on.

"It was a robbery bro, I think maybe we robbed this guy's family," the response was blurted out rapidly and with a certain amount of relief as if Pretty Boy felt unburdened at last.

Panhead suddenly and quickly produced a flick knife from the back pocket of his jeans, he pressed the release button and the blade was up to Pretty Boy's throat in a flash.

"No normal man kills because his pad got done over, the truth brother, now or I cut and gut you, tear out your eyeballs and piss in the holes," he pressed the point of the blade into the flesh of Pretty Boy's neck.

With fear all over his face and his eyes filling up with tears Pretty Boy looked directly into Panhead's eyes.

"I think we did his family, I... I think we did his bitches."

"You killed his family?" asked the VP.

"No, no," stuttered Pretty Boy, "worse bro, much worse."

***

At 6pm that evening, Ian pulled up outside of Murphy's house. He got out of his van locked it and checked twice that the rear doors were securely locked before walking down the short pathway to the front door and ringing the bell.

Gus opened the door, his face was pale and it was obvious to Ian that the cop was worried.

"Everything ok?" he asked, knowing that it wasn't.

"All fine," replied a lying Gus, "tea, coffee?" letting Ian into his house and closing the door after quickly looking up down the street to see if anyone was watching.

"Beer, brandy?" replied Ian.

"Don't you think we should all keep a clear and sober mind tonight?" Gus asked.

"Listen pal, I have just driven from Wales with a van full of explosives hoping to fuck that I didn't get stopped by one of your esteemed colleagues, now get me a beer." Ian didn't want to die without at least one last beer being consumed.

"They're in the fridge, fill yer boots."

"Where's the fridge?" asked Ian.

"It's in the kitchen where else would it bloody be?" Gus answered, not sure if Ian was taking the piss or not.

"How would I know? I live in a fucking van," said Ian making his way to the kitchen. "Full of fucking bombs," he shouted as he found the fridge and pulled out a bottle of beer.

Holding the bottle against the side of the kitchen worktop Ian struck the top with his fist and flipped off the top, much to the disgust of the house proud police sergeant.

"You ready for this?" asked Ian.

"No, not one bit," replied Gus truthfully.

"Fantastic," said Ian laughing, "nothing better than a copper out of his comfort zone."

***

At 8pm that evening, Grant mounted his motorbike. His knife was tucked into his right boot, hidden under his jeans, the firearm was inside an internal pocket of his jacket. He made his way out of the woods not certain that he would ever see this place again and headed off down the road for his meeting, not absolutely certain what was waiting for him.

At the same time, as planned, Gus pulled the van over to the side of the road about half a mile away from The Crippen's clubhouse. Ian quickly got out of the van taking with him two satchel bags which he had transferred from the back of the van to the cab before leaving Gus's house. In his jacket pockets were the smoke grenades. He began to walk up the road towards the clubhouse heading for the narrow alleyway that ran alongside the back wall of the clubhouse. Gus drove past him, as he did so Ian pulled his right hand out of his pocket and gave Gus a thumbs up.

Gus carried on up the road and once again pulled up to the side of the road just beyond the corner of the side street where the entrance gates to the clubhouse were located. He turned off the engine and waited. His arrival had not gone unnoticed. Just inside the gate a member of The Crippens stared through the gap between the two gates. He waited a few minutes watching to see if anyone got out of the van, when nobody did he ran back to the clubhouse to inform Tankslapper of the vehicles arrival. The club secretary was stood by the clubhouse door, he nodded his head upon hearing the news and instructed the biker to return to the gates and keep watching. Tankslapper made his way to the 'The Church' to pass on the message.

No one had seen the drop off of Ian half a mile down the road, nor his approach and entrance into the alleyway. He looked for a place to hide until he had to make his move. He spotted a large green industrial wheelie bin against the wall of the factory that stood opposite the clubhouse wall, it was the only place that was any good so he settled himself behind the bin, pulling it back as close to the wall as he could while leaving himself enough space to sit down behind it.

It was beginning to get dark and a spattering of rain began to fall as he settled himself down trying his best to find the most comfortable position possible in the tight space.

He pulled the mobile phone that 'Ordnance' had given him, wondering whether or not to switch it on. He decided not to right now, the last thing he wanted to do was hit the wrong key while sat so close to two primed and ready satchel bombs.

***

Tankslapper entered the meeting room.

"The van is here," he said.

The people inside the room, The Priest, Pretty Boy, Panhead, Cowboy and Emma all looked towards him.

"Where?" asked the President.

"Corner of the street at the front," replied Tankslapper.

"Is he here?" the club President asked again.

"Not seen," replied the Treasurer, "just the van, don't know who's in it."

The Priest rubbed and pulled his goatee. "Early," he said, "he's not here yet." Then looking at Emma he smiled and said, "Almost time to say goodbye."

***

At ten minutes to nine Grant put his bike into neutral and looked down the road, He could see the white van parked on the corner of the street, he was about a quarter of a mile away. He had to assume that Ian was in place and he also guessed that Gus was a bundle of fear and nerves sat behind the wheel of the van.

He sat on the bike and allowed the bike to gently rumble, sat upright he stretched and arched his back raising his arms upwards and placing his hands on the back of his helmet trying to stretch out the tension that was building up in his body. He looked at his watch: 8.52p.m.

He pulled in the clutch and engaged first gear. Releasing the clutch slowly he moved forward and rode the bike slowly down the road, it was dark enough to need his headlight but he left it off. As he approached the van he could see Gus watching his arrival, the man looked nervous, afraid even. Grant didn't acknowledge him, he rode past and without signalling, he turned right into the side street. Less than a hundred yards ahead of him outside the front gates, stood three bikers and Emma. He slowly rode past them and then did a u-turn manoeuvre and stopped the bike.

Looking around he could see nobody other than the four figures he had just ridden past. He moved the bike forward slowly and once again brought it to a standstill right opposite the small gathering. Pointing at The Priest and Panhandle in turn Grant shouted, "You two, inside the gate, just Pretty Boy and Emma stay!"

The Priest turned towards his VP and flicked his head indicating that he could return back into the courtyard inside the gates, then looking back at Grant, he called back, "I stay, at least give me a chance to see and talk with the individual who has the balls to give himself up for this wretched cock-snogging spunk chariot." His use of language that he detested was purely an effort to unsettle and hopefully anger Grant. An angry man made mistakes.

Grant nodded and moved his bike back up the street and stopped it about halfway between where the bikers and Emma were stood and where Gus had parked the van.

Leaving the engine running he got off it and glanced at his watch: 8.58 p.m., so far so good.

Grant removed his helmet and gloves, placed the latter inside the former and walked towards the three awaiting people.

As he came to a stop he looked towards Emma and nodded, the young girl simply smiled and silently mouthed the words 'thank you'.

"At last, we meet," said The Priest, "but I notice that you leave your bike running which tells me you have no intention of staying and enjoying our hospitality."

Grant nodded in the direction of Emma.

"The bike is for her. I stay, she rides away. Before that happens though, you fuck off; Pretty Boy and I have a need to speak to each other."

"Is that what this is all about?" asked the club president. "You kill one, possibly two of my brothers just to have a chat with my Sgt at Arms. If that is all you want, let the girl ride away now and we can all go inside and have that chat you want, I would like to hear why you are so interested in confronting him."

Grant glanced at his watch again: 9.02 p.m.

"So you've not shared your secret with your brethren Pretty Boy? With your leader?" Grant asked the nervous-looking biker.

"I have no idea who you are," he replied.

"You know of me, you know why I'm here, you know what you fucking did!" shouted Grant angrily.

"Is time of some importance to you Grant?" asked The Priest.

Grant smiled and then laughed almost hysterically.

"Time? Time stopped for me a year ago," he replied. Grant could feel the anger and hatred he felt towards Pretty Boy boiling inside him, it was taking over and making him lose his focus.

"Let her go and let's get this done," Grant demanded of the bike club leader.

"I'm intrigued by this secret, if one of my brothers has offended you without my knowledge, without my authority then the punishment of that individual is mine to administer," The Priest was honestly interested now.

"Punishment?" screamed Grant. "This is not about punishment or revenge, I want to know why. I need to hear this piece of shit tell me why."

Once again he looked at his watch; 9.08 p.m.

***

Ian looked at his watch, eight minutes past nine. He moved out of his hidden position and walked to the clubhouses' rear wall, placing one of the satchel bombs against it. The alleyway was no more than eighteen feet wide and he had nowhere else to hide other than back behind the large waste bin. He made sure the explosive device had the side marked with a big arrow and the numbers 666, drawn there by Ordnance, facing the wall and then returning to his crouched position behind the bin he turned on the mobile phone that he had considered switching on earlier.

The phone screen lit up and once again Ian checked his watch: 9.09 p.m. *Fuck it*, thought Ian and pressed the number six button three times and then the green 'call' button.

The explosion had a bigger impact than Ian expected, the force of the bomb going off pushed the wheelie bin backwards against the wall pinning Ian between the two. Momentarily stunned he suddenly felt the pressure of the bin against him ease as it bounced back into the alleyway towards the clubhouse wall. For a few seconds, which to Ian felt like a lifetime, he fought to get his breath back after being winded by the impact of the bin.

He moved away from the factory wall and was faced with a cloud of debris dust, the alleyway was littered with pieces of brick. Covering his eyes with one arm he made his way towards the wall and discovered a huge hole in it, the rear clubhouse courtyard covered, like the alleyway, with a scattered mess of brick and dust. Clambering through the hole he noticed two large motorbikes lying on their side having been blown over by the explosion.

Moving fast he ran over to the back wall of the clubhouse itself and laid the second satchel bomb against it, this was also had an arrow drawn upon it with the numbers 999 below it. He ran back towards the outside wall intending to go back through the breach and hiding on the other side, pressing 999 as he ran he accidently, in a moment of panic, also pressed the green 'call' button.

The blast hit him hurling him through the hole that had been blown into the outside wall just a minute earlier. He lay in the debris-covered alleyway feeling like his back was on fire and watching consciousness disappear, slowly return as a blur and then disappear again.

***

At the front of the clubhouse the blast came as a surprise to everyone except for Grant, as the two bikers and Emma instinctively ducked Grant shouted as loud as he could, "Emma, the van... RUN!"

The barmaid didn't have to be told twice, running as fast as possible she headed for the van when the second blast went off forcing her to hide behind Grant's bike. She looked towards Grant watching as The Priest took shelter by the wall next to the gates and Pretty Boy momentarily dropped to one knee. She heard someone shouting her name and looked over her shoulder.

Gus had opened the van's passenger door and was screaming at her.

"Emma, Emma… quick, run, get here quickly."

Getting to her feet she continued her escape running towards the open door of the van.

Grant turned quickly, even he had been surprised at how soon the second explosion had followed the first. A cloud of dust could be seen rising into the night sky from the area above the clubhouse building. He watched as Emma ran towards the van and, happy that she was as good as safe, he turned back to face the two bikers and unzipping his jacket pulled out the gun.

Pretty Boy had reacted quicker than any of them and reaching Grant before he could get the pistol fully out from inside his jacket he bundled him to the floor but much to Grant's surprise didn't follow up with an attack instead deciding to chase after Emma.

He heard the now familiar voice of the club President and watched as he stood up and sweeping his long leather coat to one side he reached behind his back and brought forward two pistols extracted from the waistband of his jeans.

"Now you go to hell, I hope Lump and One a Year are waiting to give you a warm welcome!" he yelled at Grant.

He reached into his jacket, his pistol was not there, frantically he felt deeper inside the jacket but could not find it. He looked around and as he saw the black Glock pistol shining in the dark from its position about three feet away from across the road he also heard two shots go off as The Priest fired both weapons in his direction.

Grant squeezed his eyes closed waiting for the pain to kick in but both bullets missed him, he moved towards the Glock quickly, grabbing it and rolling he raised it in the direction of the biker and pulling the trigger. The bullet embedded itself in the large wooden gate about two feet from the two gun-toting biker who scooted to his right and grateful to see that Panhandle had left the gates slightly ajar he leapt through the gap to use the gates as shelter.

A few bikers had run out of the clubhouse into the front yard, they were covered in dust from the second explosion that had ripped open the back of the building and started a small fire from the combustible material that had been used to build the back rooms. Flames licked their way up cheap wooden timber framework.

Outside the gate, Grant got to his feet and took the chance to run to his bike either as a getaway or a place of greater safety than the middle of an open road but as he got up he saw Emma struggling to open the back doors of the van. In her panicked state she had totally missed the fact that the passenger door was sitting open, the rear doors were closer to her and that is where she had instinctively headed but now Grant could see that Pretty Boy was just thirty feet or so from her position.

Getting to his feet Grant was unsure what to do, firing at Pretty Boy could result in anything, missing, hitting him or worse case scenario shooting Emma. His mind was made up as out of his peripheral vision he saw The Priests head pop out from behind the gate, he once again aimed his gun in that direction and fired over and over again. Bullets rained into the heavy wooden gates forcing the club president back inside and scrambling across the floor to seek shelter behind the solid brick wall as a bullet pierced its way through the gate.

Grant turned his attention to the van and began to run trying to close down the distance between him and the running biker before he reached Emma, an impossible task but one that he had to try. He could not and would not allow this man hurt another woman.

Pretty Boy reached Emma and grabbed her by her hair, spinning her round to face him and pushing her head backwards banging it into the van doors. He changed his grip of her letting go of her hair and wrapping his hand around her throat, his other hand reached into a pocket and pulled out a Stanley knife. Grant watched in horror trying his best to run faster as he watched the biker raise the knife towards Emma's face and push out the sharp razor blade, he just knew that this was the same weapon that had been used to cut open his wife's face a year ago.

Bikers were now pouring out onto the street from the clubhouse gates led by The Priest who viewed the scene in front of him and once again took aim at Grant with both weapons.

The next few seconds were a blur, Grant having no control over anything that happened but every event had an impact on the entire situation, the final outcome being one that Grant could never have dreamed of happening.

As The Priest fired both weapons; one bullet screamed past him hitting the side of the van, the impact delayed Pretty Boys progress with the knife giving Gus the seconds he needed to punch the biker squarely in the back of the head. Pretty Boy flew forward striking his forehead against the doors of the van and collapsing onto the floor, the knife dropping from his grip and hitting the road with a metallic clinking noise. At the same time, two dull 'pops' sounded off behind Grant followed by a fizzing, hissing noise as the smoke from the two grenades was released. A dazed and injured Ian stood next to a parked car watching the smoke cloud give shelter to his two friends and the young girl from the shots being fired in their direction. A mixture of thick green and red smoke formed a formidable cloud preventing the bikers from seeing what was happening on the other side of it and more importantly not allowing the enraged screaming club president to see where he was shooting.

Grant watched as the cloud slowly blocked out his view of his good friend, his last view of him being to watch him slump to the floor and lean against the parked car. He mentally thanked and wished his friend well before quickly making his way to the van. By the time he got there Gus had bundled a terrified Emma into the passenger seat and was making his way around the back of the vehicle to get into the driver's seat.

"Help me get him into the back of the van!" yelled Grant.

"Leave him, it's over Grant, we have done what we came here to do," replied Gus.

Grant raised the Glock and aimed it at the cop.

"No, we haven't, now help me get him into the van." Gus had no doubt that Grant was willing to shoot him.

Opening the doors they picked up the biker and threw him into the back of the van.

"Now go!" yelled Grant slamming the doors closed.

Grant ran back to his bike hearing the van tyres squeal on the wet road, its engine screaming as Gus gunned the engine. Jumping onto his bike he did exactly the same, he had to momentarily close the clutch and drop the throttle as the bike tyre threatened to veer out of control as it struggled to grip the road.

As he rode away he looked back at the smoke-filled area behind him hoping to see Ian coming through it, instead, he saw the slowly emerging figure of The Priest. The pistols were being held down at his side pointing to the floor, he made no attempt to raise them and take aim. He just stood there glaring at Grant and screamed,

"I'll kill you, I'll kill you all!"

Grant took one last look backwards, no sign of his friend. He twisted the throttle and turned left following the van, helmetless the wind whipped into his face causing a streak of water to wipe its way down his cheek from his eyes, or maybe it was the tears of a man who had just lost a speck of light in his life.

The Judas Cradle

The bikers followed their president back into the clubhouse. A few had been sent to walk the local streets to search for whoever had thrown the smoke grenades; by the time the smoke had cleared whoever it had been had disappeared.

The Priest stood by the doors of 'The Chapel' and turned to face his brethren.

"We must all now leave here, let this place burn to the ground," he looked at one of the bikers and said directly to him, "make sure it does."The biker nodded and walked away to get as many petrol cans as he could find.

"The rest of you get on your bikes, get on the back of bikes if yours are damaged and go from here. Never come back. We will reach out to you when the time is right and we have a new home to return to. Until then your aim is simple: find this man, find his accomplices and find that girl… and kill them all."

He waved Panhead over to him and placed his arm around his shoulders as the VP stood next to him.

"It has come to my attention that you spoke with Pretty Boy earlier; did he give some explanation my brother?"

"He mentioned things boss, no details but something bad went down," said Panhead.

Nobody is sure if he would have wanted his last words on this planet to be something more meaningful but most people don't get a chance to plan those words.

The Priest reached backwards with one hand, the arm around Panhead's shoulders pulled him in a bit tighter, and pulled out one of the pistols from his waistband. He placed the muzzle of the gun in front of the VP's face and pulled the trigger. His face exploded in a mass of torn flesh, bone and blood, some of all those ingredients splattering all over the club president's face. Panhead's dead body dropped to the floor.

"Now go, be loyal to me and this club," he said to the crowd of bikers without flinching or wiping the bloody mess from his face. "Oh, and before you go, let's all congratulate Cowboy on becoming our new VP."

The crowd remained silent as everyone looked in the direction of the once club secretary and the new club VP.

Only the sound of The Priest clapping his hands together could be heard.

The Crippen's left and journeyed in different directions generally in small groups of between two and five, the last to leave were The Priest and Cowboy. Their leaving emblazoned with a background of flames as their former clubhouse was razed to the ground by an all-consuming fuel-driven fire. People from the nearby houses were stood on their doorsteps or in their front gardens watching on as the bike gang members rode out of town leaving behind them a trail of destruction. Many, if not most, were happy to witness their final ride out. A young child stood between his parents innocently waved as the final two bikers rode by, The Priest responded with a two fingered 'imitation gun' hand gesture at the child. The two parents' only response was to shepherd their child back into the safety of their home.

***

About eight miles out of town Grant overtook the van and between pointing gestures towards Gus and then at himself and mouthing the words 'Follow me,' he was confident that he had made his message clear. This was confirmed when Grant indicated left and turned his bike off the main route back to Milton Dryton and watched in his mirrors seeing Gus follow him.

He was relieved that the van had followed him because he knew that he couldn't complete the last phase of his journey without the assistance of both of its occupants. He had no idea what Emma would think about this but with the absence of Ian, he would need her involved otherwise it would prove impossible.

Studying the Judas Cradle on his last visit to 'the factory' he had worked out that it would need three people to make it a success, with Murphy and Ian on board it had seemed easy then. Now he just had to hope that Emma was angry enough to let her raw emotion overcome the horror of what he was going to ask her to become involved in.

Riding very steadily, relying on the headlights of the van behind him Grant took about thirty minutes to get to the woods that were now so familiar to him and then around another ten minutes looking for a suitable but fairly well-hidden entrance that could accommodate both his bike and the van and keep them out of view of anyone passing by. He had no doubts in his mind that he was not the only biker on these and other surrounding roads tonight.

It was nearly 22.00 hours when he came across the type of inlet he was looking for. Noticing it at the last moment he turned into it quite sharply, having to put his inside foot down on the bracken covered dirt track to stop himself losing control of the bike and ending up 'shiny-side down'.

He rode the bike as deep as the forest would allow him trying to give room for the van to park and be unnoticed from the road. The van pulled in behind his bike and the passenger door flew open. Before Grant could even dismount from his bike Emma rushed up to him and threw her arms around him.

"Thank you so much, you have just become my hero."

Grant wanted to respond kindly but the pain from losing his friend cut deep.

"Your hero should be your father," he snapped back at the grateful girl.

Emma let go of her grip and stared at him.

"My father," she responded, "I don't know my father."

"Try looking behind the wheel of the van and before you get all gooey on him tell him I need his help to drag that leather-clad wank stain from the back of the van and into a world of pain like he has never known." Grant was not in the mood for girly emotion.

Emma stared back towards the van looking directly at Gus.

"You're my fucking Dad?" she screamed.

Gus climbed out of the van and shrugged his shoulders; he had no idea how to respond and stuttered the single word, "Sorry."

"Can you both sort out this issue once I have finished what I came here to do!" shouted Grant, becoming more and more impatient.

"And what was that, you never did tell me," Emma almost hissed the words, almost pure hatred threaded through her question.

"To avenge my family, my wife, my daughter!" screamed Grant, all the hurt, pain and vile detestful anger leaving his body in a few words. Looking at Gus he said, "What has it been like Gus, looking on from a distance as your daughter grew up, watching her make mistakes and never being able to do a thing to help, never being able to hug her and tell her everything will be ok?"

Gus once again just shrugged his shoulders but this time he hung his head in a symbol of shame.

"Well let me tell you this," continued Grant, "it will never be as painful as never being able to do that again. Once you've tasted that and lost it, it hurts forever, hurts like pain you wouldn't wish on your worst enemy. Except I have learned that the last bit isn't true, not one fucking bit. The pain I want to inflict on my worst enemy is beyond your most horrific dreams and that enemy lies in that van."

His face was flushed with fury, he looked ready to kill and despite the two deaths he had already inflicted, for the first time he actually wanted to kill.

"Now it's time to bring this to a finish but I need help from both of you."

Neither Emma nor Gus could look at Grant or each other, they were both looking down at the ground, unable to speak.

"Well?" asked Grant, slightly calmer this time.

"What do you need us to do?" The first words from Gus since switching off the engine of the van were those of somebody who had given up on caring and just wanted all of this to come to an end.

"Brace yourselves would be a good start," said Grant looking at them both with an intensity that said more than any words could possibly say.

He made his way to the back of the van and swung open the doors. A dazed Pretty Boy looked at him and attempted to sit up only to be met by the heel of Grant's right hand, breaking his nose and spreading blood and snot across his face. The biker collapsed once again unconscious onto the floor of the van.

"Not yet you prick, not yet," said Grant rubbing his hand, the pain felt good.

Drops of rain began to fall as Gus and Grant began to pull the unconscious body of Pretty Boy through the woods, Emma followed silently. Eventually, after stopping twice to let a very unfit Gus get his breath back they made it to the wooden building that up until that moment Emma and Gus had not been aware of.

"What's this place?" asked Emma.

"Ian called it 'The Factory'. I've renamed it 'The House of Redemption," replied Grant, his voice once again emotionless as he began to move into the zone that allowed him to do what he was about to do.

Dragging the biker inside, the two men dropped the biker's feet to the floor with a thud. Gus looked at Emma but she was not returning his gaze. He looked around in the direction of Emma's stare and became as stunned and confounded as his daughter.

"What the hell is that thing?" he asked Grant.

"That my friend is redemption," he replied.

"I don't know what it's for but I don't like the look of it and I don't think I can be involved," said Emma now visibly afraid.

"Then in that case, we walk away, I fail my family, we all fail my family. We leave this piece of scum to come around and get back in touch with his mates and they come to find you... I think you can work out the ending to that touching tale," said Grant.

"There is no need to be so horrible Grant," Emma responded, her eyes shiny with water that was just seconds away from transforming into tears.

"This is what I am Emma, this is what I was forced to become. I hate what I am and who I am. Look on the bright side, after today you never have to see me again. I have to live with me for the rest of my days." Grant looked at them both. "Now are you both ready to do this?"

"What do we have to do?" asked Murphy.

Grant spent five minutes explaining the very simple workings of the Judas Cradle. At the end of the explanation, Emma walked outside and threw up.

It's becoming a bloody vomitorium out there, thought Grant to himself.

***

Throughout the cold and increasingly wet night bikers who had once been members of The Crippens rode the streets and roads searching for a white van and lone motorbike. All mobiles were switched on and every now and then they would stop their bikes and check their phones looking for an order, some direction, a message from a fellow brother, anything really to bring this road trip to a conclusion.

After about three hours of riding one message reached them all which they picked up at their next individual stops.

'Anybody found him yet'?

The text message was from The Priest.

Not one biker responded, nobody wanted to be the first to say 'No' and be on the receiving end of the wrath of that mad man.

It was half an hour later when the club president sent one more message, a very clear statement.

'Find him or become nomads for life'

The temporary nomadic Crippens continued their search.

***

Pretty Boy had been secured into the chair, still unconscious his head slumped forward. He had been elevated to a height of about three feet above the pointed pyramid with relative ease thanks the expert engineering of Ian and his rope and pulley system.

Grant silently thanked his lost friend, pulled up a chair and waited for consciousness to return to the suspended Crippen.

Emma and Gus went outside and for a few minutes just looked at each other.

It was Gus that first broke the silence saying, "I'm sorry but it was for the best and it was what your mother demanded of me."

"That conversation can wait," she replied, "are we really going to do what he asks?"

"Do we have a choice?" answering his daughter's question with a question but then following with the answer. "If we don't what do you think he will do to us, he can only let us go if we are as guilty as he is of this crime."

"Grant wouldn't hurt us," Emma replied.

"Emma you don't know what he has already done up to this point, this is a man torn apart by a nightmarish act of evil, he is capable of anything." Gus didn't look or sound like he didn't believe what he was saying. He was certain that they were both in a position of be involved or be killed.

A voice from inside the building called out to them, Grants voice was just loud enough to be heard but they could still hear the tone of a person who was on the verge of completing a job.

"Oi you pair, stop kissing and making up for mistakes made, it's time. Pretty Boy has joined the party."

Emma and Gus walked back into the shack, Pretty Boy swung in the chair above them, spittle flew from his lips as he greeted them.

"You are both going to fucking die. I'm going to drag you down the road bitch until even the crows wouldn't be interested in what is left of your body."

Grant laughed. He laughed loud and raucously, a laugh that had been waiting for over a year to be released.

"Pretty Boy, look at your situation, you are only going to ride one more thing in your life and it stands just below your arse and when I am finished the crows won't come within a mile of your rotting corpse."

"Do you think I don't know what this is all about?" asked the dangling biker although they both knew that it wasn't really a question that needed answering.

"First it was One a Year and then Lump. I knew you were coming and hey look you got lucky. What now, do you expect me to beg you for your forgiveness, plead for my life? Well fuck you. Fuck you like I fucked your wife and daughter. They begged for it, believe me they wanted to be fucked rough by old Pretty Boy I can tell you that for free."

Grant held back the rage that was rising inside him, every sinew of his body wanted to beat him to a bloody pulp but he controlled himself, knowing that the final words he would hear from this man would be words of pain and sorrow.

"Gus," said Grant and nodded towards the copper.

Gus walked to the secured end of the rope and untied it from its coupling. No further instructions were needed as he began to lower the chair.

265

"Hope that thing is sharp enough to go through my jeans, hope you have really thought this through," said Pretty Boy who despite his situation seemed not to be afraid or in a state of panic.

Grant held up his hand and Gus held the rope tight stopping the descending movement of the chair.

"I may look like an amateur but if you were really as focused as you are making out you would have noticed by now that your underwear has been removed and your jeans have been cut open, bearing your arse to the Judas Cradle," said Grant.

"And you have a really tiny prick," screamed Emma holding up her right hand and wiggling the little finger towards Pretty Boy.

"Big enough to fill your hole bitch," replied the Crippen, laughing at her.

Grant once again raised his hand and Gus began, once more to release the rope slowly through his hands, the pulley system making it extremely easy to do this with an almost pleasurable slow pace.

The tip of the Judas Cradle reached the buttocks of Pretty Boy and the tip disappeared into the rip in his jeans. Gus waited for Grant's hand to rise up again but it didn't happen.

The first bit of pain hit Pretty Boy as the tip entered him.

"You fuckers, you are all going to die!" he screamed and the pain showed across his face.

Grant once again raised his hand, much to Gus's relief who once again took the strain and stopped the lowering of the chair.

"The only person who is going to die is you Pretty Boy and your brotherhood will find your rotting body and will understand that things can be achieved by a single person and that violence for the sake of vengeance will be seen as the right thing in years to come," said Grant almost turning a short speech into a prophecy. "And don't expect your friends to burst through the door to rescue you either."

At that point, the door burst open.

Grant stood up from the chair and spun around to face the door reaching for the gun in his waistband even though he knew it wasn't loaded.

Ian staggered into the shack and fell to his knees.

"Does it work?" he asked before collapsing face down. The shirt he was wearing was ripped to shreds exposing a badly burnt and bleeding back. The second explosion had caused severe damage to Grant's friend but despite that he had managed to make his way round to the front of the clubhouse and let off the smoke grenades and then somehow evade the searching Crippens and make his way to the woods.

Pretty Boy stopped screaming, firstly because he actually thought his brothers had come to his rescue and then because of the state of the man who had entered the building he started to laugh.

"Watch him die and see your future you fucking wanker," he groaned at Grant.

Grant ran towards Ian and held his friend in his arms.

"Ian hold on bro' I'll get you to a hospital," he pleaded. "Emma, Gus help me please."

Emma made her way towards the two men but holding on to the rope Gus was at a loss for what to do, his focus diverted by the ongoing events the rope slipped slightly inside the grip of his hands and Pretty Boy released a piercing scream of pain as the whole of the metal tip of the Judas Cradle entered his body ripping into his rectum.

Stilling cradling Ian's lifeless body looked towards the pain stricken biker.

"For violating my family in a way that no human deserves," he said and then looking towards Gus he shouted, "lift and drop Muttley!"

As Gus heaved backwards on the rope he looked at Grant and angrily responded,

"Don't ever call me that."

He pulled Pretty Boy about two feet above the pyramid, blood dripped out of the bikers arse as he rose higher. The biker looked towards Gus and silently mouthed the words "Please don't."

"Go to hell!" shouted Gus and released the rope from the grip of both hands.

The full weight of the chair and biker combined to drop them both like a stone. The sharp peak of the pyramid ensemble of the Judas Cradle tore its way into the rear orifice of the stricken biker and impaled him onto the structure. The force of the drop hitting it split the seat of the chair allowing the body of Pretty Boy to drop a few more inches causing even more internal damage. Blood gushed out of him and dripped down the four angled sides of the lethal pyramid. The biker let out a blood-curdling scream of excruciating pain.

Grant heard it all but saw none of the final throes of death of the man who had caused him, and his family especially, so much agony. He was concentrating on his friend, the friend he had thought he had lost and then in a few short moments of mayhem imagined he had got back but quickly faced the realisation of losing him all over again. Even in death Pretty Boy was witness again to the agonising loss of someone in Grant's life.

"It's done Grant," said Gus solemnly.

Grant, kneeling on the floor, didn't look up. Tears rolled down the cheeks of his face and gently fell onto the face of Ian.

"I don't care," he replied quietly, "I don't care about anything anymore."

***

It was at least thirty minutes later before Grant released the body of Ian and gently laid him back on the floor. He removed his jacket and placed it over the shoulders and head of his dear trusted friend.

At last, he stood and turned to look at the scene of Pretty Boy's death. The biker sat atop the blood-covered Judas spike, the broken chair maintaining his balance and preventing him from falling to the floor. His face was frozen in a deathly portrayal of the pain he had endured in his final minutes, for death had not been immediate. It had taken about twenty minutes before death came to take him, luckily for Pretty Boy the initial pain had been so excruciating his body's pain reactors had kicked in and allowed him to fall into a state of unconsciousness and not feel the blood drain from his body.

"You didn't suffer like my family you bastard, you made them suffer until the end. You got off too easily," said Grant at the unhearing dead body.

Emma approached Grant and hugged him, no words were said; the act of affection and gratefulness said everything. Gus joined the pair of them and placed his hand on Grant's shoulder.

"We need to go mate and destroy this place before we leave" he said.

Grant shook his head, "No, let them eventually find their brother. Let them get the message."

"OK Grant, whatever you want," Gus replied, too tired to argue.

"Help me put Ian into the van then do me one last favour," said Grant.

Gus nodded, "Anything, just ask."

"Place him on the side of a road, somewhere easy to find then call for an ambulance," Grant said, a sadness in his voice that belied his real deep sadness. "Use the phone in his pocket, it's unregistered. Then burn out the van, destroy the plates, scrape off the identifying numbers, you know the drill Gus you are a cop."

"OK, no problem, anything else?" asked the Gus.

"Yeah, go home, get to know your daughter properly, love her every day and protect her for longer. Be the best father you can be, be a better father than me." Grant hung his head as if ashamed of himself.

Emma began to cry but through the tears she managed to say, "You have been a good Dad Grant. You did what no father should have to: avenge your daughter's death."

"Thanks… for everything, both of you," replied Grant. "Forget about me now, it's over."

The Final Ride Home

Grant stood by his trusty bike and watched Gus reverse the van out of the woods and back onto the road. Emma waved but Grant did not respond; she knew it was her final goodbye and would never see this man again. She had mixed emotions as Grant disappeared from her sight, a man capable of so much evil but full of so much good. It was a certain reminder of what pain mixed with a need for revenge could result in.

Gus put the van into first gear and began the journey home. Emma placed her hand on top of his which was still holding the gear shift stick.

"Let's go home Dad," she said.

Gus looked at her and smiled, he had waited years to hear that.

Grant returned to the shack and collected together the belongings he had left there. He did not look in the direction of Pretty Boy's dead body, not once. He had no idea what he was going to do now but the one thing he did know was that he did not need a final reminder of what had gone on. That had happened once before about a year ago when he had stood in his bedroom at home and looked around, the signs of what had happened still obvious despite the police and forensic staff's best efforts to clean up. That memory, those images had led him to this path of destruction.

It was late so Grant laid himself down on the floor and covered himself with his jacket that had earlier covered the body of his friend. Despite the deathly scene around him, he fell into a deep sleep quickly, the stress of having to finish the job now lifted.

He awoke at around five in the morning. He decided that he would look for a rest stop with washing facilities on his journey. He took one last look around the building to make sure he was leaving nothing of his behind. As he walked towards the door his peripheral vision caught sight of the bloody scene that sat beneath the dead biker's body, no emotion, no feeling of guilt rushed through him.

He left the building for the last time securing the door behind as best he could and walked back to his bike never looking back. The time for looking back was over even though the future looked as uncertain as ever.

Packing everything away into his throw over panniers Grant fired his bike up and headed out on the road. At the entrance to the woods, he rode past an abandoned bike lying on its side. Ian must have used this to make his escape from The Crippens, he could only assume that it belonged to one of the bike gang. He pointed his bike north not sure of where he was heading but certain that it was still not the time to return to what had been his family home. He was certain of one other thing too: he was in dire need of a coffee.

He had ridden for about twenty miles on the still slightly damp roads before he came across a place to stop for a coffee. An independent petrol station stood next to a small café, ideal thought Grant this was a great opportunity to refuel himself and the bike all in one stop.

He filled the bike's tank with fuel and went into the garage to pay, picking up a chocolate bar in case he needed an energy boost later. '*Any excuse to pick up a chocolate bar'* he heard the voice of his wife say. He smiled and noted that he hadn't done that for a while when remembering her sweet voice. He took the time to have an ordinary conversation with the old man behind the payment desk, it felt good to be doing normal things again. Had he not had that conversation, had he not taken those extra few seconds to select a piece of confectionary, had he not returned to the till and deposited his change in a charity collection box then maybe, just maybe he would have seen the leather clad figure stood at the corner of the café building. Then he would have recognised the leather cut and the patch on the back of it as the biker turned around and made his way round to the back of the building where his bike was hidden from site. He may have even seen the biker get his mobile phone from the front pocket of his cut and start to make a call. But he didn't because he was happily engaged in ordinary events like chatting, buying chocolate and giving a few pennies to a charity.

***

The biker, road name Crinkle because of the many crinkly creases in his forehead, made the call that The Priest had been waiting for.

"Found him," said Crinkle, a pause as he listened to the voice at the other end of the call, "Reynold's place next to the Jolly Diner café," he replied.

More instructions followed and finally Crinkle said, "Yeah no problem, I'll keep an eye on him."

As he ended the call he heard Grant's bike engine roar into action and travel the short distance to the Jolly Diner, luckily for Crinkle Grant decided to park his bike at the front of the building, pushing his bike back, to park in a space allocated for bikes, so that it was left facing towards the exit back out onto the road. As he walked towards the entrance door he noticed a sign on the door window.

BIKERS WELCOME

Always a good sign he thought.

Grant ordered and subsequently tucked into a full breakfast and made full use of the free coffee refills by having three mugs. He ate and drank heartily for the first time in months, enjoying every mouthful of the fatty fried food. He savoured the textures and tastes and thought about where to head. He had always wanted to visit Scotland so made an almost instant decision that this would be his destination, visiting a variety of unplanned places on the way. *Take it as it comes* he thought.

While Grant was enjoying his breakfast and thinking about his onward journey, Crinkle had moved his position to the back of the garage. Hidden from view from anyone entering or leaving the café but able to clearly see Grant's bike it was the perfect vantage point to wait and watch undetected.

Just short of an hour after arriving Grant said thank you to the waitress and left the café getting back on his bike, ensuring first that all luggage was secure and fastened away. He pressed the electric start and revved the engine loudly, loving the feel of the rumble of the engine travelling through the seat into his body.

Only an idiot would place an engine next to a container of petrol put one wheel at the front of it and one at the back and then sit on it, his wife had once said to him. He was happy being an idiot if it meant riding.

He set off as the hidden biker got back on his phone but this time, there was no reply, Crinkle could only think that his brothers were on their way.

***

"Hello, which emergency service do you require?"

"I've just seen a body on the edge of the Blackwood Road heading towards Milton Dryton."

"Who is calling please?"

"Fuck you, get an ambulance there now."

Half an hour later Emma stood in the house of her father for the first time in her life.

"Wanna stay?" asked Gus.

Emma nodded her head.

"We'll talk in the morning, yeah?"

Emma again nodded her head and hugged her Dad.

One thought echoed through her mind:

Thank you Grant, and good luck.

***

Ten minutes after Grant had ridden away from the Jolly Diner the horde of bikers rode into the forecourt of Jim Reynolds garage. Crinkle ran out to meet them and headed straight for the bike of his club president.

As Jim Reynolds walked to the door of his little garage shop to turn the sign around to read 'Closed', The Priest was informed that Grant had left ten minutes earlier and Panhead curled his fingers and thumb of his left hand and waved it up and down in the well-known hand gesture of 'wanker' in the direction of the old garage owner.

The bikers roared off in formation behind their leader and Crinkle joined them at the rear.

The Crippens were back together and going full throttle.

About fifteen minutes ahead Grant was taking in the views as he rode the bike steadily, he had eventually picked up the A41 and had decided that he would make his first stop in Chester. He had promised his family that he would one day take them all to Chester Zoo to see the white tigers but like most things in his busy life he had never gotten around to it. It was time to keep his promise now. Not wanting to be confined to the larger roads and potentially miss out on some great hidden sights he started to look for a turning that would take him in the general direction of his destination, his thoughts being to ride along the route of the River Dee which he hoped would keep him northbound towards the ancient town.

The A41 was a long winding road with some lovely stretches of straight tarmac for a biker to relax into his ride and not worry about sharp bends, Grant had taken full advantage of this. Maybe if there had been more bends and more traffic he wouldn't have relaxed so much and then maybe he would have looked in one of his mirrors and seen in the far distance behind him a collection of individual travellers that could only have been bikers.

The Crippens, led by their president and newly appointed vice president had gambled on Grant looking for a main route to get a few miles under his belt. The direction he had headed from the Jolly Diner took him directly towards the A41 so that is where The Priest led his brothers. Now looking way ahead of him he hoped his guess was correct as far in the distance he spotted a lone biker, tiny in the distance.

They had just taken the long right hand bend in the main A-road close to Milton Green when they all saw Grant slow down and turn left off the main road.

The Priest raised his left hand and waved his hand, first finger raised, in a circular motion. As one the bikers, numbering in the twenties, throttled their bikes and increased their speed considerably.

Going for the quiet route are you?, the bikers leader thought to himself, *'perfect'*.

Grant had turned into a narrow road named Pratt's Lane which heading West should naturally take him towards the River Dee where he hoped he would be able to head North again and follow the line of the river.

Pratt's Lane was not as smooth as the main A-road he had just left, much narrower and a few more turns to concentrate on, it was also still quite wet and slippery from an earlier rain shower, all which combined to convince Grant to slow down a bit. He had just taken the second bend in the road when something caught his eye reflected in his left-hand side wing mirror. Just a flash of movement and colour, he slowed slightly and watched as the image of the group of bikers appeared in the mirror. He had no doubt at all who it was and without a second thought turned the throttle fully open and increased his speed down the lane. The road ahead was fairly straight and he made as much use of it as the bike would allow.

As Grant approached the end of the straight stretch of Pratts Lane all those conditions that had a few seconds earlier combined to slow him down plus the fact that The Crippens were now in close pursuit all acted against the speed and weight of the 1300cc cruiser as he was suddenly faced with an extremely sharp right-hand bend.

He eased on the brakes, maybe a touch too much, and leaned the bike hard over to the right. The loose wet surface refused to offer any grip to the bikes wide rear tyre and before he had a chance to react Grant felt his back tyre go into a massive slide taking the bike away from him.

Grant tried hard to hold on but as the bike slid sideways to the left the weight of it increased its momentum and he felt his arm torn out of the shoulder joint. He hit the ground with a crash, his injured shoulder shooting a lightning bolt of pain through his upper body. He remembered losing sight of his bike as it slid away from him and tumbled into the wide ditch at the side of Pratt's Lane. Grant himself rolled two or three times, his helmet striking the road violently several times. Thankfully, his clothing protected most of his skin and flesh and had it not been for a good pair of boots his ankle would have certainly been broken as he tumbled across the surface of the road. His left knee wasn't so lucky though as the final time he twisted through the air and hit the road at an awkward angle causing his knee joint to twist and snap.

He lay broken and in pain on the wet road, dazed from the impacts taken by his helmet he lay for a few seconds longer before trying to crawl towards where he had seen his bike disappear. The pain as he moved was excruciating and his progress was slow but it was quickly brought to a halt as the front wheel of a bike appeared directly in front of him about an inch or two from his head.

Grant lifted his head as much as his shoulder would allow and watched the bike wheel turn slightly right and then lean over in the same direction. A few seconds later a pair of black cowboy style boots stood in front of him next to the bikes wheel.

"You do look to be in a sorry old state Grant."

He recognised the voice of The Priest immediately.

"Been in worse," replied Grant discovering that even talking increased the level of pain he was experiencing.

"I very much doubt it, you clearly haven't given enough thought to the situation you are in," the club president said.

The Priest leaned downwards and grabbed the collar of Grant's jacket with both hands and hauled him upwards.

Grant groaned in pain as more electric sparks of pain from his shoulder shot down his body. Then the pain from his knee kicked in as his upward movement caused it to move. His groans transformed into an anguished scream.

"Where's Pretty Boy, what have you done with him?" asked The Priest.

"Sent him to fuck arse hell," replied Grant sniggering for about a second before he discovered that this hurt him even more. He coughed and the upper body movement made his shoulder feel like it was on fire. Grant coughed again and spat out a large globule of blood.

The Priest released his hold and dropped Grant back to the floor, another groan as the impact of body hitting road sent pain shooting through every avenue of his body.

"Time to join him," and although Grant heard the words of the maniac his attention was drawn to the growing crowd of feet and legs that were surrounding him.

The first act could have been mistaken for an act of kindness as one of The Crippens roughly removed Grant's bike helmet and threw it in the general direction of his smashed up bike. The second act proved that it was no act of kindness as a large boot swung into the side of Grant's head.

As his head flew violently away from the direction of the kick his mind's eye was flooded with sparks of speckled light, he momentarily forgot all about the pain in his knee and shoulder and then wished he could just feel that pain again as the kicks and strikes reigned in.

After the headshot, the next kick was into his lower stomach and groin region quickly followed by a stamp of a large foot onto his head.

The strike into his lower spine felt nothing like a connecting kick which was not surprising as it had been caused by a heavy wood baseball bat.

Grant fought the urge to let unconsciousness take him away from these savage blows and over the next thirty minutes he endured more pain than any one man could survive.

Kicks, punches, stamps and baseball bat strikes were interspersed with cries of "This is for One a Year you bastard" and "My brother Lump would like you to have this."

One of the last things that Grant experienced and remembered was the tearing impact of a motorbike chain ripping through the side of his face.

Throughout the duration of the assault, The Priest stood back, his arms raised towards the skies. His words could hardly be heard because of the screams of his horde.

"Be savage my brothers.

Be savage like those that were savage to me

Cleanse this place of another

Who believes he can better me"

The assault slowly dissipated as the bikers both became exhausted and bored with kicking a limp ragdoll-like body.

Grant's body lay on the road twisted, broken and bleeding. The angle of some of his limbs and joints were unnatural, his facial features were unrecognisable distorted and covered in blood.

As the bikers dispersed and began to return to their bikes The Priest walked towards the broken lifeless body and looked down at it. He unzipped his jeans, pulled out his penis and began to urinate over Grant, swaying left to right to ensure almost total coverage.

As he tucked himself away and pulled up his zip he noticed the fingers of Grant's right hand flick open and then closed again.

"A fighter to the very end, respect. Wish you had become a Crippen," and then The Priest stamped heavily onto the curled up hand crunching every bone within it.

He turned and returned to his brothers, mounting his bike and slowly they manoeuvred their bikes around and rode away. The final biker at the back of the leaving formation looked over his shoulder and smiled at the motionless body. Dead, left for dead, whatever, the biker didn't care, respect to their lost brothers had been paid.

Grant watched as the bikers left and then slowly closed his eyes. He whispered the words "See you soon girls," before the darkness took him.